MW00930590

Lynn H. Elliott was born in Cardiff, Wales. After studying in Nottingham, he completed his masters and doctorate at the University of California, Santa Barbara. He taught English literature and creative writing at California State University, Chico. He is an award-winning playwright and screenplay writer. He has written a number of books for children. His *Another Child's Christmas in Wales*, written in both prose and dramatic forms, is autobiographical. He is a father and grandfather. He and his wife, Dani, live in Chico, California.

For my wife, Dani, who helped again and again and again; and my parents, who shared with me their love of storytelling.

Lynn H. Elliott

The Crossingway

Austin Macauley Publishers™
London • Cambridge • New York • Sharjah

A CIP catalogue record for this title is available from the British Library.

ISBN 9781528942553 (Paperback)
ISBN 9781528942560 (Hardback)
ISBN 9781528971195 (ePub e-book)
ISBN 9781398418462 (Audiobook)

www.austinmacauley.com

First Published (2020)
Austin Macauley Publishers Ltd
25 Canada Square
Canary Wharf
London
E14 5LQ

My thanks also to Ruth Younger, who helped with an earlier version of the manuscript; and to Martha Yates, our guide through Navajo, Hopi and Zuni territory.

1. Bully Harold Bully and the Blind Boy

I dangle upside-down—again—my ankles held in Bully Harold Bully's iron grip as his two cronies dance around me, chanting.

"Witch, witch, your mother is a witch.

Hunt her down, tie her up and throw her in a ditch."

As I swing back and forth, I stare at my topsy-turvy town. In the distance, cars zoom north and south on the freeway, disobeying gravity as they cling to the freeway above them. Just below, restaurants, coffee shops and boutique stores sell smelly incense, crystals, tarot cards and other weird stuff. Below them is the railroad with an upside-down train dragging the upside-down boxcars, stopping all the wrong-side-up cars from crossing the track. A sudden jerk. My hair sweeps the ground in a half-circle, and I face the mountain that gives our town its name: Mount Shasta. From the base of the mountain, a two-lane road zigzags downwards toward the snow-covered peak. And below all is the blue sky, dotted with puffy clouds, dangling from the top of the mountain.

A punch in the arm. "Go on, say it! Witch, witch, my mother is a witch."

"Did you like that photo I posted on Facebook?" Pug the Pyro joins in. "Already two thousand likes."

"I never look at Facebook," I lie. Three witches—my mother, my sister and me—stirring a large cauldron.

"Say it, Hhoowwll," the third bully, Sloppy Jack joins in. 'Witch, witch, my mother is a witch.'"

My name is Howell. Bully Harold Bully and his cronies prefer to call me HHHH-OOOO-WWWW-LLLL. A pack of wolves.

"Say it!"

"Never!" I shout. I stare at Bully Harold Bully's muddy shins, scraped knees, mismatched socks and dirty, untied sneakers as he swings me back and forth, my curly red hair sweeping the ground.

"Do you want Pug to set fire to your hair?" Pug the Pyro enjoys setting fires: boys' backpacks, lunch bags, homework, or toilet rolls in the bathroom.

A sudden jerk and I face Pug the Pyro's untied black boots. Two sizes too big, making his legs look even skinnier. Pug's large shirts always hang down to his knees hiding his skinny body and arms. Bully Harold Bully is the opposite: a tight black T-shirt shows his muscles. Pug has stringy dirty blond hair. Bully has a tight buzz cut, like his father and two brothers. No hair dares grow more than one eighth of an inch on any of their heads.

"Admit it," Pug the Pyro growls. "Your mother's a freak."

"My father says he's going to videotape her dancing naked on the mountain with goblins, werewolves and trolls in that strange language and put it on YouTube." Sloppy Jack snorts.

Tall, thin and scrawny, Sloppy Jack decorates himself in mustard or ketchup or whatever he's eating. Even if stuff is wrapped in a plastic bag, it will find him. Sloppy Jack has a high, squeaky voice. A mouse caught in a trap.

"You are all so stupid," I yell. I struggle to get loose, my fists swinging at Bully Harold Bully's filthy knees.

My mother does spend a lot of time alone in this one particular meadow on the side of Mount Shasta, especially before her trips to New Mexico.

Sometimes, I'd accompany her. We'd sit quietly, not talking, listening.

Finally, she'd say, all is balance. Good, evil, right, wrong. One day you'll understand that, Howell.

And that was all. She'd stand and throw some coins into the running stream. Then we'd return to the car and drive back down the mountain.

By now my pants are sliding up my thighs. My shirt sags down over my face showing my naked belly to the world, and my head is inches from the ground, my hair sweeping the gravel parking lot. I desperately need some help if my head and brain are not to bounce up and down in the next thirty seconds.

"Your mother won't help," Pug the Pyro adds. "She's gone to one of her hippie-dippy retreats in New Mexico. Dancing naked around some pole all decorated with flowers."

I struggle to free myself. Nobody is going to say things like that about my mother.

"Maybe your weird Uncle Tal will come and save you," Sloppy Jack giggles. "My dad says he should be in a loony bin."

"Your Uncle Tal and his crazy Volkswagen bus covered with its flowers and strange signs," adds Pug the Pyro.

Sloppy Jack and Pug the Pyro laugh.

Bully Harold Bully doesn't.

My arms reach out, protecting my head and body as my ankles are released and I crash to the ground. Bully Harold Bully screams in pain. He is bent over double grasping his boy parts, a white walking cane jammed between his legs.

"Lo siento mucho. Yo no veo," says a different voice.

Before us stands a young boy, dressed in a white shirt and baggy pants, skin browned by the sun. He wears sandals on his feet but no socks. On his head sits a rounded hat that looked like a pot. He wears large sunglasses.

"Speak English, you moron," Pug the Pyro yells.

"He can't hear you," Sloppy Jack says. "He's blind."

"Fool," I respond, pushing Sloppy Jack in the chest. "Blind people can hear."

"I say sorry. No see you." As he spoke, the blind boy turns and the white cane smacks Sloppy Jack in the knees. He collapses, lying next to Bully Harold Bully.

"Lo siento mucho. ¿Te lastimé? I very sorry. I hurt you?"

Pug the Pyro crouches like a prize-fighter and winds up his fist. "Get ready for a knuckle sandwich, blind boy."

But before Pug the Pyro's knuckle sandwich can land, the blind boy grabs Pug's fist. A twist of his arm and Pug the Pyro flips over backwards landing on top of the other two.

The white cane points at me. "Ir rápidamente!" the blind boy calls out.

No need for a translation. I turn and run as quickly as I can. "Nos vemos de nueve proto," the boy calls after me. "We meet again soon."

When I am out of the schoolyard, I look back. The three bullies are on their feet, fists tight, turning in circles, looking for the unknown boy, now nowhere to be seen.

Bully Harold Bully stares across at me and shakes his fist. "We'll be waiting for you after school tomorrow, Howl, and the next day and the next."

I know they will.

2. The Man in Black

I duck down an alley, a short cut to my home. A figure blocks my way. It is a man, dressed in a full-length black leather coat buttoned up to the neck and tied at the waist with thick string. Heavy, biker boots with six-inch platforms poke from under his coat. He pushes back the leather hood pulled over his head. His face is white, skeletal with a long-beaked nose. His right eye is large and blood red. A black patch covers his left eye, and, in the middle of the patch, glows a yellow spot. It travels up and down my body like a laser.

"The time is near," he hisses. "Who will it be?"

"Who will what be?" I blurt out.

"The boy doesn't know." He laughs, the foul breath from his mouth threatening to knock me over. "His mother hasn't told him yet. Well, we'll see if it is him. Soon."

Head down, eyes closed, I bustle past him and dash down the alley.

What hasn't my mother told me? I think to myself.

Man in black, man in black—the image races before my eyes.

As I rush down the street to our home, I think back on all the stories my mother told me. Was there a man in black?

Each night, my mother tells my sister, who everyone calls Sister Sarah, and me stories from Welsh mythology. When Sister Sarah got "too old for fairy tales," I sit alone at my mother's feet as she tells stories of Merlin, or Myrddin as my mother called him, and the enchantress known as the Lady of the Lake. She often ends with some enigmatic statement.

"Who knows? Maybe we are long-distant relatives of Myrddin." A smile on her face, a twinkle in her eye. Who really knows?

Man in black, man in black—the image dances before my eyes.

I walk faster, looking before and behind me.

I once asked my father why my mother left Wales, following him to California. He smiled and said, "Protection."

"For you?

"No. For you and your sister."

"From what?" My father smiled. The question was never answered.

I arrive home.

Time for answers.

3. Tommy Foxglove

I rush up the driveway of our home. A quick glance down the street to make sure the man in black with strange eyes is not following me. I creep quietly through the front door. I want to talk to my mother, to tell her about the blind boy and the man in black. She'll have answers. She always does.

But she's not home.

She left Northern California a week ago travelling to the State of New Mexico. One of her meetings in the desert. About what I don't know. She makes this drive six times a year. Things change when she's away. My father, Stuart Evans, doesn't cook, so it's a steady diet of cereal, fast food or take-out.

Within hours of my mother leaving, Sister Sarah brought her creepy new boyfriend, Tommy Foxglove, to the house. I don't like him. I don't like the way he fixes me with his steel-grey, unsmiling eyes, never blinking. A snake hypnotising its prey. What does Sister Sarah see in him? Whatever it is, she demands I be nice to him—or else.

I tiptoe quietly past the living room. Father and Sister Sarah, take-out meals balanced on their knees, sit staring at the television watching a rerun of last night's *Dancing with the Stars*. I turn to creep upstairs to my bedroom and bump into Tommy Foxglove. He blocks my way.

"Here you are sneaking in quietly," he hisses. "Were you hoping we wouldn't see you?" The smirk on his face says he wants to know what is troubling me—if he doesn't know already! I curse quietly, push him aside and rush upstairs to my bedroom. I've only known Tommy Foxglove a few days, but I already hate him.

Safe inside my bedroom, I grab my laptop and dive under my dinosaur-covered comforter.

Tomorrow Bully Harold Bully and his two cronies will catch me. Maybe my blind protector will reappear. I hope so.

I take some deep breaths and log on to my laptop. Sharing with friends on Facebook, writing in my diary and playing Grand Theft Auto will help me relax. I type in my password and check my diary. Yesterday's entry. Nothing unusual. My fingers tap the keys as I record what happened today.

Blind boy saves me from the bullies. Says he'll see me again. When? Where? The man in black with the yellow glowing eye. Did I really see him, or was it a hallucination from blood rushing to my head after being held upside-down? Or maybe something I ate at the school cafeteria disagreed with me. And then there's those horror movies Sister Sarah makes me watch, and those scary video games like Resident Evil or Silent Hill she forces me to play with her.

I close my diary and open Facebook. My body stiffens. On the screen is the figure of the man in black. He turns slowly. I see that same white, skeletal face.

I slam the laptop lid shut, breathing heavily and throwing off the comforter. Tingles of hot sweat slide down my forehead, burning my eyes. My hands sweat. I wipe them on my comforter.

My index finger inches forward and opens my laptop. A sigh of relief. Before me is a selfie sent by my friend, Erin Powell. She looks so cute dressed in her cheerleader outfit. Then my fingers shake as the screen darkens and is replaced by the man in black's face. The yellow dot that is his left eye moves slowly across the screen. It's watching me!

I slam the laptop lid shut again. A knock on my bedroom door.

"Tommy says you seemed upset when you came in," my father says entering. "Would you like to talk?"

"It's nothing."

"Are you sure? Tommy was concerned about you."

Tommy Foxglove stands at the open door. His steel-grey, dead eyes pierce through his rimless glasses. A manic smile spreads across his face. The evil clown in the sewer. Not one ounce of concern.

"Why don't you come in and join us, Tommy," my father offers.

Tommy cautiously puts a foot inside. A sudden bang as the painting above my bed jerks sideways, almost falling. Tommy Foxglove whips his foot back quickly into the hallway.

"I think it best if I stay out here," Tommy replies, glancing at the painting.

I look from Tommy to the painting of a lady dressed in white, riding a white horse across a mountaintop. However, much I jump around on my bed, that painting never moves.

I stand on my bed, ready to straighten the painting, my eyes fixed on Tommy Foxglove. Before I can touch the painting, it jerks back into place.

I see it; my father doesn't.

"What can I do to make you feel better, Howell?" he asks.

Get that creep out of my sight! I think to myself. *Maybe Sister Sarah sees something in him, but I don't. And why did he wait until my mother was gone before coming to the house?*

True. Even though Sister Sarah and Tommy Foxglove met three weeks ago, none of us, except Sister Sarah, had ever seen him. My mother insisted Sister Sarah bring him to the house. She even made a special dinner so we could all meet—but he never came. Always last-minute excuses. That night, my mother came into my bedroom. She sat at the end of my bed and asked me about my sister and Tommy Foxglove. Had I seen him? No. Had Sister Sarah said anything to me about him? No. Then she stood up, kissed the top of my head and said, "I think he'll come here when I leave." And with that warning, she left my bedroom.

I didn't think of what she said until a week ago. Just an hour after my mother left to drive to New Mexico, Tommy Foxglove appeared on our doorstep for the first time saying how disappointed he was at missing our mother.

He lied. My mother was right. He'd waited until she left the house.

"Maybe some ice cream," my father says, breaking the silence. "I'll get you some."

Tommy Foxglove stays in the hallway, his eyes flicking back and forth between me and the painting on the wall. His question slithers across the room.

"Do you know why your mother attends these meetings in New Mexico?"

"Yes," I lie. I don't know, but I'm not going to admit that.

Sister Sarah once told me that our mother told her everything about those meetings. I don't believe her. The night before my mother left, I sat on the stairs, listening to my mother and father talk in the living room.

"The Drygoni know the time is near," my mother was saying. "They'll do everything they can to stop it before it happens, to prevent Howell stepping through the Crossingway. They'll use those bullies to test Howell, to prevent the transfer."

What is she talking about? I thought to myself. *Bully Harold Bully and friends being used to test me? And what is a Crossingway, a transfer, and a Drygoni*? I made a note to look up those words in Wikipedia.

"Maybe it's not Howell!" my father snapped. I was surprised. My father rarely raised his voice, especially to my mother.

Why was this transfer thing, whatever it was, so troubling to my father?

"I know it's him," my mother replied calmly. "He's the one who'll need protection. I'll contact Tal."

No! Don't bring Uncle Tal here! I thought to myself. *I'll be the laughingstock of the school.*

I was ready to burst in and tell my parents what I thought.

"Once again the category for final jeopardy is unsolved mysteries," the television boomed. Too late. I crept back upstairs.

My thirteenth birthday is soon. November 1. When my mother comes back from her trip to New Mexico, I'll ask her about this Crossingway, transfer and these Drygoni things. She'll tell me.

"Here's your ice cream, Howell." My father holds out a bowl filled with caramel ice cream. As I reach for the cone, Sister Sarah yells from downstairs.

"Tommy, come down. Entertainment Tonight is on."

I remember when Sister Sarah used to dress in tight jeans, cowboy boots, a rodeo dress shirt covered with blingy stuff, and a leather jacket with fringes. Her heroine was Annie Oakley, some female sharpshooter in the Old West.

Then Tommy Foxglove entered her life and she changed overnight. Tough-talking, shoot-from-the-hip Sister Sarah started wearing dresses and jewellery and slopping makeup on her face.

And now that same Tommy Foxglove is staring at me through his rimless glasses, smirking as he waits.

For what?

4. Deeper and Deeper Down the Mountainside

As I reach for the bowl of ice cream, something slams into my back. I am hurled across my bedroom, slamming into the wall. My father jerks back open-mouthed. Another blow and I'm thrown sideways, collapsing over my desk.

All this time, Tommy Foxglove crouches in the doorway, panting and rubbing his hands together. "Yes, yes," he hisses through his teeth.

Suddenly, the floor under my desk opens beneath me. I cling to my desk as it drops downward, deeper and deeper. I am hurling down a mountainside. Trees flash past me on both sides. Their branches slash at my face. Then the desk wobbles, threatening to throw me off. I open my mouth to scream for help, but no words come out. I lose my grip and pivot in the air, watching as the desk falls faster beneath me deeper and deeper.

A hand reaches out from above and grasps my wrist, saving me from falling deeper. A young, dark-skinned girl with pale blue, almost white eyes, her hair shaped in cornrows grasps my wrist, preventing me from falling. "*Ou mande èd. Mwen vini*!"

What is she saying?

"You ask for help. I come!" she translates.

I don't remember asking for help, but I'm glad she came.

"Thank you," I call out as the girl drags me out of the pit. She points to her lips and gestures with her hand. My saviour is deaf.

"*Nou rankontre ankò byento*. We meet again soon," she murmurs.

Exactly what the blind boy said to me earlier.

When? Who are you?

But before I can ask those questions, the pit and the girl disappear. I am lying flat on the bedroom rug.

My father grabs my arm. "Help me, Tommy," my father begs. But Tommy won't move. He stares at the painting on the wall. He can't enter my bedroom.

As I stand, I see my reflection in the mirror: a pale white face and curly red hair spattered in blood.

"What happened, Howell?" my father cries. "You were saying something about falling, mountainside, branches smashing windshield, tree crash."

"And what about that mumbo jumbo nonsense he was blabbering?" Tommy interrupts. "Sounded like some foreign language."

"I didn't hear that, Tommy. What did all that mean, Howell?"

Before anyone can say another word, the downstairs phone rings.

"Answer that, Sarah," my father calls out.

"I'm watching TV," Sister Sarah yells back. "Use the upstairs phone."

"Will you be okay, Howell?" my father asks. I nod. He sets me down on the bed and leaves my room. Tommy Foxglove stays, manic clown grin pasted on his face.

Silence as my father listens. Then he screams into the phone, "Who are you? Why would you say such a ridiculous thing?"

He slams down the phone and re-enters my bedroom. A forced smile. "Kids playing a sick joke."

My father helps me downstairs. He puts an icepack on my bruised face.

Tommy Foxglove slithers onto the sofa beside Sister Sarah, his dead eyes stare at me, unblinking. The snake sizing up its victim.

Suddenly a bang on the front door. "Turn down the volume on the TV, Sarah," my father calls out as he exits the living room to answer the door.

I peer down the hallway. Police, one has his hand on my father's shoulder, stopping him from falling. A moment later, the police leave and my father staggers down the hallway to the living room, clutching his chest. His face is pale, and tears run down his cheeks.

"The phone. It wasn't a sick joke. It was the truth."

Sister Sarah joins us. Tommy Foxglove remains seated in the recliner, the evil smirk still pasted on his face.

My father takes my face in his hands. "The mountainside, the crash, the trees. How did you know?" he whispers.

How did I know what?

5. Wolf Girl

The next day, a bitter wind sweeps down from Mount Shasta, its peak shrouded in a dense white cloud. Icy cold fingers slither around alleyways and in through shop doors.

Father insists I go to school. "Staying away will not help the Sierra Nevada search-and-rescue team find your missing mother," he says. Tommy Foxglove says he'll help. My father and sister thank him. I don't.

I glance around, expecting Bully Harold Bully and his friends to leap out from an alleyway. Hopefully, my blind friend will be there to save me.

I pull my hoodie tighter over my head and push on toward school. As I walk down South Mount Shasta Boulevard, I see a young girl, walking down the middle of the street, accompanied by a huge grey wolf, white, from head to tail. A shaft of sunlight splits the falling snow and protects her and the wolf from the icy wind. I panic as the wolf's head turns and its cold white eyes stare at me.

What should I do? Rush to the police and tell them a wolf is loose, prowling down the middle of South Mount Shasta Boulevard? And what about the girl? Isn't she afraid of the wolf?

The girl's skin is dark brown, and a long, dark braid reaches down her back. A beaded headband circles her head. Her linen dress is brightly coloured, and on her feet, she wears moccasins. Not the clothing for icy wind and snow. The girl turns her head, looking at me. A smile. Her white teeth gleam against her dark skin. She holds up a large eagle feather, waving it in my direction. I look up and down the street before giving a quick wave back.

I hear a voice, "Aoo' yá'át'ééh. Howell."

How does wolf-girl know my name? And what language is she speaking?

"Look at stupid, stupid, Howl." It's Brenda Blackstone and her two friends. "The witch boy is waving at the cars as they drive by," Brenda sneers. Her friends laugh and imitate me waving. "Hello SUV, hello truck, hello his stupid uncle's crazy Volkswagen bus! Crazy! Bonkers! Just like your mother." Brenda continues.

Something's different. Brenda's thin face is always twisted into a snarl. Her thin lips, up on one end and down on the other, hide her crooked teeth. But today her form is dark, shaded over like I'm seeing her as a negative in a photograph. Same with her friends, the mean girls.

"Harold and his friends say they're going to give you such a beating today that you won't get out of the hospital for a year," Brenda yells at me.

They head off down South Mount Shasta Boulevard toward school, snorting and laughing as they look back at me chanting, "Whacko, witch boy!" Suddenly, without warning, all three girls stop and throw up, all over each other.

"You made us do that, witch boy," Brenda screams.

I look to the middle of the street. The girl and her wolf have stopped. The girl is facing Brenda and her friends, holding up her feather.

She turns back to me and waves.

"We meet again soon," she calls out.

Again!

And then she's gone. Disappeared.

Blind boy, deaf girl and now wolf-girl, I think to myself. *Did they come because I needed help? And why do they all say we'll meet again soon?*

I rush past Brenda and her friends as they shout curses at me, threatening to tell Bully Harold Bully what I did.

6. "I Stepped Through the What?"

"So Ralph, the central character of *The Lord of the Flies*," the teacher calls out, "has two choices: to stay with Piggy or join Jack's gang. What would you do?" Some hands go up. Not Bully Harold Bully or his gang. They don't read.

I rub my eyes. *What is the matter with them?* Bully Harold Bully and his friends are clouded over, just like Brenda Blackstone and her mean-girl friends. Through the mist, I see Bully Harold Bully snarling at me as he smacks his fist into his hand. He points to the clock. An hour before school ends. An hour before he and his two hangers-on attack.

If I call my blind saviour, will he come?

Suddenly, slicing through the teacher's ramblings comes the sound of dogs howling. I glance out at the schoolyard. No dogs.

Then, mixed in with their howling, I hear the voice of Uncle Tal, my mother's brother. His real name is Taliesin who was supposed to be some mystical Welsh poet and friend of King Arthur. When my mother told me that story, she ended, as she does most times, with a twinkle in her eyes and a question. "Do you think your uncle could be related? Or maybe he's the original Taliesin and hundreds of years old." My Uncle Tal is strange looking but doesn't look like someone who's lived for one thousand years.

I call my uncle Tal for short. And this is definitely his voice I am hearing. "Your mother crashed on a mountain road two hundred miles away," he whispers. "Her car rolled down the hillside. At the same time a pit opened in your bedroom and you fell in. It wasn't coincidence."

I whirl around. Classroom, playground, outside streets. No Uncle Tal.

Where is the voice coming from?

"You stepped through the Crossingway," his voice continues.

"I stepped through the what?" I blurt out.

The teacher and students turn and stare at me.

"Did you say something, Howell?"

My head drops and shakes back and forth. When I look up, Bully Harold Bully twirls his finger around his temple. "Crazy witch boy," he mouths.

"The Crossingway," Uncle Tal's voice continues. "The thin veil between here and there."

That makes no sense. I plug my fingers in my ears, trying to shut him out.

Then I see him, outside in the schoolyard, leaning against his purple Volkswagen van decorated with painted sunflowers, daffodils and mathematical symbols. He is dressed, as always, in his shining emerald green pants and purple shirt. A multi-coloured cloak, covered with strange symbols, dangles from his shoulders. He waves a large bright green silk handkerchief in my direction.

How did Uncle Tal and his crazy Volkswagen van get here? Mother told me before she left that Uncle Tal was back home in Wales, Great Britain, in that small town where he and his sister came from. That's six thousand miles away!

Even with my fingers stuck deep in my ears, I hear him. "They took her. She was focusing on the transfer instead of watching for them. Now they have her."

"Stop," I whisper.

"Speak up so the class can hear you, Howell," the teacher says.

I shake my head. No one will understand.

Through the mist I see Bully Harold Bully and his gang snickering, pulling faces. Twenty minutes and school is over.

I try to focus on the teacher, but Uncle Tal's voice returns.

"They'll test you," he murmurs. "Something tells them it's almost time for the transfer."

What is he babbling about?

"A test using Bully Harold Bully and his two friends."

My mouth drops open. *How does he know about them?*

"The shades are on them," he continues. "You see it."

Yes. The shades are on them. I see them.

Yes. The shades are on them. I see them.

Although I press my fingers deeper into my ears, I can still hear Uncle Tal's voice. He whispers something in my ear, it's one of those long Welsh words. A real tongue twister, all consonants and only one vowel. He repeats it a second time, a third. "Remember this word. Use it when they attack."

I don't need a useless word. I have my defender.

"You'll need more than the blind boy," Uncle Tal responds.

How does he know about the blind boy?

Bully Harold Bully points to the clock and smashes his fist into his palm.

Five minutes.

7. "Call Them Off"

"Say it, Hhoowwll! Say, 'My mother is a witch,' or I'll turn you upside down and bounce your head so hard on the ground, your stomach will pop out through your eye sockets!" Bully Harold Bully snarls, his eyes glowing and his words hissing through his teeth.

The three bullies circle me, punching me in the stomach and back. Something is different. Their forms are darker as though they are moving through blackened smoke. They crouch lower, their arms almost touching the floor. As they circle me, I hear a low whistling sound.

Uncle Tal's voice rattles around inside my head. I want to call out to tell him to leave me alone. To not get inside my head. But he's there, ordering me to say the word.

So I say the word.

Bully Harold Bully grabs my shoulder, pushes his knee into my spine and bends me over backwards as if I'm a pretzel. "Hit him hard, Pug. Right in the gut." Pug the Pyro walks back three steps and swings his arm around, winding up ready to rush at me and hit me so hard in the stomach that his fist will smash through my spine.

"Louder," Uncle Tal's voice shouts.

As Pug the Pyro rushes toward me, I shout out Uncle Tal's word.

I close my eyes, waiting for the blow.

Nothing.

I open my eyes. Pug the Pyro, Bully Harold Bully and Sloppy Jack are dancing around, yelling and slapping their hands front, back and to the sides.

"Call them off!" Pug the Pyro yells.

"Call what off?"

"Them," Bully Harold Bully cries, dropping his hold on me. "Them. The dogs."

"I don't see any dogs."

I check around, puffing out my chest. Did anyone see me take on Bully Harold Bully and his cronies? Did anyone see the way they ran from me, screaming and yelling? They won't dare cross me again. I'll be a superhero, leading a long line of kids scared of Bully Harold Bully and his gang to and from school. I picture Erin Powell, the cutest girl in my class, dancing up to me and grabbing my arm, the smell of her strawberry hair shampoo swirling around me. Howell, her champion, her bodyguard.

That image doesn't last long.

8. Y Lodes Wen A'r Y Ceffyl Gwyn

Uncle Tal's multi-coloured Volkswagen bus sits parked outside our home.

I open the door and walk into the living room. "Our weird Uncle Tal is here," Sister Sarah whispers. "All the way from Wales. He flew here on his fiery red dragon with his crazy van tied to the dragon's tail. When you grow up, you'll be crazy just like him, Howell."

I dodge around her and run upstairs to my bedroom. Safe inside, door locked, I sit on the bed and open my laptop. I'm ready to tell the world how I battled Bully Harold Bully and his gang—and won.

My Facebook page doesn't have time to appear before Uncle Tal sits at the foot of my bed. A locked door never stops him from entering or exiting when and where he wants.

Uncle Tal gazes at the painting above my bed. "*Y lodes wen a'r y ceffyl gwyn*," he says. Welsh. Uncle Tal and his sister, my mother, are from a small island off the coast of Wales. Anglesey in English, Ynys Mon or Mother Island in Welsh. My mother told me it was the last outpost of the Druids before the Romans slaughtered them.

I hear her voice and see the smile on her face after telling me this, "Maybe we're descendants of the druids, Howell."

"Maybe we are," Uncle Tal blurts out. Not even thoughts are secret from him.

"The white lady on the white horse," Uncle Tal translates pointing to the painting. "Do you know who she is, Howell?"

"She's Rhiannon Adar, Rhiannon of the Birds, Princess of Faery," I answer. "My mother said she was named after her." I continue, telling how the evil Gwawl tricks Pwyll into promising Rhiannon to him in marriage. How she, in turn, tricks Gwawl, marries Pwyll, and how Gwawl gets his revenge by stealing her baby.

Suddenly I stop. I picture my mother, sitting at the foot of my bed, telling story after story: Bran the Blessed, the magic cauldron that returns dead warriors to life.

My mouth twitches, my body shakes and the tears flood down my cheeks. It's not my mother at the foot of my bed. It's Uncle Tal. My mother's car crashed down the side of a mountain in the Sierra Nevadas. My mother is lost.

Uncle Tal holds me close. "You miss her, don't you?" I nod. The lump in my throat grows larger, almost stopping me from breathing. "We'll find her," Uncle

Tal assures me. A pause and then he says, "Tell me more how Rhiannon Adar met Pwyll, Prince of Dyfed."

I take a deep breath, fighting to push the lump lodged in my throat down into my stomach. *Why does Uncle Tal want me to tell him the story? He must know it already.* I stumble on. "Pwyll the Prince of Dyfed first saw Rhiannon Adar when she rode her white horse across the sacred Mound of Arbeth in South Wales. Pwyll had his hunting dogs with him that day." I pause. *Hunting dogs!*

Uncle Tal leans closer. "You heard them today, didn't you, Howell?" I nod. "They came when you called them. When you said the word."

Hunting dogs. Bully Harold Bully and his cronies screaming, 'Call them off.' It was me. I was the one who called them by using Uncle Tal's word.

Uncle Tal stares at me with his piercing green eyes. They slide around my brain seeking information. He smiles. He's found the answer to his question.

"The word worked," he states. "Your mother was right. It's time."

"Time for what?" I demand.

Instead of answering my questions, Uncle Tal fixes those piercing eyes on me again.

"There's something more you need to tell me."

I can't stop the thoughts from popping into my head. *The tall stranger dressed all in black with the glowing eye patch. The blind boy, the deaf girl, and wolf-girl. He'll think I'm crazy. Maybe I am. Maybe I just imagined it all.*

Too late.

"Tell me more about the tall stranger with the glowing eye patch," Uncle Tal insists.

It's no good. I can't hide anything from him.

I tell him about meeting him in the alley and how he reappeared on my computer.

Uncle Tal strokes his beard. "He knows it's time. He wants to see if it's you. He'll use those bullies."

I clench my fists and puff out my chest. "I'll be ready for them next time." Visions of my classmates cheering as I call up the invisible hounds to scare the three bullies in the schoolyard.

Uncle Tal shakes his head. "The word won't be enough. He'll protect them."

"Then give me another word."

But Uncle Tal isn't listening. He stands and paces the room.

"Your sister's new boyfriend. Your mother never met him, did she?"

I shake my head.

"He arrived in town a few weeks ago," Uncle Tal growls, "and made up some story about coming here for work. But none of you knows where he works. He watches you all the time. Won't enter your bedroom. Afraid of the painting above your bed. We won't be seeing this Tommy Foxglove," Uncle Tal continues. "Not while I'm here."

A pause as he ruffles my red hair.

"They won't give up," he adds.

"Who?"

Uncle Tal stares at me with those piercing, brain-scouring eyes.

"The sooner we leave here, the better," he continues. "I'll talk to your father. No more school. They've kidnapped your mother and now they're determined to capture you before it's time for the transfer. We must be in New Mexico before your birthday. That gives us one week to prepare you. Be ready to leave when I say."

So many questions bounce around my head: *my mother kidnapped, my birthday, the transfer, prepare for what?*

Before I can demand answers, Uncle Tal digs into his pocket and places something in my hand. "A gift for you. An early birthday present." And with that he disappears through the locked door.

In my hand sits a broken compass, its glass so smashed I can barely see the N E S W. "Another useless gift," I grumble. I toss it in the bottom drawer with the other "gifts" my weird uncle gave me in the past: a mangled credit card, a rusty ball bearing, and other junk.

I plop down on the bed, put my head between my hands and growl.

"Before you consider slipping out through your bedroom window in the morning to go to school," Uncle Tal says, from outside my bedroom door, "you might want to take a look outside."

I creep slowly to the window and draw back the blind. Outside in the street I see three dark-grey figures circling wildly, growling. Humans or animals? They look like the bullies—sometimes. But, as these figures dance and shriek in a circle, their body outlines change. Now they're roly-poly, now skeletal and drawn-out—their bodies shape and reshape themselves. First one thing then another. And always the hideous clown faces gazing up at me.

The faces of all three contort in a mixture of dread and terror as Uncle Tal exits the front door. As his arms extend outward and upward, his form grows, shaping and reshaping into a huge red dragon hovering above the three. A boom as it breathes out a fireball, which roars down from the sky toward the three forms. They scuttle off, squealing on all fours like animals, pursued by fireballs.

I stare open mouthed as the red dragon shrinks and reshapes itself into the figure of my Uncle Tal, standing at the front door.

Did I just see what I saw? Uncle Tal becoming the Red Dragon? Y Draig Goch? The one on the Welsh flag?

Uncle Tal looks up at me and smiles before re-entering the house.

What is happening? Bullies shaping and reshaping themselves, half-human, half-animal. Talk of a transfer and New Mexico. And now my uncle becoming a fire-breathing red dragon.

If only my mother were here. She'd have answers.

9. No Birthday Party, No Water Slides, No Howell

A sudden glare from my overhead bedroom light wakes me.

Uncle Tal rips off my dinosaur comforter. The cold air swirls around my body. I roll into a ball, trying to stay warm. "Get up, Howell. We don't have much time," Uncle Tal snaps. "Get your things together? We must leave now."

I crawl out of bed. "You're my uncle, not my father. What about…?"

"That birthday party you were promised? If you stay, you'll never see another birthday. No party, no water slides, no Howell. And you'll never see your mother again." And with that he's gone.

I dress quickly and rush downstairs determined to find out what my father thinks. He sits with his head in his hands talking to Uncle Tal. "The police say they found the car, but not her. They think she walked into the forest. They have search and rescue patrols looking for her. They'll find her soon."

Uncle Tal puts his arm around my father's shoulder. "Did the *Safonals* find footprints in the forest? No."

Safonals? Another word to look up in Wikipedia.

"I'm sorry, Stuart," Uncle Tal continues. "Police, search and rescue—they don't know how or where to look."

"And you do?" my father responds.

"She's not in the forest. They've taken her."

My father gives a deep groan. Uncle Tal takes my father's hands and looks deep into his eyes. "You knew our family was different, Stuart, when you married my sister. Powers passed down through the generations. Think, Stuart. She's driven that road many times. She knows every twist and turn. But this time they caught her. Now they want Howell, to prevent the transfer. I must take him tonight."

"How do you know it's Howell and not Sister Sarah?"

"It's that boy, Tommy Foxglove. Sister Sarah didn't react to him. Howell did, and he to Howell," Uncle Tal replies.

"My wife is missing, Tal, and now you want to take my son. Can't we wait a day or two for the police and search and rescue to l find her."

Uncle Tal pulls me to him. "The boy has already seen things. Remember the man in the black leather coat? The one you saw in the mountains of Wales? Your son has seen him. And many other things. They know where and what he is."

"And what am I?" I ask.

"Your mother brought you to this place to protect you—until now. On your birthday, you are destined to receive some of your mother's Doeth power," Uncle Tal answers. "That is the transfer. The Drygoni will do everything they can to prevent that happening. They want that power to be transferred to one of their own. To make it theirs and upset the balance."

"Balance," I blurt out. "That was the word my mother used when we sat together on Mount Shasta."

"Peaceful Meadow," Uncle Tal adds. "Dôl Heddwch."

That's what my mother called it. Her special place.

"And what if this balance is upset?" my father interrupts.

"Night with no day," Uncle Tal continues. "Sickness with no health; anger with no joy; hate and revenge with no love or forgiveness. Without *Doeths, Safonals* lose choice. No balance."

Doeths, Safonals, balance? What does it all mean?

Before I can ask, the house shakes with a thunderous overhead explosion. "We've talked long enough," Uncle Tal continues. "For the transfer to occur, you must be at the right place at the right time. If not, you and your mother are in real danger."

My father pulls me to him and strokes my curly red hair.

"You look so much like her," he whispers. He holds me tight. His tears dampen my hair. "You're sure of this, Tal?"

Again, a blazing lightening flashlights the street, and the thunder roars, shaking the whole house.

Uncle Tal holds my head and stares into my eyes. "Time to go, Howell. Now!"

Suddenly the telephone rings. My father picks it up. "Hello. Who's there? Answer me! I'm calling the police." He drops the phone and covers his ears as a loud low hollow whistling echoes around the room. Uncle Tal grabs the phone and slams it on the receiver stopping the noise.

"They're coming. Help the boy pack," my Uncle Tal barks. "I'll be waiting outside."

Another flash of lightening and boom of thunder.

I follow my father up the stairs. "Get dressed and throw on your heavy jacket, Howell." My father stuffs my Sudoku for Kids book and clothes into my backpack. I give him my laptop. He shakes his head, "they can trace your laptop. Leave it."

No point complaining. Dad isn't listening, and that low hollow whistling sound continues to ring in my ears. My father is in the bathroom rifling through the toothbrushes and toothpaste. "Yours is the red one, right Howell?" Shirts, socks, and underwear—all are crammed inside my backpack. Finished, he rushes down the stairs, dragging me after him.

Outside Uncle Tal stares up at the black and red clouds tumbling across the night sky.

My father hugs me. "What about my birthday party at the Redding Water Park?" I ask.

"If you still want it, we'll have it when you return, Howell. I promise."

"We must leave," Uncle Tal calls out.

My father pushes me into the Volkswagen van just as the heavy raindrops explode on the van. He throws my overstuffed backpack onto my lap.

"Seatbelt," Uncle Tal commands.

My father pokes his head in through the side window. "Listen to your Uncle Tal at all times. And don't phone home." He chokes back a sob as he takes my face in his hands. "I love you, Howell. Bring your mother back!"

My father's plaid shirt, beige Dockers pants and brown slip-ons are soaking wet from the pounding rainstorm. He rushes back into the house.

Lightning flashes, thunder cracks and rain beats down on us. The mountain is lost in thick, dark clouds.

Uncle Tal walks around the Volkswagen van three times in a clockwise direction, muttering something, before leaping into the driver's seat.

"Get some sleep, boy. We have a long journey ahead. We're leaving just in time."

"Where are we…?"

My question is cut short as a series of lightening streaks flash across the sky, lighting up the whole street and splitting a nearby tree. A boom of thunder follows, rocking the van.

The last thing I remember is Uncle Tal's long fingers curling in a circle before my face.

And I fall asleep.

10. Stranger Than Strange

"I don't like the look of this."

Uncle Tal's long fingers dig into my shoulder, shaking me awake. "What do you think, Howell?" My eyelids open a fraction. Uncle Tal is crouched over the steering wheel of the van staring at the road ahead. "Very strange," he mumbles.

You call this strange? I think to myself, still half-asleep. *Getting thrown around my bedroom at the exact moment my mother disappears in a car accident two hundred miles away. That's strange. All this talk of saving my mother and transfer. Seeing bullies change shape before my eyes. Meeting three strangers who all say, 'We'll meet again.' Getting dragged out in the middle of the night so I'll be 'protected' from things called Drygoni—whatever they are. All of those are really strange. So what is it this time?*

My body lurches forward, jams against the seatbelt then collapses back. My head thumps against the headrest as the van screeches to a halt.

Uncle Tal's fingers tap my shoulder. "What do you see, nephew?"

Red lights flash on both sides of the road. Signs. Slow. Single lane traffic. Absolutely no passing. Signs. Too many signs.

"Roadwork in the middle of the night," I croak, still half-asleep. I peer into the darkness ahead. "I don't see any workers."

Uncle Tal nods. "Exactly. Why does the traffic stop when there are no workers?"

Uncle Tal's van edges forward, stopping a car's length from the pickup in front of us. I hear the growl and hiss of an eighteen-wheeler pulling up close behind. Too close behind.

Uncle Tal holds up his finger. "Do you see any drivers in the cars and trucks ahead and behind us?"

The full moon slices through the towering Douglas firs and lights the roadway. No drivers. Just a line of cars, pickups and trucks. The thick, choking exhaust fumes from the pickup in front slides into Tal's van and slithers into my nose and throat. I roll down the window, but the stench of hot tar at the side of the road sickens me. I roll the window, but the stench of hot tar at the side of the road sickens me. I roll the window back up quickly as I lean forward, hacking and coughing.

"The pickup truck in front of us is moving backward," Uncle Tal mumbles. "It's going to jam us in."

"He can't do that. I'll get out an…"

Before I can finish my sentence, Uncle Tal rams his foot on the accelerator.

"Hang on!"

The van lurches to the left, barely missing the rear bumper of the pickup. On we rush, past driverless cars, pickups and trucks. Uncle Tal crouches over the steering wheel, his nose inches from the windshield, his eyes wide open, and his lips moving wildly as he mutters strange words to himself.

I stare ahead and behind, waiting for the Highway Patrol to give chase, lights blazing. *Double fines in construction zones.*

What I see sends chills through my body, making my body and arms shake. About twenty yards behind us, lined, up side-by-side, the ever-changing shapes of Bully Harold Bully, Sloppy Jack and Pug the Pyro skim along not touching the road.

I thrash around, choking. There isn't enough oxygen. Uncle Tal grabs my wrist. "What you see is not real. They're morphs. That's how the *Drygoni* attack."

That word Drygoni again.

Uncle Tal's van roars down the strip of road. Both of my hands press against the dashboard; my knuckles are white. I glance at the speedometer. Ninety miles an hour! The van shakes, threatening to rip apart.

On we rush. To our right, parked alongside the forest, huge bulldozers prevent us from veering off into the forest. Thick steaming tar bubbles slithers into our lane. The sticky slap-slap of the tires grows louder as the tar grabs at them.

"What happens if we're forced to stop?" I yell.

"You don't want to know."

No, I don't.

I look across at Uncle Tal. *How did he know we would be trapped?*

With a final burst of speed, we roar past a red stoplight, free from the bubbling tar that now covers the roadway. The Volkswagen van jerks back as Uncle Tal takes his foot off the accelerator.

"We're safe—for now. You can relax, Howell!"

Relax? Not knowing if the morphs of Bully Harold Bully and his friends are still slithering along behind us, ready to crash through the back of the van and grab me. Relax, when all I want is to be home in bed, instead of sitting in a Volkswagen van listening to my Uncle Tal humming a melody? A sleepy melody. A very sleepy melody.

11. The Veiled Lady

In my dream, I am inside the painting above my bed, scrambling up the side of the sacred Mound of Arbeth in Wales. From above, on the flat field at the top of the Mound, I hear hoof beats. I drag myself up, grabbing and ripping at grass and bushes.

She's there: the lady dressed white, face veiled, riding the pure white stallion.

I wait for the white veil covering her face to blow back so I can see her. Is it Rhiannon, my mother? She gallops past. I leap to my feet, pursuing horse and rider. The hoof beats keep the same rhythm, but I get no closer. I run faster, but the distance between us stays the same.

This is exactly what happened to Pwyll in the Welsh story my mother read to me. No matter how fast his horse ran, he could not catch up with the lady in white.

I trip over a rock and fall. The veiled lady stops and turns. Slowly the veil lowers. But the face is not my mother's, not that of Rhiannon. It is Sister Sarah. Her eyes are wide open, sad and terrified. Her face sickly and pale—not the sister I left at home.

Then I hear that same low hollow whistling I heard before. It's growing louder. I jam my hands over my ears, trying in vain to block out the noise. A sudden rush of air and shadowy, hunchbacked figures hurtle past, knocking me to the ground. They chase the horse and rider who gallop away. As they move, the figures change shape. Now fat, roly-poly figures waddling on short chubby legs. Now skinny, striding forward on long skeletal legs. Now animal figures racing along on all fours. The gathering mist soon swallows up horse and rider. The figures stop at the edge of the mist, raise themselves up, open what must be mouths and release a deafening shriek. Then they turn slowly to face me, their eyes glowing red. They slither slowly forward toward me.

My mouth is open, but no sound comes out. A scream locks itself in my throat. I want to breathe but can't. A hand grips my shoulder and shakes awake. I gulp in the cold night air.

"Breathe, Howell, breathe!" Uncle Tal shouts. "Tell me about your dream."

"I chased the woman on the white horse across the hill of Arbeth. Although I ran faster, I could not catch her."

"Pwyll, Prince of Dyfed in South Wales, chases the Fairy Queen Rhiannon," Uncle Tal interrupts.

"But it was not her," I reply. "When the veil blew back from her face, it was Sister Sarah."

"Your sister?" Uncle Tal queries. "Are you positive?"

"Yes."

"So that's their plan," Uncle Tal groans. "Their task is set. We must be ready. Soon you'll meet the others. You'll need their help."

I want to ask about the others, but a huge ball of dry sand is lodged in my throat. I cannot speak.

12. A Tree Talks to Me

Although the heater in the Volkswagen blasts away, cold air slides through the cracks in the door, under my blanket and up my trouser legs. My forehead slumps against the icy side window, and my eyelids flutter. I don't want to sleep, don't want to return to that dream again.

Roadside trees flash by in the half-light. I jerk upright and stare into the darkness. Something is out there. I rub my eyes and stare again. In the trees, Bully Harold Bully, Sloppy Jack and Pug the Pyro, horrible grins pasted on their faces, leap from tree to tree like white-faced monkeys. I jam my fingers in my ears as they screech, "Howl, Howl, Howl!"

I taste the blood in my mouth as Bully Harold Bully's fist punches me again and again. "Your mad uncle thinks you're ready," he laughs. "You're not ready, Howl. Not ready for the task."

I shut my eyes tight and jam my fingers in my ears to keep out the howls of laughter. I want to be home in my bed, to hear my mother singing a Welsh lullaby:

Holl amrantau'r sêr ddywedant,
Ar hyd y nos.
Sleep my child and peace attend thee,
All through the night.

The low hollow whistling attempts to rip through the lullaby. I open my mouth and sing louder.

Uncle Tal pats me on the head. "That's the way, Howell. Trust yourself to defy them. Others will help, but, in the end, it's up to you." He hums along with my singing of the lullaby.

Suddenly the seatbelt digs into my stomach as the Volkswagen fishtails, jerking to a sudden stop. Uncle Tal leaps out and walks down the road.

What now? Why leave the safety of the van? Why walk out where Bully Harold Bully and his gang wait?

Outside the full moon lights the trees lining the sides of the road. Warning signs alert motorists of an upcoming dangerous curve. The barrier protecting motorists from the sheer right-hand drop is buckled. Suddenly my arms and legs shake uncontrollably. I pant, sucking in freezing air. This is the place where she crashed. Where my mother missed the curve and hurled down the mountainside.

Uncle Tal calls me to him. I leave the van and walk, checking around nervously for the bullies, to where Uncle Tal leans against a tree. "Why did she take this road?" I call out. "Why not Interstate 5? It's much faster. Why here?"

Uncle Tal puts his arm around my shoulder and squeezes me gently. "She always chooses this route, thinking they won't find her. But this time they did. Now we need to know what happened." He guides me to a tall pine tree at the side of the road. "Put your forehead against the tree, nephew."

I lean my head against the tree's rough bark. It digs into my forehead. Overhead the pine needles and leaves rustle as Uncle Tal begins chanting in a strange language.

The pain in my forehead slowly disappears and images, at first blurry and out of focus, appear. Then I see it clearly: mother's car moving slowly, cautiously, toward the curve.

I am sitting in the back seat of her car, watching as my mother brakes, preparing for the dangerous curve ahead. Twenty miles an hour and dropping. Suddenly the car lurches forward. Something rams it from behind. I turn, expecting to see a truck smashing into the back of her car. But I see nothing. My mother panics as the car races forward. She slams her foot on the brake and rips down through the gears. The gears grind as the speedometer leaps up to sixty then seventy miles per hour. My mother pulls at the handbrake, trying to steer the car to the side of road. But the steering wheel locks in place. Nothing can stop her headlong rush toward the barrier.

The car spins out of control as it crashes into the barrier and plunges headlong into the canyon below. I grab the front seat. My heart thuds and I pant in terror as we dive deeper and deeper into a black pit. I shout for help, but no noise escapes my mouth.

The car rips through the brush before coming to a crunching stop, the hood buckled around a large tree. The driver's door is flung open. I see a black leather coat tied at the middle with thick string. An arm with long skeletal fingers reaches inside, clutches my mother and drags her from the car. Before leaving, the figure leans down. The face is hard to distinguish beneath the darkened hood, but I see one blood red eye, the other covered with a dark patch with a centre point that glows yellow. The form utters a deep, guttural laugh before it drags the limp body of my mother up the hill.

My forehead aches where it presses against the tree's rough bark. Tears stream down my face and my body shakes violently.

"That's what I saw in my bedroom," I wail. "It wasn't her fault. Something pushed her over the edge. And then he was there, his face hidden but his two eyes, one red, one yellow. He dragged her from the car."

Uncle Tal wraps his cloak around me. "He's still out there—looking! Trying to determine if it is you."

"Why didn't whatever-it-was push us over the cliff too?"

"Because it's not time—yet," Uncle Tal replies, leading me back to the van.

I crawl to the van, climb inside and slam the door. Again Uncle Tal walks three times, clockwise, around the van, muttering some strange words before climbing into the driver's seat.

I pull my coat around myself. The something that grabbed my mother is out there waiting.

And it's looking for me!

13. Here Is Always Here, Even When It's There

"Wake up, Howell."

My eyelids open a fraction—and shut instantly, pierced by the glare of the early morning sun.

"Time for breakfast," Uncle Tal continues, ruffling my hair as he unbuckles my seatbelt.

The dusty smell of farmland replaces the scent of fir and pine trees. We've dropped down from the tree-lined mountains of the Sierra Nevadas into California's Central Valley, which is, at this moment, a strip of road running between fields of tall sunflowers.

The van is stopped outside a tiny, roadside trailer, about ten feet long and four feet wide. Most of the creamy-yellow paint has peeled off the trailer, revealing patches of aluminium. The tires are flat, and one end of the trailer is much higher than the other. Towering sunflowers surround the trailer on three sides.

"Are you serious?" I blurt out. "Breakfast here? In this place? Why not iHop or Denney's?"

Uncle Tal stands before the trailer doing his morning exercise: some Tai Chi forms mixed with stretching his arms up in front of him then squatting down on his heels. As he repeats these, he closes his eyes and turns to the sun, his lips uttering some silent words.

I stare at the words written on the sign dangling by one hook from a post. A jumble of letters, some right side up, some upside-down, that don't make sense.

Uncle Tal taps me on the shoulder and points to the three broken wooden steps that lead to the door of the trailer.

I follow Uncle Tal, stumbling up the creaking stairs and poke my head inside the dilapidated trailer. A quick glance and I immediately lurch back outside again. The inside is huge.

I pace the length of the trailer. Ten paces long and four wide. An oblong. And one end is definitely much higher than the other.

I'm about to push my way into the sunflowers to pace the back of the trailer when they lean down toward me. What's happening? Sunflowers always face the sun. But where is the sun? It has disappeared behind the one black cloud in an otherwise blue sky. A cold wind shivers up my trouser legs and whirls around my body.

I hear Sloppy Jack's high-pitched whine: *"Eat here? A filthy trailer?"*

"You must tell all your friends about this place when you come home, Howl—if you come home. If your crazy uncle doesn't lose you," Bully Harold Bully adds.

Shrieks of laughter.

I spin around, expecting to see the three bullies. Nothing. Just sunflowers—everywhere. And the freezing cold. Again that low hollow whistle. My nose twitches at the sickly smell of melting tar.

Something shifts in the sunflowers. I glimpse the shadowy, hunchbacked figures from my dream. I panic. Suddenly sunflowers, blocked on all sides, surround me. They lean down, trapping me inside them, cutting off the light and air.

I scream for help. Where is the entrance? The exit?

A blur of white as a large grey wolf, white from head to tail, crashes through the sunflowers and circles me, snarling and snapping at the plants. I run down the path the wolf has made in the sunflowers. The trailer is before me. I dash to the front door and glance inside.

The restaurant is ten—no fifty times—the size it is on the outside. The floor is completely flat, not raised at one end. There are booths around the windows (windows *not* on the outside), a long counter, and a cooking area (complete with huge exhaust fans to carry away the smoke) that stretches to the back of the trailer.

I shut the door of the trailer and think. I have a choice: stay outside with the grey wolf, the howls and squeals, and figures slithering among the claustrophobic sunflowers, or continue inside where the walls of this huge trailer may collapse and crush me.

An older dark-skinned woman, wearing a loose-fitting yellow blouse and ankle-length brown skirt covered with flowers, lines and multi-coloured symbols, walks toward me. A long white braid of hair stretches down to her waist. She wears necklaces of turquoise and silver, and bracelets of the same material nearly cover her arms from wrists to elbows. *Did she see the wolf?* I ask myself.

The woman smiles, "Don't stay out here. Danger." She grabs my hand and pulls me with her inside the trailer.

Uncle Tal sits at a booth. He waves, inviting me to sit with him. The woman releases me and heads to the kitchen.

I want to ask so many questions: sunflowers, darkened figures, a large wolf, but nothing escapes my mouth. After a few minutes staring at Uncle Tal, a question blurts out of my mouth, "Is this place one of those crossing things?"

"Crossingway? Could be. We're here to eat breakfast." He looks deep into my eyes and smiles. "You'll get used to it, nephew. Here is always here, even when it's there."

That doesn't make sense!

Uncle Tal waves to the dark-skinned woman who pulled me into the trailer. Her dark brown eyes twinkle with a smile as she waves to us from the kitchen.

My mouth waters at the smell of bacon, toast and eggs. I rub my hand across my lips to make sure I'm not drooling. Suddenly I have this terrible thought: *What if everything in this place expands like the trailer? I pop an egg in my mouth and suddenly it's the size of a turkey. My cheeks expand like a chipmunks and I can't shut my mouth! And then my throat and stomach expand like a helium-filled balloon!*

"Where are the menus?"

"No need. The cook knows what you want."

The woman with the long, twisting white braid places a steaming cup of black tea with milk in front of Uncle Tal, and for me a hot chocolate with whipped cream floating on the top. Exactly what I want.

A strong smell of sage floats in the air as the older woman places the cups on the table. It swirls inside my nose, clearing out the sticky stench from outside in the sunflowers. The woman watches as Uncle Tal draws some mathematical signs on a napkin. He passes it to her. She stares at me, catches hold of my head and kisses me on both cheeks before returning to the stove.

I place my hands around the steaming cup of hot chocolate and sip it slowly.

"Looks like we're going to get some company, Howell." A young girl talks to the older woman who pulled me inside.

My mouth drops open. It's her. The girl I saw walking down South Mount Shasta Boulevard surrounded by sunlight in the bitter cold. Wolf-girl. We meet again. Just like she said we would.

"What language are they speaking?" I stammer.

"They're Navajo. Diné bizaad. Both from New Mexico. The young girl is headed over here. You two will become very good friends. You'll need each other as you face what's to come."

What is to come?

14. My Greatest Enemy—Myself

The girl skips across the room, smiling. She holds out her arms to hug me. "Yá'át'ééh, Howell. Hello."

My head drops. I blush, red. Bright red. *Doesn't she recognise me?*

The girl laughs and turns to my uncle. "So, you're the famous Taliesin. My mother told me so much about you. *Aoo'*. Welcome. *Yinishyé*, Dani Walks-Her-Pony."

"*Aoo'*, Dani Walks-Her-Pony," Uncle Tal replies. "The young boy staring at the floor with the beet-red face is my nephew, Howell."

"Welcome, Howell!" I glance up. It's definitely her: Wolf girl.

A long, dark braid flows down the girl's back. As she smiles, I remember seeing the white teeth that gleamed against her brown skin. Like the other woman, the girl wears a turquoise, loose-fitting blouse. Her ankle-length skirt is covered with flowers, lines and multi-coloured symbols.

She thrusts out her hand to me. "We meet again, Howell."

Uncle Tal taps me on the shoulder. "Close your mouth, Howell! Shake hands! Be polite!" I put out my hand. The young girl grasps it in both of her hands and jiggles it up and down. My arm flops like a dying fish.

Instantly my head drops, staring at the linoleum floor, pretending to trace patterns with my fingers. Trying to hide my bright red face, neck and ears. The young girl grasps my drooped head and moves it gently upward. I gaze into her beautiful, large dark brown eyes. "Your eyes are soft and beautiful, just like a deer," I blurt out.

"I have hooves like a deer too," she replies. "My people, the Diné, call me Deer Woman. I trample men to death."

She laughs aloud as I jerk back and look at her moccasin feet. "They are quite ordinary feet, thank you," she assures me. Down goes my head for the third time.

"You'll get along famously with her," Uncle Tal whispers, as the young girl dances back to the counter. "Pity you didn't get a good long look at her, Howell. She's very pretty."

True. Even with one or two quick glances, I can tell she's much prettier than Erin Powell, the girl in our school all the boys like. I turn slowly toward the kitchen. The young girl waves to me. The corners of my mouth twitch upward, forcing an uncomfortable smile. The floppy fish at the end of my arm jerks a wave up and down.

"When I was outside, I saw a..."

"A large grey wolf." Uncle Tal smiles and ruffles my hair. "You wandered off on your own. You needed protection." Before I could ask my question, Uncle Tal blurts out, "Our food is coming."

Dani crosses to us, plates in her hands. I didn't order anything.

Bacon, eggs, hash browns and sausages cover Uncle Tal's plate. Waffles, drenched in syrup and three sausages on the side, fill mine. Exactly what I want. My mouth drools. I poke at the sausages, wondering if they'll grow in size.

Dani returns to the kitchen, and the older woman joins us, sitting beside Uncle Tal. "I'm Dani Walks-Her-Pony's mother, Esther Evening Star. I know your mother, Rhiannon, Howell. A special woman and very proud of you. You have a sister, right?"

"Sarah," I mumble.

Esther Evening Star turns to Uncle Tal. "You're positive it's him and not the sister?"

"He's been tested," he mumbles through his food. Both stare at me before Esther Evening Star places her hand on my head and mumbles some strange words before returning to the kitchen.

"Eat up," Uncle Tal mutters. "The van is rested. She's ready to press on to the State of New Mexico."

"The Land of Enchantment," I murmur, reciting something I'd learned in a geography class.

Uncle Tal quickly finishes his food, leaps to his feet and heads for the door.

I gobble down the scraps of food left on my plate. As I stand, Dani Walks-Her-Pony runs across the room, throws her arms around me, and gives me a hug. She kisses me on both cheeks and slips two Hershey chocolate bars with almonds, my favourite, into my shirt pocket.

"Shouldn't we pay for the meal?" I whisper to Uncle Tal as we exit the trailer.

"It's bartering, Howell? They do something for us; we do something for them."

"What can I do for them?"

Uncle Tal looks around before adding, "Let's not discuss such things out here, Howell. Someone might be listening."

My head jerks around. *Do those sunflowers have ears?*

Suddenly the three bullies are back, snarling in my ears. *"What will you do in New Mexico, Howl? Fight dragons? Swim fiery moats? Rescue a fairy princess? Battle creepy things that crawl around in sunflower fields?"* Shrieks of laughter.

As I head for the van, Dani Walks-Her-Pony races out of the tiny trailer. She hugs me and kisses me on both cheeks—again. "Ahe'ee!" she says as she hangs a turquoise and silver necklace around my neck.

"Be careful, Howl," the voices cackle. *"Remember: deer woman is very beautiful. While you stare into those beautiful eyes, she'll trample you to death with her sharp hooves."*

I can't stop myself. I glance down at Dani's feet—again. Totally normal human feet.

Dani stares into my eyes, her face inches from mine. "My people say, 'O Great Spirit, help me to overcome my greatest enemy—myself. The enemy out there is dangerous." Then she taps my forehead. "But the voices in your head are just as dangerous."

With that she turns and runs back to the trailer.

Before entering the trailer, Dani calls out, "Bye, Howell. Remember: the lady on the white horse waits for you—when and if you're ready. See you soon."

My head spins. *The lady on the white horse? She knows about the painting?*

15. A Change in Direction

I look to Uncle Tal, but he is already standing beside the van wiping the mud-caked windscreen with his large bright green silk handkerchief. Before I can ask how Dani knows about the lady on the white horse, Uncle Tal waves to a short thin man emerging from the trailer.

Where did he come from? I didn't see him inside the trailer.

The man's dirty white shirt and baggy pants, both of which are much too large, droop over his body. He wears sandals on his feet, no socks, and a rounded grey hat that looks like a pot on top of his head. A young boy, about my age, shorter than the man but similarly dressed, clings to the man's arm. He holds a white cane in his right hand.

My mouth drops open as I stare at him. It's him: the blind boy who protected me from Bully Harold Bully and his cronies in the schoolyard.

"Where did those two come from?" I ask Uncle Tal. "I didn't see them in the trailer."

"They were working in the fields, picking strawberries, about fifty miles back," he replies.

"How did they get here? I don't see a car."

Uncle Tal points to two donkeys quietly standing in the shade at the side of the road.

"They rode their donkeys fifty miles in the time we had to eat breakfast?" I blurt out.

"Yes. Both were working in the fields," Uncle Tal repeats, smiling at me. "Those are the same donkeys," he continues, "they rode from Oaxaca in southern Mexico. They are both members of the indigenous Mixtec people, which dates back to 1500 BC. The image on their T-shirts are that of the eleventh century Mixtec king and warlord Eight Deer Jaguar."

I hear the three bullies laughing. *"Are you listening to him, Howell? He's a joke! And don't forget he's related to you! Crazy runs in the family!"*

"And I supposed you're going to tell me that they rode those same donkeys all the way from Mexico," I cry out.

"As a matter of fact they did," Uncle Tal responds. "Up through Mexico, crossing the deserts of New Mexico and Arizona, along the Devil's Highway, and on to California, where we saw them working in the vineyards."

I couldn't stop myself from bursting out laughing. "And all that—hundreds of miles through the scorching heat of the desert—on two donkeys? That's impossible!"

Uncle Tal ruffles my hair and smiles. "It is if you think that was there and then. Not if you think this is here and now."

"That doesn't make sense," I reply defiantly.

"Unless…" Uncle Tal responds with a smile. He gently taps my head with his finger. "Remember: The Crossingway."

The man and young boy stop in front of our van. The boy places his hands on the hood.

"Now what is he doing?"

"Telling us something."

Finished, the boy walks around the van three times. He whispers in the older man's ear. The older man faces the van and makes signals with his arms.

"It's called semaphore. It was once used in the navy, signalling from ship to ship, before cell phones. His arms and body make shapes. Each shape is a letter. No words in case someone or something is listening."

I watch the young boy whispering to the old man who then makes gestures with his arms. Uncle Tal watches intently, spelling out letters and words silently.

"What's he saying?" I ask.

"If I tell you, they'll know," Uncle Tal replies.

I look at the sunflowers surrounding the dilapidated trailer. *Are they listening?*

Uncle Tal leans across and whispers in my ear. "A change in directions." He finishes and puts his index finger to his lips. No speaking.

I stare ahead at the long strip of asphalt dividing the fields, a dark line stretching to the horizon, shimmering in the heat of the sun.

A change in direction? There's only one road! I think to myself.

Before we drive off, I look back to the trailer. A lone grey wolf prowls back and forth, watching, protecting.

16. Something Beginning with 'C'

Uncle Tal leans over the steering wheel, eyes fixed on the road ahead as the van chugs forward. We've gone about ten miles when he suddenly turns to me. "They're tracking our every move," he grunts. "Time to confuse them." Without warning, he jerks the steering wheel to the left, crossing the road in front of an oncoming eighteen-wheeler, horns blaring. We fly over the drainage ditch at the side of the road and bump up and down along a dirt path. Dust swallows the van.

"How can you see where you're going?" I shout.

"I don't need to see. The young boy gave the van directions. It's following them."

A van following directions?

I wait for the van to crash into a building or drop headfirst into an irrigation ditch. The dust is so thick I can't see the path (if there is a path) or crops (if there are crops). Dust in my eyes, my mouth, up my nose, and lodged in my ears.

We bump up and down for about half an hour before Uncle Tal slows down. The dust settles. We are rolling along an asphalt highway passing a large tractor.

I look back at a huge vineyard with grapevines strung up on taut wires between large poles sticking out of the ground. *How did we pass through the wires without slicing the van and us in two?* I wonder. *And there are also deep channels for water irrigation. Did we leap those?*

Uncle Tal chuckles. "Acceptance is an important step along the road of life."

"Write that down, Howl," Bully Harold Bully snickers. *"Acceptance blah, blah, blah. Be honest. This trip is a long ride to nowhere. A journey to Crazyville. Leave, Howl, while you're still sane, and not crazy like your uncle."*

"Shut up!" I yell to the voice.

"Keep fighting, nephew. They'll give up soon," Uncle Tal grunts.

Good.

"But others, far more dangerous, will take their place."

Not good. Terrifying.

We race down the narrow strip of road, lined on both sides with acres of grapes, then acres of strawberries, then acres of corn. Groups of farm workers flash by, some bent over in the sweltering sun, some standing next to a fruit and vegetable stand at the side of the road. Seeing them breaks the monotony.

"Let's play a game," Uncle Tal says. "I spy with my little eye, something beginning with C."

"Corn," I blurt out. "Corn, corn, and more corn."

"No. Not corn. Give up? Church. That begins with C."

"I know church begins with C," I groan.

Uncle Tal glances at me before stretching out a long, skinny index finger, pointing.

At the side of the road, standing amongst flattened cornstalks, stands a gleaming white church. The building itself looks like a long flat box, barely tall enough for someone to enter, but the steeple rises up and up, towering over the cornstalks. Three people stand on the steps outside, poised for a wedding photograph. But there's no photographer.

The three stare at us.

"How did they get there?" Uncle Tal asks. "Two men and one woman," he continues. "Bride, groom, minister. Anyone you recognise?"

"Your uncle is playing games with you, Howl," the voices giggle. *"A church in the middle of nowhere and you're supposed to know these people."*

"Pay close attention," Uncle Tal continues. "You will meet those people again."

"When?"

"You'll know."

What sort of answer is that? Someone I know but don't know and will meet again, but I don't know when.

I let out a sigh of exasperation before digging inside my backpack and pulling out my Sudoku for Kids book. My pencil is poised, ready to write down a number, when Uncle Tal slams on the brakes. My pencil slides off the page onto the floor.

"Now what?" I shriek.

"We're there, Howell," Uncle Tal replies. "Excited?"

17. A Headful of Useless Information

My mouth drops open I stare out of the van. We're in the middle of the desert! I look back. Two seconds ago we were in California's Central Valley, staring at a church surrounded by cornfields. Now it's baked, cracked earth broken up with cacti, sagebrush and tumbleweeds surrounding us as far as the distant mountains.

"Are we already out of California? What about Arizona? We travel through Arizona to get to New Mexico."

"You missed it," Uncle Tal answers.

Missed Arizona? It's a huge state! And I missed it while searching my backpack for a pencil and my Sudoku for Kids book?

I check my watch. Impossible. *We left our home around eight o'clock last night. Now it's noon the following day. Sixteen hours. No way.*

I once checked the distance on Google maps. One thousand five hundred miles straight down California Interstate 5, crossing to Interstate 40 and east through Arizona. Nineteen hours non-stop in a brand-new Ferrari with no cars, trucks, Highway Patrol or Tule fog to slow you down. And no need to stop for gas! Yet here we are. Sixteen hours on back roads, never the freeway, with Uncle Tal's Volkswagen van, sputtering and coughing up the smallest of hills. Plus stopping for breakfast.

Without warning, Uncle Tal throws the steering wheel to the right. We bump off the strip of road onto a dirt path, throwing up clouds of dust that hide the outside. Five minutes of this and Uncle Tal jams on the brakes, jerking me forward. He leaps out of the van and does his Tai Chi, arm-stretching and leg-squatting once more. Finished, he holds up his arms to the distant mountain and utters some words in Welsh before turning to me. "A wonderful morning! Hurry, Howell. Get your backpack. We don't want to miss the school bus."

"School bus? Here? Your Uncle Tal's playing mind-games with you, Howl," the voices call out. "*Soon you'll be as loony as him."*

I swallow hard, growling deep inside remembering my father's words: "Listen to everything your Uncle Tal tells you." *When he said this, did my father know I'd be standing in the middle of a baking hot desert, backpack in hand, surrounded by tumbleweed and waiting for a school bus?*

Immediately I hear the babble of Bully Harold Bully and his gang:

"Did you hear about that fool, Howl?"

"Highway Patrol helicopter found him sitting alone in a Volkswagen van in the middle of the desert. Seatbelt fastened, alone, mummified, baked to a crisp. Toasted on both sides!"

"Come join me, Howell!" Uncle Tal calls out. "Do you know what those large cacti are? The ones that look as though they're watching you?"

"Spooky, spooky! Howl and his weird uncle being stalked by large cacti. Spooky!"

"They're called saguaros," Uncle Tal continues. "And what about those large bushes?" he adds.

"Why is he telling me these things?"

"That's a trick question," Uncle Tal continues. "They're not bushes. They're actually cholla cacti. If you cut off the top of the cactus and skin the sides, the meat inside is like a cucumber. If you wrap that in a cloth and squeeze it, you get water. Very important to know in the desert. And you can eat the berries."

"Those berries may be the only thing you do eat, Howl. You'll puke and have diarrhoea until there's nothing left of you," the voices giggle.

"See those bushes?"

How can you miss them, Howl? They're everywhere."

"Tumbleweeds. But their true name is Salsola. Some call them wind witches."

"*Oh, wind witches. More spooky, spooky!"*

"Shut up, shut up!" I yell, collapsing to my knees to the hot desert floor and jamming my hands over my ears.

Uncle Tal kneels down and cradles my face in his hands. He stares deep into my eyes. "They're searching—in here," he says, tapping my head. "Softening you up. They want you to doubt yourself and me."

For a moment, as our eyes meet, the voices are silenced. But, when we stand, they begin again.

"Be careful of that boy-eating cactus that wraps itself around its victim like a boa constrictor," mocks Bully Harold Bully.

"Or those wind witches that hurl themselves at you, disappearing down your throat and choking you," all three yell.

The bubbles of rage start in my belly and move slowly up through my chest and throat. The voices are right. I'm stuck in the desert listening to advice from my know-it-all madcap uncle.

Uncle Tal points at the cholla cactus and wind witches. "You need to know how to protect yourself in the desert, Howell."

I spin around. "Protect myself from what? Maybe that yellow thing over there?"

"A prickly pear cactus flower," Uncle Tal answers.

"Whatever," I scream back. I can't stop myself. I crouch, like a chimpanzee, scratching under my arms, running around yelling, "Look out! That yellow plant is going to leap up and attack me. I'm scared, I'm so scared."

Uncle Tal grips my shoulder and stares into my eyes. "Don't let them win, Howell." He hugs me tightly and repeats, "Don't let them win." Then he turns away. "I need to park the van."

I struggle to control myself, but the words pour out my mouth. "Park the van? Where? Underneath a pile of wind witches?" I shriek, joining in with the yelps of laughter in my head. I stretch out my arms and revolve in a circle. "Desert here, desert there, desert everywhere. No wait! There are mountains about a thousand miles away. Perhaps you can park the van behind the mountains and walk back. It'll only take you about fifty years."

Uncle Tal jumps into the van. He leans out of the window. "Be careful, Howell. You're on your own until I return. You don't know who or what you'll meet out here."

I march toward the van, ready to demand he take me home—now. Instead Uncle Tal drives off, the van blowing a large dust cloud in my face. When I stop coughing and rubbing my eyes, I look around. East, west, north, south. Uncle Tal and the van have disappeared.

Where did he go?

I sit down, my jaw stiff and my teeth clenched. All I can think about is how ridiculous this all is.

"Phone your father. Tell him to come take you home," the three hiss. *"But how can you do that? You don't know where you are?"*

Shrieks of laughter.

18. Encounter in the Desert

Thirty minutes later and I am still sitting on my backpack, arms dangling by my sides, and head drooping between my knees. A different voice now enters my head. *"Come home, Howell."* It's Erin Powell. *"Let's look at your closet and choose what you'll wear to your birthday party. That red shirt is so cute on you, especially with those long navy-blue pants. Wear those to your party, please. I'll be there."*

I close my eyes and call out loud. "If I count to ten, then open my eyes, I'll be standing in front of my closet at home picking out my red shirt and long navy-blue pants."

"Six, seven, eight, nine, ten," I shout. My eyelids open a fraction. Desert. I punch my fist into the baked soil.

Again. "Six, seven, eight, nine, ten."

Open eyes. Desert.

My mouth is dry, and my lips are cracking. I lick them frantically, but I have no more spit in my mouth. I glance at the various cacti. Which one has water?

Overhead I hear the faint cry of an eagle. A dot high in the sky. "Eagles fly high," my mother once told me. "They see everything, study from afar. Sometimes," she added, "you must see like the eagle. Other times, like the mouse. Everything up close, in detail."

Is she looking down on me now? Watching her son, the mouse, lost in this scorching desert?

No sooner do I think this than the voices of the bullies intrude. *"Are you lost, Howl?"* snorts Pug the Pyro.

"Phone your father, Howl. He can find you with the GPS on your phone," squeaks Sloppy Jack.

"But wait!" Bully Harold Bully shouts. *"You don't have a phone, do you? Nobody knows where you are."*

I look up and down the strip of the road. Nothing. No road sign or billboard advertising Taco Bell or McDonald's or Motel 8. No Indian casino around the next corner. Not even a next corner in sight.

A cold shiver creeps down my collar and circles my body. *What happens when the sun slides behind the mountains? What happens when night comes, and the icy cold winds find me? I'll be alone with no shelter and no Uncle Tal. I'll die out here.*

I stand up and squint into the sun. Someone is walking down the strip of road. I wave my arms. "Help!" I scream. "I've been abandoned."

I stop. The figure has a long, loping stride that brings it closer to me rapidly. Who would wear a black, full-length leather coat buttoned up to the neck and tied at the waist with thick string in the heat of the desert? And those thick, biker boots?

It's him!

I sit back down quickly, scared, grabbing my knees, scrunching myself into a ball, not wanting to attract attention.

In minutes, the man stands over me. The same tall, thin skeletal face, long-beaked nose and pasty-white hands and fingers. He leans down until his face is inches from mine. He stares deep into my eyes with his one, large blood-red right eye. The yellow dot on his left eye patch glows as it shifts across my body. A grimace slowly creeps across his face, revealing yellow fang teeth. The stench of his foul rancid, gym socks breath threatens to bowl me over. His eyes stare at me, trying to pierce my brain. He throws back his head and snickers. "You've been left here, alone," he hisses. "A test. And you're failing. So, it can't be you." He slaps his ice-cold hand against my forehead, pushing me backward onto the burning desert floor. The low whistling sounds ring through my ears.

He turns on his heel and strides down the road, laughing.

I lie on the desert floor, hot air burning my lungs, not daring to make any sound in case he returns.

A test and I'm failing.

A quarter-hour passes before I dare move. I stand up slowly and look around.

About twenty yards away, Uncle Tal stands next to a bus stop waving frantically. "Hurry, Howell! Grab your backpack! The bus is coming!"

19. From Nowhere to Somewhere That's Not Anywhere

I see nothing except a small dust cloud in the distance.

"Hurry," Uncle Tal calls. "The bus driver is a real grouch. He won't wait for you."

The dust cloud draws closer—rapidly.

I stagger to the bus stop, spitting out mouthfuls of desert dust, as a rickety orange school bus covered with obscure multi-coloured signs sputters toward us.

I grab Uncle Tal's arm and shake it. "Did you see him? The tall, thin, one-eyed man in a long black leather coat?"

"Did he speak to you?"

"He laughed and told me it couldn't be me. That I failed."

Uncle Tal gazes down at the desert floor. "Good."

Good? Why good?

"He thinks you're alone. Not protected. Vulnerable. That gives us a little more time."

Before I can ask any more questions, Uncle Tal shouts, "Watch out for the bus!" I turn. The bus lurches, heading straight toward me. I grab my backpack and dodge to the side, but the bus slithers still heading straight at me. Back and forth I dodge. Each time the bus corrects itself to follow me. Finally I close my eyes, blinded by the cloud of dust, and wait for the impact. The bus squeals to a stop barely an inch in front of me. As the dust settled, the side door springs open.

A voice booms from inside the bus, "Why did you keep jumping back and forth in front of me, foolish boy? Could have knocked you flat. 'Why did you knock him flat?' they'd ask me. 'Because he kept jumping around in front of me,' I'll answer."

Uncle Tal boards the bus. I spit out dust and follow him.

Behind the driver's wheel sits a small, squat man with a small, baldhead that makes his head look like an oversized Ping-Pong ball. Beginning at his neck, rolls of fat flow from his many chins. From his flushed, red face, two watery grey, unblinking eyes glower at me.

"Jumping back and forth in front of my bus. Foolish boy," he growls. "Are you going to stand there all day gawking at me? Get on!" I place my foot cautiously on the first step, expecting the bus to disappear, leaving me flat on my face in the dust. "Move it, move it!" yells the driver. I climb the stairs.

"Sit down! Got to get this bus moving again. Can't be late. 'Why are you late?' they'll ask. "Some silly boy jumping back and forth in front of me," I'd answer. And don't expect air-conditioning, foolish boy. No. They won't give me air-conditioning. Not them," the driver grumbles. "'Open the windows,' they say. 'That's your air-conditioning,' they say."

Uncle Tal grabs my hand and pulls me down into the seat next to him. "Good to see you again, Joe," he calls out to the bus driver who grunts in return. He's not happy to see anyone.

Uncle Tal leans forward. "Do you have everyone?"

"I don't know, do I?" scowls the driver. "Gave me a list, they did. But did I look at it? No. Not like they gave me photos. Besides, I can't look and drive at the same time, can I? Crash, I would. Then they'd say, 'Why did you crash the bus?' And I'd answer, "Because I was looking at your stupid list of names.' And do I have everyone, you ask. I don't know, do I? And I know they'll blame me if I do miss someone. 'Are you sure you stopped at every stop?' they'll ask. 'Are you sure you waited long enough?' But they don't tell me how long to wait, do they? Could be five minutes, could be five days. Nobody tells me. They tell me to go here or there and wait. So I go here or there and wait. And if I miss someone? Not my fault. Still, right or wrong, I'm always the one they blame."

"Who is this 'they' he keeps talking about?" I whisper to Uncle Tal. "Our bus driver seems very scared of them."

"He's told who to pick up, when and where, by the Council of *Nerth Doeths*, the Superiors, like your mother and me," Uncle Tal replies. "And no, he does not need to be scared of us," he chuckles. "Still, he likes to grumble and complain."

Uncle Tal taps the grumpy driver on the shoulder. "My nephew here says he saw him."

"Which him? Long black leather coats and boots, blood-red eye and shifting yellow dot? That him? Boy sure it was him? Still, couldn't be any other him, could it? Scares me that one. What would I do if he was waiting at one of the bus stops? That's what I ask myself. Wouldn't stop, I tell myself. No, wouldn't stop. Not for him. Not good if the boy saw him. Not good. Must be looking for someone. Could be him or could be someone else. Not good. No more talking now. Driving."

Uncle Tal leans back in his seat and gives a heavy sigh. Time to block out the ramblings of our bus driver.

Where's this grumpy bus driver taking you, Howl? Seems to us you're going to nowhere from somewhere that's not anywhere.

Screams of laughter.

20. The Hounds of Annwn

The bus rumbles across the desert, swerving back and forth to avoid clumps of sagebrush, and bumping up and down over dried-out riverbeds. We are headed for the hazy mountains in the distance.

A poke in the shoulder. Dark brown eyes and white teeth gleaming against her brown skin. Sitting across the aisle from me is Dani Walks-Her-Pony. Next to her sits another dark-skinned girl, but her eyes are pale blue, almost white. While Dani's hair is a long braid that flows down her back, the other girl's hair is neatly shaped in cornrows. She smiles revealing the whitest of teeth. Dani leans closer to me and whispers, "This is my friend, Dazmonique. Look at her when you speak. She'll read your lips."

My mouth drops open. "I know her," I reply. "She saved me from falling into the pit in my bedroom."

Before I can explain, the grumpy bus driver flaps his many chins and yells at us, "Sit straight up. No leaning. No talking. One bump of my bus and you'll fall flat on your face. Then what will I tell them? 'Young lady fell flat on her face,' I'll say. 'Her fault,' I'll say. But would they listen to me? No they wouldn't. Never listen to me. 'Shouldn't let her move,' they'll say. 'Shouldn't let her talk. Do you always let silly children talk on your bus?' That's what they'll ask. They won't blame the silly girl or boy. 'You're the one to blame. The bus driver is always the one to blame.' That's what they'll say. Right or wrong, I'm always the one they blame."

A sudden uproar breaks out at the back of the bus. The bus driver throws himself backward, holding onto the steering wheel as he rams his foot down hard on the brake. The bus fishtails back and forth, threatening to spin in a circle, throwing up huge clouds of desert dust before we screech to a halt.

In an instant the bus driver leaps out of his seat and waddles down the aisle. "If I've told you once I've told you a hundred times. No fighting. What will they say if they knew there was fighting on my bus?"

"Mother gave me, Jimi One, that red sweater, and him, Jimi Two, this red sweater." Standing in the aisle, facing the bus driver is a small boy with spiky, black hair pointing in all directions. He has a round face and rimless glasses, which perch on his nose. He wears black shoes, long grey socks, grey shorts, a grey shirt and a bright red sweater.

I rub my eyes as another, absolutely identical small boy stands up next to him.

"I'm Jimi One, not him, and Mother told me that my red sweater was on my bed," says the second boy. "He stole my red sweater. The one I'm wearing is his."

Both boys suddenly face each other, open their mouths wide, push their tongues down to their chins, put their open hands up to the sides of their heads and wiggle their fingers. "Stupid brother emoji," they both call out.

The bus driver grabs both Jimis. "I don't care who is who, or who makes the most stupid face," he screams. "Nor do I care which one of you has which red sweater. Any more problems and I throw you both off the bus. I don't care what they say. I'll leave you alone in the desert with the rattlesnakes, scorpions and poisonous spiders. Do you understand?"

"The Jimis understand," they repeat together.

The bus driver growls. He dumps one identical in a seat in the back of the bus and drags the other to an empty seat at the front. The closest Jimi—One or Two—folds his arms, sinks his head into his chest, pulls faces, and mutters about the nasty things he's going to do to his brother when he has the chance.

Before returning to his seat, the driver takes a deep breath, sucking all the air in the bus into his huge chest, and bellows, "No standing, no fighting, no leaning this way and that, and no talking. Everyone face the front. That's how I want it, and that's how they want it."

I turn my head quickly, looking straight ahead. Uncle Tal sleeps, undisturbed by the din.

On rattles the rickety orange school bus, bumping and rocking its passengers from side to side across the hard, sun-baked desert floor, getting closer and closer to the mountains. Whenever we hit a large rock, all of us, including the driver, go flying up six or seven inches out of our seats. All except Uncle Tal who sleeps soundly, never moving.

Across from me, Dani signs words for her deaf friend. She points out of the window, her hands telling the girl about plants and roots and trees and things. Not that I have any idea what she's saying. Dani looks at me and writes down some words on a notepad. "Mormon tea, oleander, wild plum, foxglove" and on and on. Then she signals with her thumb. Up, down as she writes alongside, "Good to eat. This bad."

"Poor Howl," the voices whisper. *"Now you have to learn what's safe to eat and what's deadly. Never had to think about that in the local Safeway."*

A monstrous bump ends the voices and sends me sprawling right on top of the grumpy driver.

"Get off me. Want me to crash, do you? Write on the report, I will. 'Boy fell on top of me, he did.' Make me look ridiculous in front of them, wouldn't it? Get off!"

I fall back into my seat.

We now leave the flat desert covered with sagebrush and slip and slide along a dry, sandy riverbed.

On either side red canyon walls reach up, higher and higher as we bump and shuffle our way deeper into the canyon.

A tap on my shoulder. I turn my head and see—myself! Or rather two little myselves. Two Howells staring back at me—my reflection in a pair of large sunglasses.

"*Mi nombre es Leonel*," whispers the boy behind. His hand dangles over the seat. I grab his hand and press it.

"Howell."

"We've met before," I whisper.

"*¿Hemos*? Have we?"

"Twice."

"*¿Dos veces*?"

"You fought the bullies hitting me in the schoolyard. Then we met at the breakfast trailer. You gave us directions. And the older man with you signalled with his arms. Semaphore. A warning. Don't you remember seeing me?"

Leonel lifts his sunglasses, showing the milky white pools that are his eyes. He smiles. "*No veo*. I don't see."

"I'm sorry!" I mutter.

"Don't be. *No lo sientas*. I don't want my new friend to be sorry."

We both laugh. As I turn to the front, I see the little pig eyes of the bus driver focused on me in the rear-view mirror. I sit up straight, staring ahead at the canyon walls growing higher and higher, closing in on us.

To my right, Dani continues to sign words before writing them and showing me. She points to the trees and shrubs. "Tamarisk or salt cedar. Bad. That one too. Russian olive. Choking other trees."

A series of four huge bumps sends the bus bouncing up and down and skidding back and forth. Even Uncle Tal, still asleep, grabs hold of the seat.

Then I see them. A pack of hunting dogs, pure white except for red tips on their ears, running and barking at the sides of the bus.

I look across at Dani. She stares straight ahead, not noticing. But the girl next to her, Dazmonique, gestures to me. She writes the word "Dogs" on a sheet of paper.

I tap Dani on the arm. "I thought you said your friend was deaf."

"She is." Her eyes twinkle mischievously as she adds, "That doesn't mean she can't hear things."

"But if she's deaf…" The beady eyes of the bus driver glare at me. No more talking.

His eyes still shut, Uncle Tal whispers, "*Cŵn Annwn*. The Hounds of Annwn. The hounds Pwyll took hunting when he saw Rhiannon. Remember? The lady on the white horse? The picture above your bed?"

"Are they the same dogs that attacked Bully Harold Bully and his cronies in the playground? The dogs I didn't see?"

"Probably. Now isn't this exciting?" he murmurs, changing the subject. "Wait until you see our school."

The bus continues to lurch back and forth in the dry sand, threatening to throw us all out the windows and onto the desert floor.

School? Here? Deep in this canyon?

Without warning, the driver suddenly throws his weight backward, gripping the steering wheel and ramming his foot on the brake once more. The bus fishtails back and forth and spins in a half-circle, facing the way we came. Clouds of sand and dust billow in through the open windows, making us all cough and choke. When the sand and dust finally settle, I look out.

We're trapped inside a narrow canyon with steep red-coloured cliffs rising on either side.

Uncle Tal jumps to his feet and rubs his hands. "Camp *Corwynt.* That's what I call it. Camp Hurricane. What is it? A camp, a meeting place, a school—all of these and none of these."

Uncle Tal can call it what he wants, but I see nothing. No camp, no meeting place, no school, no buildings, nothing.

"Here is where the task begins," Uncle Tal continues.

"Is this where my mother is held captive?" I ask.

"No. Not here. Far to the south," Uncle Tal replies.

"If you know where it is, why don't we go there now?"

"Too dangerous and not the right time."

"But you could change into a dragon, like you did before and…" Uncle Tal shakes his head.

"What about if I became a fighter like the Irishman Cu Chulainn, the Hound of Ulster, who could defeat an army single-handed?" I continue. "Or it could be a giant like Bendigeidfran who crossed the Irish Sea to rescue his sister, Branwen. Or…"

Uncle Tal chuckles. "Enough. Nephew, your references are impressive, but you are the only one who can rescue her."

"But…"

Uncle Tal shakes his head. "No, this is not just about fighting and overcoming *Drygoni*, you're forgetting about the transfer. Her rescue depends upon transferring some of her Doeth power to you, her son."

"But…" I'm trying desperately to think of other heroes.

"Do you remember the story of Sir Gawain and the Green Knight, nephew? Sir Gawain couldn't face the Green Knight until he was proved a worthy challenger."

"So I have to become worthy to rescue my mother? Become like Sir Gawain?"

"Exactly."

"What if I'm not? What if I'm just plain Howell?" I blurt out. "No hero, no giant, no knight—just Howell?"

Uncle Tal grabs my shoulder again and stares into my eyes. "You will be ready." And with that he stands and exits the bus.

I fall back in my seat, stunned.

A pair of beady eyes stare at me. "Get off," the driver yells. "Don't want anyone loitering, you hear? 'Tried to get him off,' I'll tell them. 'Daydreaming he was.' Will they believe me? No. They never believe me. 'Look at him,' I'll say. 'Head back, open-mouthed, in a trance,' I'll say. 'You're making it all up,' they'll say. 'Get him off your bus. Now!' That's what they'll say."

21. Camp *Corwynt*

Three more adults—a man and two women—bundle past me, following Uncle Tal.

Before I can stand, I'm punched on the shoulder and pushed back into my seat. "Most important ones first," a boy calls out as he barges past me. Two other toughs punch me as they follow.

"Watch those steps," the driver yells. "Leaping out like that. Break your legs, you could. Make me write up a report, they will. Take up hours of my time."

Once the "most important ones" are off the bus, I gesture to Dani and her friend. "Ladies first."

Both smile and exit. Leonel grabs my arm. "*Necesito tu ayuda, amigo.* I need your help, friend."

I guide Leonel out of the bus one step at a time. We both sink ankle-deep in soft sand, filling our tennis shoes. I pull out one foot, hoping to find somewhere more solid to put it. I don't.

"Do you want me to carry you on my back?" Dani laughs.

The girl with cornrows grabs my arm and faces me. "Dogs. You see dogs. They come when you need them."

How did she know?

She takes Leonel and my arms and pulls us to solid ground.

Uncle Tal slaps me on the back. "Bet you thought we'd never get here, nephew."

Get where? Trapped in a boiling hot canyon covered in red dust with not a cloud in the sky or a stream or drop of water?

Dani tugs at my shirtsleeve. "Don't forget, my friend Dazmonique reads lips. Look her in the face when you talk. And make sure your face and words speak the same language."

"What does that mean?"

"If you're saying something happy, look happy. If you're saying something…"

Leonel cuts Dani's explanation short. "I hear girls' voices," he giggles. "Are they pretty? *Bonitas*?"

"This is Dani Walks-Her-Pony and Dazmonique, Leonel," I reply.

"He asked if we were pretty, Howell," Dani laughs. "Are we?"

"They're both very pretty," I mumble, hanging my head to hide my bright red face.

"I like pretty girls," Leonel chuckles. "Howell's face is bright red, isn't it? Me llamo Leonel, Dazmonique and Dani." Leonel holds out his hand.

"Wrong direction, Leonel," I laugh. I turn him to face the girls. "Dazmonique is deaf. You must face her."

"*Creo que los dos están muy bonita,*" Leonel continues. "I think you're both very pretty."

"*Di ou mèsi,*" Dazmonique replies.

Leonel shakes his head. "What language is that?"

"Creole," Dani answers. "Dazmonique was born in Haiti. She now lives in Louisiana."

Dazmonique speaks slowly, her mouth forming each word carefully. "*Di ou mès*i means thank you, gracias."

"How do I sign beautiful?" Leonel inquires.

"Hold your right hand to your forehead," Dani responds, "and circle your face clockwise. That's the sign for beautiful. And don't look down when you say it. Remember: your face says the same as your words."

Leonel and I both hold up our heads and gesture "beautiful," smiling at the two girls, even though my face is red with embarrassment.

The two girls look at each other. "We think you and Howell *tou de bèl jenn gason,*" Dazmonique says. "Both handsome young men."

She stretches out her hands and silently traces the shape of my and Leonel's heads.

What is she doing?

She holds her fingertips about an inch away from our foreheads and closes her eyes. A pause before she smiles and kisses each of us on the cheek.

"*Ou bon moun,*" she announces. "You good people. We stay together."

"How did you know about the hunting dogs, Dazmonique?" I ask.

"Dazmonique *konnen anpil bagay,*" she replies.

"She says, she knows many things," Dani translates. "You'll find out."

Leonel grabs my elbow. "Describe this place, amigo."

"A small canyon jammed between high plateaus. Red dirt and sand everywhere. We're standing in a dry riverbed." I whirl around, amazed. "And the school bus has gone. Disappeared."

"What about the school? Is it huge with tall spires and things that go bump in the night? Long, winding staircases filled with secret passages and demons and monsters?"

Dani laughs. "You've been reading too many books. There is no school. Not yet."

Not yet? Where is it?

"How many of us are there?" Leonel inquires.

"About fifteen," I answer. "Everyone's looking around wondering where we are—if we're anywhere."

My mouth drops open. The "most important" boy glares at me. He looks identical to Bully Harold Bully. Not the roly-poly one back in Mount Shasta, but the morphed Bully Harold Bully, the thinner one with fewer freckles and tight, mean lips. And the two other toughs look exactly like the morphs of Pug the Pyro and Sloppy Jack.

"What are you staring at?" the first boy yells.

"It's rude to stare," the second boy growls, pushing his face into mine.

"I know boys who look just like you," I say.

"Oh, do you?" the third boy laughs. "Aren't you lucky?"

The boy who looks like Bully Harold Bully confronts me, resting both arms on his hips. "Never seen a Special-Special One before?" he snorts. "Well don't get used to my face because you won't be staying here long. You'll be sent home soon—for stupidity! That's unless the *Drygoni* or some giant lizard catches you, eats you and spits you out!"

The three boys imitate me getting eaten and spat out before giving each other high fives.

A girl dressed all in black—black sweater, black skirt, black, stockings and black shoes—with red bangs in the front and red hair flowing down her back stares at me. Her face is pale, and her large glasses magnify her bright green unblinking eyes.

Dressed all in black in the heat of the desert? I stare back at her. I've seen her before. But where? In an instant, she has disappeared. I look around, but she's nowhere to be seen.

All this time, the adults gather in a tight-knit circle, talking to each other. Now and then, Uncle Tal points at me. The other three turn and stare. Why, I don't know.

I recognise Esther Evening Star from the breakfast trailer. A man separates himself from the other adults and speaks to the group, "*Mi nombre es Señor Cuitláhuac. Dejamos en cinco minutos. Estar listos todos ustedes.*"

I turn to Leonel. "What did he say?"

"His name is *Señor Cuitláhuac*. We leave in five minutes. Be ready—all of you."

Great! I think to myself. *We're going on a hike down this never-ending canyon in the blazing heat to find a non-existent school led by someone with an unpronounceable name who only speaks Spanish.*

"You don't need to translate for me," announces the "most important" boy. "I speak seven languages fluently."

"*Si no recuerda mi nombre, me llaman Señor Quit, que nunca hago*," the man calls.

I look at the important boy. "What did he say?"

The boy turns his back. "Like I'd tell you."

I turn to Leonel who translates for Dani. "He said, 'If you can't remember my name, call me *Señor* Quit, which I never do.'"

Señor Quit walks to a small sandy flat area about fifty yards away. "You waste our time, you spend night alone. Outdoor. In canyon."

So he does speak English.

Señor Quit laughs at his own joke. We join in, half-heartedly, hoping he's only joking.

"Cuitláhuac was the name of a famous Aztec king," Leonel whispers. He chuckles. "I don't think that's him. That king died 500 years ago."

Well that's comforting! Trekking down a never-ending, boiling canyon with a 500-year-old ghost who only speaks a little broken English is not my idea of fun.

I stare at *Señor* Quit. "He's the man who was standing beside you at the breakfast trailer, Leonel."

"If you say so," Leonel responds. "He's mi tío, my uncle."

Señor Quit waves his arm. "*Sígueme*! Follow me!"

Dani and Dazmonique grab Leonel and my hands.

"Where's my iPhone?" yells the Special-Special boy. "I'd like to take a photo of the girls guiding the two little boys."

I mutter the magic word Uncle Tal told me. Nothing happens.

The three boys push closer, laughing in my face.

Are Bully Harold Bully and his gang following me?

22. Which Is Which and Does It Matter?

My knees buckle as one of the small boys with spiky black hair pointing in all directions, and a round face with rimless glasses perched on his nose, slams into my back.

"Hi, my name is Jimi Li. J-i-m-i-l-i," he announces. His index fingers pull his lips apart. "I'm Jimi One. Happy emoji."

"No, he's not. I'm Jimi One." Facing me is the other identical. He does the same thing with his mouth and fingers.

"What are they doing?" Leonel asks. "I can't see them." I describe the twins' faces to Leonel who laughs out loud.

When the two Jimis look at each other, they pull their mouths down and poke out their tongues. A few seconds later they leap on each other and begin scuffling in the dirt.

Dazmonique grabs each by the shoulder. "*Sispann! Tou de nan ou.*" she calls out, separating them. "Stop! Both of you."

"You look very young," Dani says to the twins. "How old are you?"

"Twelve," they respond. "I'm six and my brother is six. So together we're twelve." We laugh. No one wants to argue with that.

"Why mother give both same name?" Dazmonique asks.

"Mother's father and his brother were identical twins, both named Jimi," they reply. "They moved from Japan to San Francisco's Japan town. That's where we live. Grandfathers—Elder Jimi One and Elder Jimi Two—speak to us, even though both died a long time ago." They both pull down the sides of their mouths and run their fingers from their eyes. "Sad," they say.

Dani, Dazmonique and I look at one another. Are the twins telling the truth?

"Elder Jimi One and Elder Jimi Two," the twins continue, "ask questions."

"Do they give answers?" Dani asks.

"There are answers, but they don't give them, and we don't know them," the twins assert.

I look at Dazmonique, who stares intently at the twins.

If anyone knows the answers to the questions asked by Elder Jimi One and Elder Jimi Two, I think to myself, *it's going to be her.*

"Can your mother tell you apart?" Dani asks.

"No!" they both answer.

"Why…

"would…

"she…

"want…

"to?"

"You two talk really strange," Leonel says.

"You make up questions or sentences together," I add.

"Do we?" they both respond. "But the Jimis never agree on anything."

I hold out both hands. "Good to meet you, Jimi, whichever one you are."

The twins shake my hands. "The Jimis are pleased to meet you."

I move closer to Dani. "Did you see that girl dressed all in black? Large glasses? Long, flowing red hair?"

"No," she replies. "Are you sure you saw her? There's no one like that here. And you're the only one with red hair. The desert can play tricks with your eyes."

I look around. The girl has disappeared. *Maybe the desert glare is playing tricks with my eyes.*

Dani points to the twins. They stand still, holding hands, facing each other, eyes fixed. "Elder Jimi One and Elder Jimi Two speak. They ask, 'Why should you not follow the one you follow?' That's what Elder Jimi One and Elder Jimi Two ask."

I stare at the twins. "That doesn't make sense."

"Maybe not now," Dani responds. "Maybe later."

Before I can ask what she means, the two Jimis scream and jump away from each other.

"Was I holding my brother's hand?" they both ask. "Yuck. I hate it when that happens. Whenever our Grandfathers speak to us," they both growl, "the Jimis hold hands. It's sickening." They spit on their hands and rub them in the sand, cleaning them. Then they both thrust their hands down their throats. "Vomit emoji," they both say.

23. Natural Born Leader

Before I can ask the twins about the strange question, *Señor* Quit shouts, "*Formar un solo archivo*."

"*Single file,*" Leonel translates.

Naturally, the Special-Special One has to be first in line, standing alongside *Señor* Quit and matching him stride for stride. Suddenly *Señor* Quit stops abruptly letting the 'most important' boy continue for a few steps.

"*Sé cuidado*!" *Señor Quit murmurs*, leaning closer to the important boy. "*Muchas arenas movedizas y serpientes de cascabel aquí*."

"Need help translating?" Leonel inquires.

"No," the boy snaps. "He's telling me I show initiative. That I'm a natural-born leader destined to become a Nerth Doeth very soon."

"Close," Leonel laughs. "But it sounded more like, 'Be careful. Much quicksand and rattlesnakes here.'"

The Special-Special Boy stops dead in his tracks, looking under and around his feet before edging backwards behind *Señor* Quit.

"His name is Bruce Bollsinger," Dani whispers in my ear. "On the bus, he made sure we all knew that he was the fourth in his family of that name and that he was a Special-Special One. He calls himself that. He told us his family is very wealthy. He kept repeating that he's from a long line of *Doeths*. Special children. Like the rest of us."

"Me? Special? No. I'm just a normal twelve-almost-thirteen-year-old boy," I respond.

"If you were normal, you wouldn't be here," Leonel responds.

"I'm here because..."

"Mother uncle *Nerth Doeths*. Powerful. Transfer some Doeth power to Howell," Dazmonique interrupts. "Him not normal."

"Oh, he's normal all right," interrupts the Special-Special One. "Stupid normal, Boring normal, Snoring normal and Safonal normal. That's how normal he is!"

High fives from his friends.

"*Li pa nòmal. Pwoblèm sèlman se li doute tèt li*," Dazmonique continues.

Before Dazmonique has time to translate, Brenda, a skinny girl who was always by the Special-Special One's side, dances up and down in front of her. "Oh, no. Mumbo-jumbo girl speaking her hocus pocus again."

As they all giggle and high-fived, Dani watches as Dazmonique signs. Then Dani leans across to and whispers. "Dazmonique says, Howell doubts himself! Enemy in his head! Must believe in himself!"

Before I can ask what that meant, Dani puts her finger to her mouth, silencing us. She points to the four adults who gather in a circle, holding hands. They stare down at the red earth and mumble.

Without warning, a hot wind races down the canyon, blowing up red dust, which stings our legs and faces and forces us to close our eyes.

This must be why my uncle calls it Camp Hurricane, I think to myself.

The hollow roar of the scorching wind grows deafening. We're in the middle of a sandstorm. And still, the adults chant, not caring for our safety. Leonel, Dani, Dazmonique, the twins and I grab each other's hands and crouch close to the ground not wanting to be rolled down the canyon-like tumbleweeds.

"Don't worry," Dani screams. "The adults won't let us die."

"I hope not," I yell back.

I screw up my eyelids and peer through the slits. Shimmering shapes circle us at breakneck speed.

Suddenly the roar subsides and the hot wind ceases. We raise our heads, glancing around, still holding hands. Four large single-story log huts—red, green, yellow and blue—surround us.

"Right," Uncle Tal calls out. "Red hut living quarters. Partitioned down the middle. Boys left, girls right. Adults in the green hut. Yellow hut dining. Blue assembly."

I wipe the sand from my face and clothes and describe the strange collection of huts to Leonel. "The blue hut is square, the red round, the yellow triangular, and the green S-shaped. On top of the red hut is a weathervane that spins round and round, even though there is no wind."

"Meet in the yellow dining hut in thirty minutes," Uncle Tal continues. "Enough time to find your beds, sort out your belongings and take a shower."

And with that, the adults move off to the green hut, the two men to one end of the 'S' shaped building, the two women to the other.

24. Mysterious Words

We all remain motionless, backpacks in hands, staring after the adults, wondering what just happened.

"Can't stand here all day, you fools," announces The Special-Special One. "Boys follow me; women follow Brenda!" He barges past me.

When he arrives at the door on the left-hand side, The Special-Special One stands looking down at the doorknob.

"Maybe there's rattlesnakes or quick sands inside," Jimi One and Two say.

Their hands open and circle their faces. Their mouths and eyes are wide open. "Fearful emoji," they both say.

The Special-Special One hesitates.

"*¡Abre la puerta! Hace mucho calor aquí*! Open the door!" Leonel yells. "It's hot out here."

I push past the Special-Special Boy, turn the doorknob and walk inside. "It's just a door. Nothing inside."

The Special-Special One growls at me. "I knew that. Get out of my way!"

Before he can enter, Leonel lurches backward. "*Aghh! ¿Que es eso*?" The Special-Special lurches backward pushing me into the hut. "Tell me what's inside," he screams.

I look around the red hut. Although the hut is round on the outside, inside is square. All four walls are painted light green with a red and white stripe halfway up the wall parallel to the floor. Beds and small dressers line the walls, each with a window beside it. The floor slopes down to the centre where black plastic hangs from the ceiling forming a large circular partition.

"No quicksands or snakes," I call out. "Beds along the four walls, each with a closet, bedside table and a lamp. A large bookcase against the far wall. And a large sheet of black plastic hanging from the ceiling in the middle of the room.

When I look back at the group, the twins stand each side of the Special-Special one. Their mouths hang open and their hands are on their cheeks. "Scared emoji," they both say. "Special boy look like this."

Bollsinger punches the twins, "You two are so boring. Do you hear me, pipsqueaks? Boring Tweedledum and Tweedledumber, boring faces and boring grandfathers. B-o-r-i-n-g, boring." He pushes them aside and marches to the door, knocking me aside. "I enter first," he growls. "Not you!" He pushes his face into mine, his eyes bulging and his cheeks glowing red. "What's your name, normal boy?"

"Howell."

I groan as Bruce Bollsinger and his gang dance around me, howling.

The Special-Special One points to the three beds closest to the door. "That's my bed. Biggie Pug and Jack Rabbit are next to me."

Biggie Pug? Jack Rabbit?

"You, you, you and you," he snarls, pointing to the twins, Leonel and me. "Get as far away from us as possible."

Leonel grabs my arm as we cross the room negotiating the sloping floor. "Put me next to the bookcase, amigo. I might want to stay up all night reading," he giggles.

I pull the black, plastic curtain aside and peek inside. Four toilet stalls and, in the middle, a large area with overhead showers.

The two Jimis join us at the far end of the room. As expected, they're soon battling one another. First Jimi One or Two wants this bed, and they both want that bed, always the bed the other one wants.

The Special-Special One and his gang gather around. "Hey, pipsqueaks, why don't you ask your crazy dead elders who should take which bed?"

The twins drop their heads and mumble.

"Speak up, fools," Biggie Pug yells. "We can't hear you."

"Leave them alone," Leonel retorts. "They're much younger than you."

"You are telling me to shut up, blind boy?" growls Biggie Pug, punching his fist into the palm of his hand. "You shouldn't do that if you know what's good for you."

"Don't try to spoil our fun," adds Jack Rabbit.

The Special-Special One puts his arms around the shoulders of his two friends as they return to their side of the room.

The Jimis thank Leonel. I guide one Jimi to one bed, and the other to the one next to it. But they don't unpack. Instead they stand, one in front of me, the other behind, holding hands, trapping me between them. Their eyes are open wide, and their mouths open as if shocked. "Our grandfathers, Elder Jimi One and Elder Jimi Two, saw her, the girl with the flowing red hair. They ask, 'Who is it you don't know now who one day you'll know?' That's what the Elder Jimi One and Elder Jimi Two ask."

A second later the twins break the circle, scowling at each other as they pull various faces, spit on their hands and clean them on their shorts.

I know better than to ask what the grandfathers mean. The twins won't know.

I think of their question: *Who is it you don't know now who one day you'll know?*

No answer.

My bed is next to a window, closest to the bookshelf. I reach up and pull a book, a large folio, from the shelf. It has no title on the cover, and the pages are in a language I don't understand. Same with the other books.

"How are we supposed to read these books?" I ask. "None are in English."

"Any in Spanish?" Leonel giggles. He takes one of the books, opens it and pretends to read. "Take three ripe tomatoes diced, one onion diced, two serrano chillies, thinly sliced and broiled or barbequed first, half a cup of fresh-chopped cilantro, juice of a lime, salt and pepper to taste. Combine and mix."

"Is that supposed to be funny, blind boy?" The Special-Special One shouts. "Here! Let me read it." He looks at the page, nodding his head as if he understands what he is reading.

"What does it say?" I ask.

"Like I'm going to tell you, Howling Boy," he snarls. He thrusts his finger into my chest. "Remember, Howl: We are all supposed to be special. Some, like me, are much more special. Some, like you, don't look one bit special to me. I don't know why you're even here." He flicks his towel in my face, narrowly missing my eyes, before disappearing behind the black plastic as he chases his friends into the showers.

As I help Leonel put his clothes away, he whispers in my ear, "I did read something in that book. In Braille. '*Mano derecha y el pie izquierdo primero, si usted desea pasar.*' It means, 'Right hand and left foot first, if you want to pass.' Sounds awkward," he adds. Leonel and I try walking like that to the shower.

We stand in the showers, as far away as possible from The Special-Special One and his buddies. The warm water splashing over my hair, face and body feels good after the long ride in Uncle Tal's Volkswagen van and the rickety, multi-coloured bus. Soap, shampoo, and a washcloth—everything we want appears whenever we stretch out our hands.

The two Jimis, each trying to outdo the other, hold out their hands and count the towels. Soon each is weighed down with towels that pile up over their heads.

"Enough!" I shout. All of the towels, except one for each Jimi, disappear.

"Let's hurry," Leonel snickers, "so we can see those *dos hermosas chicas*, two beautiful girls, again."

Leonel's comment breaks the ice. We laugh and flick towels at each other before rushing back to our beds to sort our clothes. Too late! The Special-Special One and his cronies have sorted our clothes all over the floor!

As we clean up, they laugh. 'They' now includes all of the boys except Leonel, the twins and me. Everyone else is a member of The Special-Special One's gang.

25. One Question Asked by Elder Jimis Is Answered

An ear-piercing bugle blast from outside the hut cuts short their laughter. We rush to the door. The girls are already lined up in front of an English butler, complete with sleeked-back greased hair, parted in a straight line down the middle, black pants, black tuxedo, pointed shoes and napkin dangling from his arm. His movements, from head to feet, are jerky, like a robot's.

"Adults request pleasure of your company in green dining hut," the butler announces. "Follow me. Two lines."

"Me first." The Special-Special One shoves some girls aside and stands at the head of the line. "You," he motions to his two tough-looking friends, "behind me."

"Hurry," the butler calls. "No time to waste. Two lines."

The Special-Special One and his two buddies can't resist imitating the butler, repeating each of his words in phony English accents.

Leonel clings to my outstretched arm as we march into the late afternoon sun.

"That girl, the one dressed all in black," Dani whispers, "She wasn't in our hut."

Neither of us notice one of The Special-Special One's cronies, a thin, scrawny boy with a mean glare—probably the one called Jack Rabbit—sliding alongside, listening to our conversation. "Hey, everyone," he shouts. "A few hours in the desert and Howl's already got an imaginary girlfriend."

"A girl would have to be stupid to fall for a geek like Howl," the Special-Special One retorts.

He jams his fingers in his mouth, pulls out his cheeks and sticks out his tongue. "Unless she looks and walks like this!" He giggles, walking with his knees together and feet flopping up and down.

Leonel grabs my arm and whispers, "*Algo esta mal.* Something's wrong, amigo. Leonel not seeing things clearly."

My mouth drops open. "You can see things? But I thought…"

Before I can continue, Leonel asks, "What colour did the butler say the dining hut is?"

"Yellow, red, green, blue, pink," The Special-Special One yells, laughing. "How can you tell one colour from another?"

"That's not very nice," I reply, clenching my fists.

"I'm s-s-s-scared," Bollsinger stammers.

"Stop talk. Keep close," the butler commands. "Not get lost. Not here."

I stare at the butler. His greased hair parted in a straight line down the middle, black tuxedo and napkin dangling from his arm shimmer before me. I rub my eyes. Is the hot desert sun affecting my eyesight?

Dazmonique steps alongside Leonel and me. Her arms are outstretched, her fingers point toward the butler. She grabs my arm. "Dazmonique want to stop."

Once again Bollsinger and his cronies slide alongside us. All hold out their arms, making fun of Dazmonique.

"Whoa!" they cry as they stagger from side to side. "Someone kooky in head. Want brain."

I lean closer to Dazmonique and mouth. "What's wrong?"

"Dazmonique did not hear man's shoes squeaking," she replies, pointing to the butler. "New shoes squeak."

So here I am, following some English butler, with a blind boy who sees, and a deaf girl troubled because she can't hear the butler's shoes squeaking. What next?

"Hey, look at Howl!" The Special-Special One shouts. "He's got the heebie-jeebies. He's shaking all over." It's true. My hands and arms shake. Bollsinger and his cronies wobble and shake, imitating me.

The butler waves his arms. "Not drop behind," he commands. "Get lost. Dangerous." Again his form shimmers before me.

Then I see the mysterious girl in the black dress with large glasses walking next to me. She whispers, "Remember Elder Jimi and Elder Jimi Two's question: 'Why must you not follow the one you follow?'" I look at the Jimis. They stare straight ahead. Same with everyone else, except Leonel and Dazmonique, who look troubled.

Leonel grabs my arm and points back the way we came. "Your uncle said the dining hut was yellow, not green. This is the wrong way."

He's right. I try to turn back but can't change direction. Some unseen force pulls us all forward. I have to stop the group. But how?

I clench my fists, grit my teeth and roll my body back and forth until I spin around. We're moving away from the coloured huts. The butler is leading us deeper into the canyon. With a sudden jerk, I thrust out my leg. Down goes Jimi One or Two in front of his twin brother. In no time, both identicals roll over in the dust, fighting, while those behind, staggering like zombies, fall over them. Soon a pile of kids lies on the ground, coughing and sneezing.

Leonel raises his arm and calls out, "The dining hut *amarillo*, yellow, not green. *No verde*. We are acting like Safonals. We're not using our Doeth power."

Safonals? Doeth power?

No time to ask as Bollsinger, who has fallen into the pile, and now screams out, "I knew it was a trick."

"No, you didn't. The Jimis don't think you're a real leader," the twins reply. "If you were, you wouldn't have followed that butler thing."

The Special-Special One grits his teeth and clenches his fists. "I wanted to see if you were all stupid enough to fall for something so obvious."

We dust ourselves down. Dazmonique still faces the canyon, her hands waving before her.

"Now what is she doing?" cries the short, squat crony. "Looking for water?"

"He gone," Dazmonique says. "Butler disappear. I no hear or feel him anymore." She turns to me. "You save us, Howell."

Bollsinger stares angrily at the two of us before snapping out his orders. "Such a simple trick, and you fools fell for it. You're so lucky I was here to save you. Back to the yellow hut, everyone. Follow me!"

I look around. The girl with large glasses has disappeared.

I slide alongside Dani. "Did you notice something different about the butler? I saw you sniffing the air."

"The smell," she murmurs. "Sliding down my nose into my lungs. Choking me. The smell was a warning."

We walk back to the yellow hut, glancing around periodically to see if something or someone is following.

What's next? we all wonder

26. The Special-Special One's Rules

We finally arrive at the yellow hut. The door bursts open, and Uncle Tal glowers at us. "Where have you been? You're an hour late!"

"An hour?" Bollsinger blurts out. "We only left the red hut two minutes ago."

"If I say you're an hour late, you're an hour late!" Uncle Tal snaps, glaring at The Special-Special One. "No need to tell us what happened. You were tested and you failed. No excuses."

The Special-Special One huffs and mutters under his breath. He never fails!

Uncle Tal ushers us into the yellow hut. The inside is not triangular as it is on the outside. It's square. The ceiling is low; Uncle Tal has to bend to walk. The walls are painted with large chessboards, each with the chess pieces in different positions. The room is empty.

"I thought this was the dining hall," I whisper to Leonel. "No chairs, no tables, no food."

"The adults have already eaten," Uncle Tal continues. "They've returned to the green hut. As for you, you may get fed. Probably not. It depends on the waiters."

What waiters?

And with that Uncle Tal leaves, slamming the door of the yellow hut behind him.

We stand silently, sheepishly looking at each other or staring up at the chessboard walls.

Except for The Special-Special One, who nods knowingly as he looks around the room. Brenda, the girl who made fun of Dazmonique, sidles up to him. "What should we do?"

"Don't you know?"

"Do you?" the Jimis shoot back.

Bollsinger turns slowly, glaring down at the twins. "How dare you question me. Of course, I know what to do. It's a test, and you fools are failing miserably. Biggie Pug, Jack Rabbit, follow me. We're going back to the red hut. I have plenty of food in my closet."

And that is when we found the door locked.

"If you're so special," Dani queries, "why doesn't the door open for you?"

The Special-Special One whirls around, his eyes flashing with anger. "Are you challenging me? I can open this door and walk out just like that," he says, snapping his fingers.

"You're stuck in here like the rest of us," I respond. Biggie Pug thrusts his face into mine. "Who asked you to speak, howling boy?" he growls.

"While I'm waiting for you fools to figure out the simple problem of how to open the door," Bollsinger snarls, "here are some things you need to know. We are all, supposedly, special children. That's why we're here. What you probably don't know is that some, like me, are far more special than the rest. And some of you," he says, "I don't know why you're even here. That fat, stupid bus driver must have picked you up by mistake.

"My name is Bruce Bollsinger," he continues, "fourth in my family with that name. That means, for those of you too stupid to comprehend, my father, grandfather, and great-grandfather were all called Bruce. And all were very gifted and very special. Since I am the fourth, I have the Roman numeral four behind my name." He thrust his index finger into my face; drawing a large "I" followed by "V" in the air with his finger. "Fourth. Someone write that on the blind boy's head, so he'll remember."

"Don't touch me!" Leonel warns.

"Oh, I'm scared," giggles Biggie Pug.

"My parents," The Special-Special One continues, "are fabulously wealthy. I was educated in the best private school in the United States. I assume you've all heard of The Lawrenceville School in New Jersey." He looks around the group. "If not, you're not worth talking to. I spent one year in Switzerland, and one year at Charterhouse in England. Again, an exclusive boarding school. All this was preparation for me to become a supreme, a *Nerth Doeth*. Maybe the greatest *Nerth Doeth* of all."

The Special-Special One doesn't seem to notice the groans and discomfort of many of those listening to his words. He stops and points a finger at Dani. "What is that girl doing?"

"I'm signing for my friend Dazmonique. She's deaf. And it's rude to point like that."

"What that boy say not true. *Bonjan pa bon pou* Doeth," Dazmonique calls out, pointing at Bollsinger.

"I thought you said she was deaf," Jack Rabbit snarls.

"Deaf, not mute," Dani responds.

"What was that gobbledygook she was babbling?" The Special-Special One sneers. "Blah, blah, blah."

Dani watches Dazmonique sign. She says, "Boasting not good for Doeth."

"Like she knows more about Doeths than The Special-Special One," sniggers Biggie Pug.

Dazmonique's eyes focus on Bollsinger. "What he say not true. Some special, no money. I no money. Parents mouri. Die. Live with *matant*, aunt. *Trè pòv*. Very poor. She *Nerth Doeth*."

"They live in New Orleans," Dani whispers to me. "In a homeless shelter."

"Is anybody really interested in hearing this deaf girl's sob story? I thought not," snaps The Special-Special One.

Everybody stares at Dazmonique as she raises her hands. "*Imilite ak konesans vre gid sou pouvwa a.*"

Bollsinger and his gang roar with laughter. "She's doing it again. Yucky-yucky mumbo-jumbo."

Biggie Pug prances around Dazmonique making guttural noises. "We speaka da English here." Soon everyone except Dani, Leonel and the twins and me join in the laughter. Dazmonique turns and signs something to Dani who turns to the four of us. "Humility and knowledge true guide to power."

I nod like I understand what that means. I really don't, although I've heard my mother say that.

Dazmonique takes my hand. "You not know what that means now, but soon you know," she whispers. "That girl you see. She help you. Like Elder Jimi One and Elder Jimi Two say, 'You think you don't know her. You do.'" I look into her deep, blue-white smiling eyes. I know who is the real special-special one in the room—and it's not Bollsinger. Dazmonique touches the necklace Dani gave me. "*Ou espesyal—men ou dwe pran anpil prekosyon.* You special—but be very careful."

Special? Very careful? Of whom? Of what?

"What are those idiots saying?" Bollsinger snarls.

"Him not special," Dazmonique leans close to me as she nods to The Special-Special One. "*Li se pwòp lènmi pi move l 'yo.* He his own worst enemy. *Li pa konnen, li teste pou nou.* He not know, he test for us."

"But I thought you said we are all special," I respond. "Because we are all potential *Doeths.*"

"*Gen kèk reyisi, kèk febli.* Some succeed, some fail," she replies.

Before I can ask her what all this means, Bollsinger interrupts. "You two! Stop talking and everyone look at me," he snarls. "Here are my rules. First: You don't talk to me unless I ask you to. Second: Only my friends call me by my first name, and I choose my friends very carefully. Rule number three: Those of you who are not my friends call me The Special-Special One, understood? And rule number four: If you don't call me The Special-Special One…"

He turns his head slowly, nodding to the two cronies sitting beside him. We hear their fists smashing into their palms.

"Biggie Pug! You're up," The Special-Special One proclaims.

The stocky boy with a round, freckled face, mouth curling down at the ends and blond crew cut stands. "Not much to say. Anyone calls me anything other than Biggie Pug, short for Big the Pugilist, is in trouble. If you want to know how I got the name, ask me. I dare you!" He high-fives Bollsinger.

"Next, Jack Rabbit," Bruce Bollsinger announces.

"They look almost identical to three bullies in my town," I say to Dani.

The Special-Special One glares at me. "When I or one of my friends is talking, you don't," he growls. Jack Rabbit, the thin, scrawny boy with the mean glare stands. His brown hair is plastered flat on his head except for one tuft at the back that refuses to lie down.

"Pleased to meet you, Mister Jack Rabbit. I shall call you by your Spanish name, *Señor Juan Conejo*," Leonel declares, holding out his hand.

"Quiet!" Bollsinger hollers, standing and shaking his fist in Leonel's face. "See what I have for you? A knuckle sandwich."

I clench my fists and face Bollsinger. He's not going to hit Leonel.

Immediately Biggie Pug marches toward me, thrusting his nose in my face. "What's going on in that stupid mind of yours, howling boy?"

Before he can continue, Leonel calls out, "Knuckle sandwich, cheese and bologna, tuna fish. One of each, please." He laughs and raises his sunglasses. "I can't see the sandwich," he continues, "but I can smell it. Someone stinks of pastrami. Really stinks."

Biggie Pug's hand shoots forward, grabbing for Leonel's shoulder. But his hand never reaches its target. Before you can say, "Pastrami sandwich," Leonel grasps Biggie Pug's hand and twists it to the side, making Biggie Pug collapse on his side squealing with pain.

"*Lo siento*," Leonel says. "Hope I didn't hurt you."

I stare at Leonel. *How does he know Biggie Pug is about to grab him? It's identical to his actions in the schoolyard. Is this one of those seeing without seeing things?*

Leonel stands still, hand outstretched, waiting for someone to shake it. "Put your hand down, blind boy," The Special-Special One blurts out. "I'll be watching out for you. Understand?"

"*Yo entiendo, Capitán Especial-Especial*," Leonel replies, saluting and clicking his heels together.

"Speak English," Bollsinger barks. He turns to Jack Rabbit. "Continue! Tell them who you are."

"Jack's the name. Another special like Bruce here." A glare from Bollsinger, and Jack Rabbit quickly corrects himself. "But not a Special-Special like him. But more special than any of you lot." As he says this, his eyes and mouth tighten. He glowers at each of us.

"You!" Bollsinger points his finger at me. "What's your name?"

"I already told you," I mumble.

"Say it again," Bollsinger yells. "We want everyone to know."

"Hhhooowwwlll!" comes the chorus from The Specials.

"Why are you here?" Bruce Bollsinger snarls, his freckled face inches from mine. Leonel is right. Both Biggie Pug and The Special-Special One stink of pastrami.

"Taliesin is my uncle," I answer.

Bollsinger laughs loudly, "Then I don't think your uncle knows what he's doing," he snarls.

Everyone, even Biggie Pug and Jack Rabbit, gasps and stares at him. Dani puts her fists on her hips and faces Bollsinger. "Never challenge the decision of a *Nerth Doeth*!" she announces.

The Special-Special One quickly changes the subject. "Where are those pipsqueaks who were fighting on the bus? Tweedledumb and Tweedledumber?"

"The Jimis don't like those names," the twins respond. Their mouths open into a snarl and their arms rise, fingers like claws before them.

"Stop pulling those stupid faces!" Bollsinger snarls.

I describe the faces to Leonel who laughs out loud. "Angry emoji!"

That infuriates the Special-Special One even more. "You don't frighten me. Which one are you?" he sneers, poking one of the twins in the forehead. "One or Two? Or don't you know? And what's all this nonsense about hearing voices of your grandfathers?"

The twins continue to face him, snarling.

"Don't…

"you…

"make…

"fun…

"of…

"our…

"grandfathers."

Jack Rabbit jumps between the twins and Bollsinger. "If The Special-Special One wants to make fun of you, he'll make fun of you and your grandfathers. Understand, Tweedledumb and Tweedledumber?"

At that moment Jack Rabbit and the rest of us learn a second valuable lesson. Leonel's quick reaction to Biggie Pug is lesson one. Now comes lesson two. Although the twins continually argue with each other, nobody insults their grandfathers.

One minute Jack Rabbit stands over the Jimis, the next there's a flash as the twins, with a frightening karate yell, leap forward, drop him to the ground and bounce up and down on his chest and stomach.

Biggie Pug and Bruce Bollsinger, eyes popping out of their heads, take a step or two or three back. Without thinking, I jump forward and grab the twins. "Stop it! Both of you. Jimi One, Jimi Two. No fighting."

They stop—which surprises me.

The Jimis stand, facing each other and holding hands, their eyes and mouths open in surprise. "Elder Jimi One and Elder Jimi Two speak again. Success is failure. Failure is success. Lessons learned. Lessons not learned. Who learns what? That's the question."

"What's that supposed to mean?" sneers The Special-Special One. The twins don't answer. They look at each other holding hands and, again, shriek, pull faces and "wash" their hands.

27. Checkmate—Almost!

The door flings open and ten English butlers, each with a broom in hand, enter and line up, facing us.

"Do you think it's a trick?" Jack Rabbit asks The Special-Special One Bollsinger swaggers forward. "No. Not this time. Beside I could knock all of these over with one blow if I wanted."

Biggie Pug jabs his finger at the two Jimis, "Lucky for you two those butlers came in. Otherwise Jack Rabbit and me would've…" He glances at Jack Rabbit who doesn't look the least interested in challenging the twins again.

The last butler slams the door shut behind him. Then the ten butlers stand in a straight line, brooms at the ready, before moving forward slowly, their brooms sweeping the floor in perfect harmony. Each time the brooms hit the floor, they call out a number.

"Ten, sweep, sweep, sweep. Nine, sweep, sweep, sweep."

A quick calculation. By the time they hit zero, we'd be flattened against the back wall—unless we could find some way around them.

A table with plates of meats, cheeses, fruit and drinks appears on the other side of the butlers. We stare at table wondering how we get to it.

"Eight, sweep, sweep, sweep."

Jack Rabbit crouches, preparing to charge the line of butlers and break through to the food and drinks. The Special-Special One calls out numbers as if he was a quarterback and Jack Rabbit the running back.

"Hut, hut, hut!" Jack Rabbit lurches forward. Crash! The wall of butlers is solid. Jack Rabbit is knocked to the floor. The butlers continue sweeping, rolling Jack Rabbit's body before them until he scrambles to his feet and backs away.

"We've got to get behind them," The Special-Special One orders. "You're next Biggie Pug."

Biggie Pug tries to sneak around the outside. Crash! A butler changes direction and knocks Biggie Pug to the floor.

"Seven, sweep, sweep, sweep."

The butlers continue sweeping, pushing us farther from the door and closer to the back wall. Will the butlers and their broomsticks crush us? Will we be flattened against the chessboard wall?

"Stop them," Brenda, the skinny girl, shouts to Bollsinger. "Tell them who you are."

"I command you to stop," The Special-Special One calls out, holding up his hand.

No response. The line advances.

"Six, sweep, sweep, sweep."

Now only about six feet separate us from the wall against which we'll be squashed like bugs. Check mate!

And that's when I see her, the girl with the large glasses and green eyes, standing on the other side of the line of butlers. She points to the chessboard painting on the wall. Then she holds up one finger and moves it to the left. I step to the left. Then two fingers and calls me to her. I walk two small paces forward, following her directions.

"Can't you walk straight, Howl?" Jack Rabbit yells.

"Watch them smash him to the floor," screams Biggie Pug, laughing.

"Five, sweep, sweep, sweep, sweep."

"He moves like a chess piece," Dazmonique calls out. "Like knight."

"A knight?" Jack Rabbit roars with laughter. "Him?"

"He's more like a one of those little pawns that gets knocked around a lot," jokes Bollsinger. He and his friends, without moving forward, imitate my jerky movements.

I continue on—two steps forward, one step to the side, etc.—until I reach the line of butlers.

"Get ready to roll in the dust, Howl," The Special-Special One calls out.

The brooms sweep toward my feet—and stop, inches before I am knocked to the floor. The heads of the line of butlers jerk. All unblinking eyes stare at me.

I move one pace to the side. One pace forward brings me face to face with the unsmiling, unblinking butler. He steps aside. One pace and I walk into the space behind the butlers. No broom touches me.

I look back. "Look at me. Follow my directions," I command, gesturing for the others to copy my chess moves. Slowly they walk forward, passing through the narrow gap I have made between the butlers.

Everyone that is, except Biggie Pug, Jack Rabbit and The Special-Special One. They are still on the other side of the butlers and almost jammed against the back wall.

"This is so stupid," Bollsinger snarls. "I knew that is exactly how to get through, but I wanted to see if howling boy could figure it out for himself. Follow me!" He leads Biggie Pug and Jack Rabbit through the butlers, copying the exact path I followed as if he'd known it all along.

We rush to the table of food, only to be stopped by Biggie Pug and Jack Rabbit. "The Special-Special One eats first," they call out.

After the three have eaten, the others in their gang are permitted to eat. Barely any food left is for my friends and me. But as we reach for the few pieces of meat, cheese and fruit left, the plates magically fill again.

Everyone stuffs food into his or her pockets—in case.

We walk to the door. I turn the doorknob. It opens.

As I leave the room, I glance back. The girl, the table and the butlers have disappeared. Ten broomsticks lie stacked against the chessboard wall.

As we march back to the red hut, The Special-Special One slides alongside me and pinches the flesh on the underside of my arm. "You think you're better than me, don't you, Howl? Think you're special, special, special. Well you're not." The fingers of his other hand grip the small hairs on the back of my neck, pulling them as he presses his lips against my ear. "Don't challenge my leadership—ever." I turn and slap his hands away, determined not to show pain.

As we approach the red hut, Dazmonique shakes my, Leonel's, Dani's and the twins' hands. "*Bon lannwit zanmi espesyal mwen.* Good night, my special friends."

"*Buenas noches, amigos,*" Leonel responds.

"*Nos da,*" I smile. "That's goodnight in Welsh. Sorry, I don't know the word for 'my friends.'"

"Wow! The Jimis are impressed. *Oyasumi* in Japanese."

"We speak English here, not mumbo-jumbo," Biggie Pug growls, sliding alongside us.

Dazmonique holds her hands before her. "*Aswè a, ou dwe brav*! Tonight, be brave!"

"Does anyone understand what that stupid girl says?" The Special-Special One snickers. "She doesn't make sense even when she speaks English."

We soon found out why Dazmonique warned us.

28. To Sleep—or Not to Sleep

Bollsinger and his gang enter the red hut, holding it shut so we can't enter. When we are finally allowed in, we see they've stripped the blankets off our beds and are staggering around, arms before them, as if in a trance.

"The Elder Jimis gave us a question," Bollsinger laughs. "Why blankets say they no want your smelly bodies making them stinky?"

They then kick the blankets around the floor before returning to their beds, snorting with laughter. The Jimis, Leonel and I help each other make our beds.

I lie down and stare out of the window next to my bed. The yellow and gold streaks of the setting sun sink slowly behind the distant hills. A last flash of light across the hilltops before darkness.

I'm exhausted, ready for sleep.

But sleep isn't ready for me—or any of us this night.

Two hours, an hour, fifteen minutes—I don't know how long. My eyes open, wide-awake. I stare at the full moon shining brightly through the window. Suddenly, a shadow crosses it. Something hurtles downward toward the open window next to my bed. Again, that same low hollow whistling sound I've heard before. A sudden whoosh and one of those dark-grey, hunchbacked shapes I saw in my dream sails through the window and lands at the foot of my bed, giggling and mumbling to itself. An arm snakes out, its clawed fingers grasping my ankle in a vice-like grip. I watch in terror, barely able to breathe, as the creature slowly shapes and reshapes itself before my eyes. Images flash before me: Tommy Foxglove's eyelids narrowing as he smirks at me; Bully Harold Bully and his cronies morphing before my eyes; the panicked look on my mother's face as her car careens down the mountainside; Sister Sarah, tears streaming down her face, riding the white horse; three figures in white—bride, bridegroom, and minister—standing before a white church; sunflowers behind the trailer leaning down, reaching for me; and, the man in the black leather coat dangling over me, the stench of his breath choking me.

I sit up in bed, gasping. My lungs burn with each breath. My ankle is covered in blood where the thing grasped it.

A gasp on my left. Leonel and the twins sit up in bed. All groan in agony.

"The Drygoni have found us," Leonel calls out.

I thrash around from side to side in my bed, my ankle burning in pain.

Suddenly the door bursts open and Señor Quit enters. He walks to the end of the room and back three times, his hands circling before him as if swimming. A loud whooshing sound, and my legs are released from the thing's grip. We fall back into our beds as the shadowy figures disappear out of the open windows.

Señor Quit turns in a circle, his arms outstretched. "*Cierre todas las ventanas y cortinas cuando la oscuridad cae.*" A flick of his wrists and all the windows slam shut, and the drapes slide across hiding the moon and anything else out there.

"*Drygoni* never sleep," Leonel whispers. "Doeths must be especially careful at night. *Señor* Quit tells us to close all windows and curtains when darkness falls."

I pull the sheets over my head. *So at no time can we rest. Doeths and Drygoni battle each other at all time. Day and night. Am I ready for battle?*

And then I think of my mother. Lost, waiting for me.

A form stands over me. My body tenses. *Have the* Drygoni *returned to suck me dry?*

I throw back the sheet, fists clenched, adrenalin pumping through me, ready to fight to the death.

Señor Quit stares down at me, smiling. "*Ellos saben quién eres y por qué estás aquí. Seguridad para dormir, joven.*"

Leonel touches me on the arm. "He says, they know who you are and why you are here. He tells you to sleep safely."

Sleep safely? With those things flying through my window and clawing at my legs? And what do the Drygoni know about me?

Señor Quit walks to the door, touches his two fingers to his lips, kisses them, before drawing his fingers in an arc. "*Buenas noches, muchachos. ¡Prepárate para mañana*!"

I don't know what his gesture means, but I do know he's saying goodnight and telling us to be ready for tomorrow.

Next morning, the red hut is silent.

*Are they outside now waiting for us? If not them, maybe one of those English butlers—*Doeth *or* Drygoni*, we don't know—preparing to lead us to our deaths in the desert? This school is definitely no fun.*

"Time to go," The Special-Special One announces. He stands, hands-on-hips, looking very confident.

Did the Drygoni visit him or his cronies?

Bollsinger jerks his head, gesturing for Biggie Pug to open the door. *Is he afraid?* Biggie Pug doesn't move, gesturing instead for Jack Rabbit to open the door.

"Why doesn't someone open the door?" Leonel calls out. "Too frightened?" He walks forward and flattens his face against the door. "I'm looking through the door and I can definitely say there are no Drygoni on the other side. *Señor* Quit got rid of them—for now."

Bollsinger's gang laughs uncomfortably. "You expect us to believe you can see through doors, blind boy?"

I don't laugh. I accept Leonel seeing without seeing, and Dazmonique hearing without hearing.

Leonel opens the door and walks out. The twins follow. "If Leonel says it's safe, then the Jimis know it's safe."

The Special-Special One is about to exit when we hear a dreadful scream from outside. He jumps back inside and slams the door shut. I leap forward. "The twins and Leonel are in danger. Let me out," I yell. "We must help them."

I push The Special-Special One aside and open the door. The Jimis stand like mixed martial arts fighters, their hands locked around each other's throats. "*Drygoni* strangling Jimisi emoji! Agh!" they bellow as Leonel roars with laughter.

Bollsinger and his gang push past us. "I knew you were playing a stupid game," The Special-Special One sneers. "Think you can frighten me? No chance. And off he marches, mumbling angrily to himself.

We follow, trying not to laugh—but we do. Each time we do, one of Bollsinger's cronies spins around, raises his fist and smashes it into his palm.

The adults are already seated at the table eating breakfast when we arrive.

Dani and Dazmonique giggle as I tell of the twins and Jimis' trick on The Special-Special One. Bollsinger's friend Brenda glowers at me. "I'm going to tell him what you said," she announces. "Expect a bloody nose." Before she can say anything, The Special-Special One, neck and face glowing red with anger, marches to a table and grabs a chair, slamming it on the ground. But, when he tries to sit, the chair moves. He falls flat on his backside. We try not the laugh. By now Bollsinger's face is beetroot red. The veins pulsate in his neck. He's ready to show someone's nose and teeth a close-up of his clenched fist.

Dazmonique walks forward, mumbles a few words and quietly sits in a chair. I stand alongside her. "Chair knows him angry. Doesn't like that," she whispers.

Does the chair know Bollsinger's angry? Really?

I take several deep breaths and prepare to sit in the chair next to Dazmonique.

Just as I'm about to sit, Dazmonique grabs my arm and fixes me with her pale blue eyes. "You no believe me. Epi ou toujou ou gen dout. And still you doubt. Your head still out there in Safonal world, not here."

Her deep blue eyes fix me in my place. "I do believe," I stammer. "I know I'm here." Dazmonique releases my arm, watching me closely as I edge my body down on the chair as I keep repeating to myself, *Stay calm! The chair knows my mood!*

The chair doesn't move.

"Now you here," Dazmonique smiles "Crossingway. Whether you here or there, up to you, Howell. *Fè atansyon: dout pran ou tounen nan mond lan nan Safonal*. Be careful: doubt take you back to world of *Safonal*."

The Special-Special One's frustration has reached boiling point. His face has gone from bright red to livid white. The veins in his neck bulge as he pants, ready to explode. He clenches his fists and bites his lip as he watches my friends calmly sit at the breakfast table. His chair will not stay still. Finally, he storms out, slamming the door behind him.

Biggie Pug, Jack Rabbit and Brenda look at each other. They're torn. Both are hungry, wanting breakfast. But both know The Special-Special One will be enraged if they stay and eat.

"Who wants stupid breakfast anyway?" Biggie Pug hisses as he, Jack Rabbit and Brenda head for the door.

We look at the adults, wondering how they'll react to Bollsinger and his crew exiting. Nothing. They don't seem to notice. They talk quietly with each other. Something is far more important than the tantrums of a few boys.

Leonel touches me on the arm. "What would you like for breakfast?"

"Scrambled eggs in a tortilla, toast and jelly," I reply, looking around for a butler. No need. The food appears.

As we eat, we wait for an adult to tell us about our night visitors. Similar things visited the girls too. Esther Evening Star drove them away. But the adults continue to speak quietly among themselves. Something is definitely troubling them.

Finally Uncle Tal stands and bangs a spoon on the table. Two butlers suddenly appear. "Find those three boys and that girl." Thirty seconds later the butlers return, dragging The Special-Special One, Biggie Pug, Jack Rabbit and Brenda by the scruff of their necks.

"Sit," Uncle Tal commands, pointing to chairs that appear.

Uncle Tal swirls his cloak around himself. "We meet in the assembly hut in fifteen minutes." His head turns, eyes fixed on Bollsinger. "I trust you remember what colour the assembly hut is." His eyes sweep the room. "Don't be late," he barks. And with that, he and the other adults rush out of the room.

That's it? No telling us what's troubling the adults? What happened last night? No answers?

29. Drygoni Are Relentless

The blue hut is square outside, oblong inside, and its walls are covered in mathematical and other symbols, none of which make sense. All four walls are windowless, stretching high above us. Tall stone pillars reach up to the pointed roof, making the whole place look like a cathedral, without the stained-glass windows or the altar. Pews line the central aisle. A wooden platform rises ten feet above the floor at the front of the room. Five high-backed wooden chairs stand behind a long oak table. The four adults sit leaving one chair empty.

We edge forward, wondering if the pews, lined up in two rows at ground level, will stay or suddenly move. We sit cautiously. The pews remain in place.

Uncle Tal stands and looks down at us. "My name is Taliesin. You may call me Tal," he booms. "You have already met *Señor Cuitláhuac*. You have not met *Madame Bouzius*." The large dark-skinned woman wearing sandals, a long white shirt and dress, and a white headscarf tied in a knot at the back smiles and bows to Uncle Tal. As she nods to us, her many seashell necklaces and bracelets jangle, wafting a delicate perfume over us. "And last but not least," Tal continues, gesturing to Dani Walks-Her-Pony's mother, "Madame Esther Evening Star." He pauses. "You notice an empty chair at the end.

My mother's chair!

All four adults glance at the empty chair at the end of the line. "One of our members is missing."

Dazmonique leans closer to me. "'Missing' not right word. *Drygoni* kidnap your mother. Now want you."

Before I can ask Dazmonique how she knows these things, Uncle Tal continues his talk. "This is not your usual school. No teachers to teach or learners to learn. What you need to know, you already know." Words—*Doeths, Drygoni* and *Safonals*—float around us, like atoms carefully bouncing away from and avoiding one another.

From inside my head comes a roar of laughter and the gruff voice of Bully Harold Bully. *"Riddles and more riddles, Howl. Does your weird uncle ever listen to himself?"*

I close my eyes. *They're here, even in Camp* Corwynt.

Dazmonique taps me on the arm. "Ou pote yo. You bring them," she whispers. "Yo pa isit la. They not here. Ou pote yo."

She knows about my mother's kidnapping and about Bully Harold Bully and his cronies' voices?

"You probably assume you are all very special," Uncle Tal resumes. Biggie Pug and Jack Rabbit high five The Special-Special One. "You are not," Uncle Tal affirms.

A gasp from The Special-Special One and his gang. Then they turn and smirk at me. They've decided I'm one of the 'nots.'

Uncle Tal points his long index finger at each of us. "You are only special when you have proven yourself worthy. At the moment, you are a little more aware than most people, the *Safonals*."

A little boy sitting next to Bollsinger leans over. "What's a *Safonal*?" The Special-Special chuckles quietly and pushes the boy away. "As if I'd tell you."

"*Safonals*," Uncle Tal continues, smiling as he looks at the little boy, "is the word we use for most people, the multitudes. They are the not knowing. The world has many *Doeths*, wise ones. Some you see here, before you. *Doeths* seek and share the natural goodness that exists in the world around us. Trees, wind, rivers, and so much more speak to them, magically sharing that goodness.

Opposing *Doeths* are the *Drygoni*, evil ones. There are far more of them than us. They are in continual battle with the *Doeths*, confusing the Safonals, offering them unneeded gifts and dragging them over to their side. As for all of you," he continues, his eyes focusing on each of us in turn, "you are all potential *Doeths*. Unfortunately, that means you are also potential *Drygoni*!"

As Uncle Tal continues, I think back to the first time I'd heard those words. Brenda Blackstone and her friends mercilessly teased, both in school and on Facebook, this girl in my class, Shirley Reese. Shirley was shy and from a very poor family. "Loser, dog face, so gross everyone hates you. Why don't you kill yourself, so we don't have to look at you?" Shirley had to put up with this every day.

"Those girls have fallen under the spell of the *Drygoni*," my mother said to my father. "In place of friendship and love," she continued, "they offer isolation and hatred." My mother tried to meet with the girl, to help her—but it was too late. Shirley Reece didn't come to school ever again. I never saw her, and her family never talked about her.

"*Drygoni* use *Safonals,*" Uncle Tal emphasises. "They use them to spread *Drygoni* power, evil power, and upset the balance of the world."

"*Koyaanisqatsi*," Dani whispers. "Word of my people. 'Life out of balance.' Dangerous. Evil rules."

"All that prevents this," Uncle Tal continues, "all that keeps the world in balance is Doeth power." He stares down at me. "Drygoni are formidable. You never know who or what they'll use to overcome us. Nor do you know when they'll attack. Some of you sitting here may soon be in the grips of the *Drygoni*."

Dani, signing for Dazmonique, stops. We all look at each other. *Who will the* Drygoni *capture?*

The Special-Special One and his gang point at me, mouthing, "*Drygoni*."

Uncle Tal smiles. "Just a warning. Something for you all to think about. Learn whom to trust. Friends, family, teachers, even yourself—all can deceive you."

Biggie Pug and Jack Rabbit and The Special-Special One give thumbs-up to each other and thumbs-down to others. In their minds, they know who to trust.

A wave of Uncle Tal's hand and the words floating around us disappear. Uncle Tal leans on the table, looking at each of us in turn. "You must each prove yourself worthy to accept an inheritance of Doeth power offered you. Be vigilant. Never let Safonal emotions doubt or weaken you. You are never safe. They may even come here, to this place, testing you, seeking some to join them." He looks around. "*Drygoni* are relentless. No one is safe from them."

He looked at the three others on the stage, then at the empty chair.

His long index finger sweeps across us. "If you fail the tasks before you, there will be no transfer of Doeth power from family or friend. No failing grade, no request to pack your bags. You'll suddenly find yourself back home sleeping in your own bed and dining with your family. If you spend time thinking carefully about what happened, you might return. If not, you're on your own. You'll live the rest of your life as a *Safonal*, knowing you could have been Doeth. That is unless you have already become a *Drygoni*."

Señor Quit and *Madame* Bouzius now stand, each addressing us in their own language. The Special-Special One snickers, "If all this stuff is so important, why can't these people speak English?"

"Look around," the voices in my head continue. *"Everyone nods, pretending to understand while these two drone on. They're boring, Howl. Close your eyes. Dream of being back home."*

Something jams itself into my neck. It's the turquoise and silver necklace Dani gave me. I jerk awake and meet the pale blue eyes of Dazmonique.

Dazmonique stares at me. "*Vwa pa bon, Howell.* Voice not good. You must get special power. *Drygoni* want it."

Dani points to the warning on the back of the turquoise and silver necklace. "Help me overcome my greatest enemy—myself."

What's more dangerous? The Drygoni *or myself?*

30. The Game We Think We Know—but Don't

Uncle Tal claps his hands, startling the room. "Why don't we play a game? Everyone outside."

We scramble to exit and line up outside. "Maybe it's like *Ullamaliztil*, that game the Aztecs used to play," Leonel offers. "The Aztec ball game with three players on each side, a hard rubber ball, and a ring up high. As the ball passes through the ring, it represents the sun passing through the day and into the night."

The Jimis jump up and down. "We know that one. But isn't the leader of the losing team killed in front of everyone? They spread out their arms before drawing one hand across their necks. Sacrificial death emoji."

The Special-Special One punches me in the arm. "That will be you, Howl. Captain of this bunch of losers. Who wants to be on Howling Boy's losing team?" High-fives and laughter.

Leonel grips my arm. "I'll be on your team, Howell."

"Oh, no!" Biggie Pug roars. "The blind boy on Howl's team. I'm so scared. My kn-kn-knees are kn-kn-knocking."

"Leonel good choice," Dazmonique answers. "Sometimes seeing, like hearing, not important. I on your team too."

"Oh, we need help! Howling Boy has the blind boy and the deaf girl on his team," Jack Rabbit giggles.

Uncle Tal waves his arms. "Gather on the baseball field."

"Baseball," Leonel says, shocked. "We could play *Ulama de cadera*. That's like *Ullamaliztil*. People play it today in Mexico and there are no blood sacrifices."

"No," I reply. "I'm sure we're playing baseball. And in this steaming hot canyon."

Bollsinger punches me again. "Your team better get used to chasing all the home runs I'm going to hit, loser."

My head hangs down. *Chasing home runs in this heat? Not much fun.*

Dani stands in front of me, hands-on-hips. "Why do you think we've lost before we've begun, Howell? That's Safonal thinking. Maybe this is a game you think you know—but don't."

I turn away, head down, not convinced.

The red ground that slopes down to the dry riverbed is now completely flat, covered in grass. No white lines, no base pads—except for the rectangle where Uncle Tal stands holding a bat.

"Two sides!" Uncle Tal yells. "Quick!"

"I've chosen my team," The Special-Special One proclaims. "Biggie Pug, Jack Rabbit, Brenda and you boys. All others are with that loser. Team Rejects." Laughter.

"We bat first." He grabs a bat and swings it. "Maybe Team Rejects will bat before sundown. But I wouldn't bet on it."

Dani walks to the mound. "Look who's pitching! Little Chief What's-Her-Name!" Bollsinger continues. He taps his hands on his mouth making a war-whoop.

"That's not very nice of you," the twins respond.

"Quiet, pipsqueaks," The Special-Special One responds. "Howling boy, you'd better send your outfield way back," he taunts. "Deep into the canyon."

"I'll play catcher," Leonel announces.

Bollsinger's team roars with laughter. "Great. A blind catcher. Your team loses before we even begin."

Madame Bouzius strides to the mound. "You not play like that. That Safonal game. We not Safonals."

Baseball's baseball, I think to myself. *A bat, a ball and bases. What else is there?*

Madame Bouzius hold her arms wide and jangles the shell bracelets. A butler, complete with black tuxedo, pointed shoes and a napkin dangling from one arm appears on the pitcher's mound.

"Him throw ball," Madame Bouzius continues before leaving the field and joining the other adults sitting on chairs, which miraculously appear.

"This is great!" crows Bollsinger. "A pitcher who looks like he's serving tables, dumb do-nothing fielders, and a blind catcher."

Leonel crouches down, catcher's mitt at the ready facing the wrong direction! The Special-Special One and his team laugh as I turn Leonel around before trotting off to where I think a shortstop should stand. Bollsinger strolls to the plate. He points his bat to the distant mountain. "Look for the ball over…"

The Special-Special One doesn't have time to complete his sentence. A thud and the ball smashes into Leonel's catcher's mitt.

"Strike one!" yells a butler-umpire who suddenly appears behind Leonel. I study the butler-pitcher. No signal, no wind up, just a ball flying at 120 miles per hour.

"Not fair," The Special-Special One yells. "I wasn't ready." He stands back in the batter's box, gritting his teeth, waiting for the butler to throw the ball. A thud as the ball hits the catcher's mitt.

"Strike two!" calls the butler-umpire.

The Special-Special One stomps away from the plate, banging the baseball bat on the ground and mumbling to himself.

"Want me to hit for you?" Leonel jokes.

"Shut your mouth!" Bollsinger screams before returning to the plate. This time the ball floats slowly through the air. I stare at it. The ball has wings! The Special-Special One waits, licking his lips. This ball is headed for the Pacific

Ocean. But just as he is about to hit it, the ball circled in front of him just out of reach. He steps forward swinging wildly as the ball circles his bat, failing to connect.

Bollsinger jerks his bat this way and that way as if trying to hit some fast-moving, radar-guided piñata. After a few seconds, the ball thuds into Leonel's mitt.

"Strike three! You're out!" yells the umpire.

"This game is stupid, stupid, stupid," Bollsinger shrieks. He throws the bat at Jack Rabbit's feet.

Knees quaking, Jack Rabbit stands at the plate. Whistle, thud, "Strike One!"

"Wow! That one almost hit you in the head," cries Leonel.

That's too much for Jack Rabbit. He runs from the home plate whining, "I'm out! I'm out!" and throws the bat at Biggie Pug.

Two balls, two strikes and a missed dancing ball leaves Biggie Pug kicking dust into Leonel's face.

"Three outs! We're up!" I yell.

"You're not," The Special-Special One replies. "Three more players on my team bat before Team Reject."

"That's not the rule."

"It's my rule."

I want to appeal to the adults, but they're huddled together talking, uninterested in the game.

"Let them bat," Leonel says. "It'll be over in two minutes."

And it is. Only Brenda manages to hit the ball—or should I say the ball hit her bat. She stands at the plate, eyes closed, the bat held out in front of her. "Bunt!" Leonel yells, running forward, his hands digging at the grass. He scoops up the ball and hurls it toward Dazmonique who stands at what she thinks is first base. "Open your glove, Daz." Leonel yells. Smack. The ball lies cradled in her glove. Brenda, the batter, hasn't moved.

"Out at first," the butler-umpire yells.

Leonel sees an invisible ball. Dazmonique hears Leonel's shout. Definitely not Team Reject, I marvel.

Bollsinger leaps forward and throws the bat at me. "Team Reject up. I'll be catcher," he yells to his team. "Thirty seconds and this bunch will be out!"

As I walk to the plate, Leonel stops me. "Remember," he whispers, "we're not in a Safonal place, and this is not the Safonal game. We're here, playing this game."

Bollsinger screams, "Weak batter! Weak batter!" in my ear. He crouches behind the plate, his gloved hand outstretched. His free hand waves about, putting a spell on me. "Hocus pocus, hear my call. Crack his head with a spit ball."

"It's coming Howl," Bollsinger yells. A whistle, a thud and the voice of the butler-umpire roars in my ear, "Strike one!"

Leonel crosses to me. "Be a Doeth. Know what the ball is going to do."

Know what the ball…?

Whistle, thud. "Strike two!"

Be a Doeth, I repeat to myself. *Know what the ball is going to do.*

"The next one will dance around in front of your eyes," guffaws The Special-Special One. "You'll chase it like you're swatting flies."

I close my eyes, feeling my hands and fingers melt into the bat. No looking, no listening. *Know what the ball's going to do*. A swing and crack of the bat and my team yells. "Run, run!" *But where?* No white lines to direct me! First base to my right. A base pad appears in front of me. Second must be at a right angle.

Brenda finally finds the ball. She grabs it and throws. "Slide, slide," Dani shouts. I do, even though I don't know where to slide. My leg slams into the second base pad that magically appears.

Suddenly the butler-umpire appears at second base. "Safe!"

"Give me the bat!" Bollsinger pushes aside Leonel and stands in the batting box. "If Howl can do it, I can."

Two strikes and Bollsinger turns and grabs Leonel. "You told him something, didn't you? What did you tell him?"

"I told him to be *Doeth*."

"What is that supposed to mean?" Bollsinger retorts. "I'm more of *Doeth* than he'll ever be." He stands, eyes slits, face twisted, wiggling his body, trying to be Doeth.

Whistle, thud, "Strike three! You're out!"

The Special-Special One throws the bat at Leonel. "Let's see what you can do, blind boy."

Leonel stands at the plate as Biggie Pug and Jack Rabbit taunt him.

"Are you sure you're facing the right direction?" they yell. "Watch you don't get yourself beaned. Infield in. No-hit batter, no-hit batter."

A whistle and crack of the bat. Leonel runs for first base. "Run, Howell, run!" Dani yells. I head for where I think third base should be. The base pad appears before me. I fly on to home plate. The Special-Special One stands, open-mouthed, totally confused as I barrel toward him. What should he do? Defend the plate? But where is the plate? And where is the ball? Suddenly a whistling sound and the ball heads straight toward Bollsinger. He throws down his glove and runs, just as I slide into home plate, closely followed by Leonel.

"Two runs score," calls the butler-umpire.

Before we can continue the game, Uncle Tal leaps to his feet. He points up to where the cloudless blue sky has changed from yellow to dark grey. In minutes, red and black clouds roil and tumble overhead.

"They're coming," he shouts. A wave of his hand and butlers, pitcher's mound and baseball field disappear. We stand in a dry riverbed of soft sand.

"Into the red hut, all of you," Uncle Tal yells. "No time to waste. They're coming!"

Uncle Tal grabs my arm and stares into my eyes. "Remember, nephew: What you need to know, you already know. The question is, how will you use or misuse that knowledge? Will it develop or lessen, particularly if we adults are not around to assist you? Only you know the answer, nephew. Now, hurry. We need to speak to all of you."

And with that he and Madame Bouzius skim across the soft sand and wait outside the red hut.

What now? I think to myself. *What is going to happen? And what did Uncle Tal mean when he said, 'If we adults are not around to assist you'?*

31. *Gran Danje.* Great Danger

Pulled by the adults, we finally stand on solid ground outside the red hut. Uncle Tal enters the boys' side, Madame Bouzius the girls', leaving us all outside with strict instructions to wait.

Dani taps me on the arm and points to Dazmonique. Her head is tilted, and her hands are cupped around her ears.

"*Gran danje.* Great danger. Dazmonique hear screams. Steel against steel. Clashing. Shouts. Ripping. Tearing. Clawing. She hear them."

Biggie Pug cups his hands over his ears. "Freaky. I hear the deaf girl talking nonsense."

Jack Rabbit joins in. "Shrieks. The crowd at the football stadium."

"Or roar of cars at Daytona 500," Bollsinger adds. "Brr, brr, brr."

Dani steps forward, her face inches from The Special-Special One. "Dazmonique hears and Leonel sees," she announces. "Get used to it! Stop thinking like Safonals."

The three puff out their cheeks, looking as if they are going to explode with laughter. "Us Safonals," they roar.

"When I look at you," Dani continues looking straight at The Special-Special One, "I see a dark shadow crossing your face."

The Special-Special One glowers and grinds his teeth, his fist clenches, wanting to hit Dani.

I stand between them.

The tension breaks when Biggie Pug and Jack Rabbit dance around Leonel and Dazmonique, chanting, "Blind boy sees, and deaf girl hears."

Bollsinger faces the Jimis who hold hands. He laughs aloud. "Look out! Another elder pipsqueak unanswerable question. Why don't you two get yourselves a crystal ball and some Tarot cards?"

"Elder Jimi One and Elder Jimi Two ask, 'What is here, soon not here?'"

"'Here, soon not here?'" shouts The Special-Special One. "I'd say it was Howl and his gang of idiots!" He punches the Jimis on the arms. "You're crazy, all of you. Speaking non-stop gobbledygook. And I know you cheated in that baseball game. No way Team Reject could beat Team Special?"

Dazmonique holds out her hands. "*Yon bagay etranj pral rive.*"

"No mumbo-jumbo!" Brenda shouts. "No gibberish."

Dazmonique stares at her. "Something strange happens."

"Well why didn't you say so? In plain English?" Brenda snaps back, pushing her face into Dazmonique's.

Dazmonique holds up her hand, finger-pointing at The Special-Special One. "*Ou pa swiv li. Danjere.*"

"Again, with the mumbo-jumbo!"

"You no follow him. Danger!" Dazmonique translates.

Brenda stares at Dazmonique as she points at me. "You no follow him. Stupid!"

Suddenly Uncle Tal and Madame Bouzius exit the respective ends of the red hut. Their presence stops the ugly chatter. "Boys follow me. Girls follow Madame Bouzius. Come! We have something important to tell you all."

We troop silently into the red hut, following Uncle Tal and gather by our beds. Uncle Tal stands at the top of the room and raises his hands. "The Drygoni are coming," he declares. "They know you are all here. As long as we adults remain, the Drygoni will stay away and you will not face the ultimate challenge: the Doeth test of inner strength. We adults must leave so they can test all of you."

Do we have to face the Drygoni *alone?* My head shakes back and forth. *I can't do that.*

"A final word," Uncle Tal says before leaving. "Remember: sometimes you succeed by failing, and sometimes you fail by succeeding."

And with that he leaves the hut.

For a moment there is silence. Then The Special-Special One bursts out laughing out loud repeating Uncle Tal's final words. "What on earth does that mean? Succeed by failing and fail by succeeding? I've never heard such drivel in my life." He and his cronies join in the laughter while Leonel, the twins and I sit quietly on our beds. We check the windows over and over again, making sure they're shut, and the drapes drawn.

Hopefully no *Drygoni* will attack this night.

Or will they?

32. The Figure at the Bottom of the Bed

I lie in the darkness, listening to the thunder rumbling overhead. Heavy raindrops splatter on the roof of the hut. A sudden thunderclap explodes overhead. The red hut shakes.

I pull the sheet over my head, mumbling prayers and wishing I were anywhere but here. A huge thunderclap follows the crackle and flash of lightning A roar as the raindrops become baseball-sized hailstones pounding on the roof, threatening to smash it, flooding our bedroom.

I clench my fists and stuff the sheet in my mouth. I don't want to cry out. Again, the lightning and thunder follow in quick succession. Too quick. Cries and squeals come from the twins.

I keep repeating, *Don't worry. The storm will pass. When we wake, the adults will still be with us.* But the storm is not passing. It is staying directly overhead.

I poke my head out from underneath the blankets. Leonel lies on his back, his eyes open staring up. *What's he looking at?*

"*Dando vueltas,* circling, circling," he chants. "*Abajo*, down. Dark shapes. Formless shapes. Shapeless shapes. *Rasgando, rasgando.* Ripping, tearing. Force meets force. Find them. Destroy them. Force meets force. *Obscuridad*, darkness. He sees them. Retreat. Gather again high above. *Formas sin forma que giran.* Shapeless shapes whirling. Obscuridad. Down they come again. He sees them. Shrieking, cackling. *Ataque*, attack."

Is he having a nightmare? Should I wake him?

I carefully pull back the sheet and place my foot on the ground. An explosion. A window shatters. Howling wind races around the room. Screams, including my own, fill the hut. I dive back into bed and wrap myself in the sheets. But something is trying to rip them from me.

In seconds, the wind retreats. I poke my head from beneath my blankets. *Who is that standing at the foot of my bed in the darkness?* A long hiss escapes its mouth. The stench of its foul breath swirls around me. A single yellow light pierces the sheets, stabbing through my closed eyelids and swirling around my brain.

"Poor Howl," a voice howls. *"Filled with doubts. His uncle thinks he's special, but he's not. He wants to return to the world of Safonals. He'll be there soon."*

I stay hidden under the blankets, crunched into a ball, praying the storm would die, and the figure leave the hut.

33. "Plas Kochma. Nightmare Place"

Finally, after a sleepless night, daylight. I peek from beneath the bedclothes. Nothing. No figure. I crawl out of bed and run to the shower. Too late.

My skin tightens and the air squeezes out of my lungs. The water is ice-cold. "Sorry, Howl. We must have used up all the hot water." Biggie Pug roars with laughter as I hop in and out of the shower, gasping for air as the frigid water chills my body.

I run back to the drying area and grab for my towel. Soaking wet. "Sorry again," Jack Rabbit sneers. "My bad. I grabbed your towel by mistake. When I realised I was touching your cooties, I threw your towel on the wet floor." He jerks his head back and roars with laughter.

"Here, take mine." Biggie Pug flicks his towel, which snaps across my stomach leaving a red mark.

All these two fools can think about are their childish tricks.

And where is The Special-Special One?

"Here," Leonel says. "Take mine! It's not that wet."

I dry using Leonel's towel while Biggie Pug and Jack Rabbit dance around shouting, "Cooties, cooties!"

The twins fight over a towel, even though it's wet. I make them agree to share, each using half the towel.

Showered and dressed, we exit the red hut wondering if one of those butlers waits for us—and if it is a *Drygoni* or *Doeth*.

No butler, but many things have changed. Overhead dark clouds block the sun. Over the distant hilltops, lightning flashes followed by thunder.

Leonel grasps my arm. "The air. It smells different. Tell me what you see."

"Everything is darker, greyer."

Leonel takes a step forward and bumps his shin against a rock.

"That wasn't here yesterday," he grimaces. "This is not the same place."

A butler appears before us. "Breakfast in grey hut."

"Grey hut?" Leonel responds. "There's no grey hut."

The butler points to what was the yellow hut yesterday. Now grey. I turn around. Our red hut is now a washed-out green.

At breakfast, we sit silently waiting for Uncle Tal, *Señor* Quit, Esther Evening Star and *Madame* Bouzius to tell us what happened in the night.

Dani slides alongside. "How are you?"

"Confused," I respond. "The Special-Special One seems to have disappeared."

"Disappeared?" Dani murmurs. "Let's hope the adults come soon and explain all this."

None appears.

The butlers place four boxes of cereal on the table. Not enough for all of us. Immediately Biggie Pug grabs three boxes and passes them to his gang members. I share the last box with my friends. Dry cereal, no milk.

A butler walks to the front of the room. "After cleaning up," the butler announces, "he say, tell them to go to brown hut, he say. Task set, he say. Don't be late."

Who's this "he" talking to the butler? And which hut is brown?

We want answers, but none of us dare ask the questions.

Dazmonique stands, puts her hands out straight and turns slowly in a circle.

"Watch out!" Biggie Pug laughs. "She's casting a spell."

"She's changing Howl and his gang into pea-brained rhinoceroses," Jack Rabbit adds.

Those two are still the same. Did they experience anything different during the night?

"Listen," Jack Rabbit giggles. "The deaf girl's mumbling something."

Dazmonique holds her hands as if feeling something. "Not same place," she whispers. "We in their place. *Plas kochma*. Nightmare place."

Biggie Pug staggers around imitating Dazmonique, mumbling. "I am so freaked out."

I must admit, Dazmonique does look strange, revolving around, and repeating her words.

Brenda stops in front of me. "Why do you stay with these crazies, Howl?"

I pause, staring back at Brenda.

Dani pushes me in the arm. "Answer her!"

"They're my friends," I mumble.

Brenda joins the rest of the gang, minus Bollsinger, as they chant, "Crazies, crazies," Leonel leans closer to me. "I know the answer to the Elder Jimi One and Elder Jimi Two's riddle."

"What don't you know that you do know?" I question.

"Not that one," Leonel answers. "That one is for you. The riddle that asked, 'What is here, soon not here?' The answer is the adults."

The twins spin around and around, looking for the adults.

"And the Special-Special One," Dani adds.

"Maybe he went with the adults," the Jimis chime in. "He said himself he was Special-Special."

"I say before," Dazmonique chimes in. "*Pa espesyal*. He not special. *Li pa ak granmoun*. He not with adults."

"Then we don't know where he is," Leonel adds.

"Biggie Pug," the twins call out. "Where's Bollsinger?"

Biggie Pug stands in front of them, fists on his hips and face contorted into a snarl. "Why should I tell you? Remember: he's a Special-Special. Guaranteed Doeth. Not like any of you."

"None of us is a guaranteed Doeth," Dani responds.

"You don't know what you're talking about Minnehaha," Brenda sneers. "Bollsinger came from a long line of *Doeths*."

"No guarantee," Dazmonique adds. "All earn it for ourselves."

"I wouldn't like to be in your shoes when I to tell him what you all said," Brenda replies.

I turn to my friends. "All I do know is my Uncle Tal told us the adults would leave," I offer, "and we'd be alone. To be tested by the Drygoni."

"What are you freaks mumbling about?" Jack Rabbit growls.

Before Leonel can answer, the butler shouts, "Brown hut now, he says. He talks in one minute, he says. Don't be late."

As we leave the red hut and head for the brown hut, Biggie Pug drifts alongside me. "You can join us whenever you're ready, Howl."

Why does he keep saying this?

34. Evil Thoughts

Biggie Pug, Jack Rabbit, Brenda and their cronies rush into the brown hut, taking the back seats. "Teachers' pets up front," squeaks Brenda. She punches Dani's arm and nods toward the front desks, "I said, teachers' pets up front, Pocahontas."

"What you say is really ugly," the twins blurt out. They cross their eyes and poke out their tongues. "Ugly Brenda emoji."

Brenda closes her eyes and holds out her arms. "What happens when the two pipsqueaks are left alone in the desert?" the stupid grandfathers ask. "They get lost and die side by side," she snarls.

The twins adopt a karate stance. Brenda runs to the back of the room hiding behind Biggie Pug.

"Plenty of room at the back with us," Biggie Pug shouts. "Any of you want to join us? What about you, Howell?"

Leonel grabs my arm. "Sit up front with me, Howell." As we sit, a barrage of paper spit balls rain down on us from the back of the room accompanied by cries of "Great shot, bull's-eye, strike!"

Naturally, Jimi One and Jimi Two want the same desk. After Dani's negotiations, they share a seat, each perched on half, dangling off the edges and glowering at the other.

"Word is you losers had trouble sleeping last night," Jack Rabbit shouts.

"Not us," Biggie Pug adds, hurling a large spit ball that hits me square in the back of my head. "Slept like babies, all of us."

We sit there, spit balls and insults piling up around us.

We wait. And wait. I glance at the clock on the wall. Although it ticks, the hands don't move.

Some boys and girls talk of what we'll learn now that Uncle Tal and the other useless teachers have left. They talk of poisons, spells, magic potions, and other things.

"When I get back home," Ellen, a girl with braces, boasts, "I'm going to change this good-looking boy, captain of the football team, who ignores me, into a pig. He'll grunt and run around the football field, covered in mud as he chases those stomach-turning cheerleaders." She runs around the room pretending to run as some boy run after her, grunting and squealing.

"You must not use your power to do hurtful things," Dani responds.

"Who listens to you anymore? Can't you see that things have changed?" Brenda yells.

Jack Rabbit turns to the rest of the gang. "Let's hear more ideas."

"More, more, more!" they all chant.

"We could make ourselves invisible," another shouts. "And then we can creep into the homes of kids we don't like, take pictures of them when they're sleeping, draw moustaches and eyelashes with magic marker on their faces, and paste them on Snapchat and Facebook. And what if we stole one of their prized possessions and hid it. Or read their diaries and then tell everyone what they're writing and who they secretly like. Or rip out pages and pin them on a notice board in the school hallway."

"We are not here to do things like that," I call out.

But they are not listening to me. The shouts of "More, more, more!" drown me out.

Two boys now leap to their feet, enacting the cruel things they'll do to their enemies: an ice-cold drink suddenly boils in someone's mouth, hundreds of cockroaches scuttle under bed sheets, seagulls rip out hair, food turns into maggots, snakes slither into backpacks, or make wasps fly into their ears. The list goes on and on. Some girls put their hands over their ears and squeal in horror, but that only makes these two boys shout louder.

"You are all so cruel," Dani calls out.

"Who listens to you, Minnehaha?" shouts one of the boys.

Dazmonique stands. "You all change," she says. "You not same as yesterday."

"We no want be goody-goody all time," cries Brenda, imitating Dazmonique.

"You're all acting like bad Safonal kids who get some silly powers," Dani adds.

"Maybe sometime we want to be just regular kids," says Jack Rabbit. "Having a little fun."

Dazmonique stands and faces all of them. "You choose their place. Too easy change."

"More, more, more!"

The boys' conversation now turns to cloaks of invisibility: plastering food over people's hair and clothing; stealing valuable items from shops; and, stealing cell phones and computers and writing hateful texts and emails, guaranteed to get them into trouble.

Dani jumps to her feet. "Enough! We are supposed to be better than this. We're special, potential Doeths."

"Hey, Chief Wampum speaks!" Brenda giggles. "Where's your peace pipe? Have you drunkum fire water today?"

The twins, fists on their hips, face Brenda. "You are a very cruel person."

"Oh, boo-hoo," Jack Rabbit sneers, raising his fists to the twins.

"Thoughts are like arrows," Dani continues, shouting above the noise. "Once released, they strike their mark."

A crowd gathers firing arrows, yelling war whoops and firing make-belief arrows.

"Evil thoughts," Dani continues, "may one day come back to haunt and hurt you." She turns to me. "What is happening, Howell? And why don't you say or do anything?"

Biggie Pug shouts above the noise. “No point asking howling boy to help. He needs his weird uncle to tell him what to do to say. Go tell your useless uncle we’re waiting—if you can find him.”

Suddenly the door bursts open and The Special-Special One strides in.

“Quiet! Sit down all of you!” Immediately everyone sits down, their eyes fixed on him. “We’re supposed to be special, yet all I hear are silly ideas. Safonal ideas.”

“The Jimis think something really weird is going on,” the twins whisper. “The Special-Special One seems so normal.” Dani, Leonel and I nod in agreement.

“*Pa gen anyen nòmal.*” Dazmonique blurts out. “Nothing normal. Changes in the night,” she continues. “*Nou tout ap viv nan mond kochma yo kounye a.* We all living in their nightmare world now. *Pran prekosyon nou*! Beware!” Her eyes meet each of ours. “*Li vini koulye a*,” she says. “He comes.”

“Are you talking about the Special-Special One?” the twins ask. “Because he’s already here.”

Dazmonique shakes her head, raises her arm and points to the door. “*Li vini koulye a.* He come now.”

We all stare at the door.

35. Professor Drago Lucian

The sickening stench of stale, rancid gym socks announces his arrival. He flings open the door, strides to the front of the class and drops a pile of books on the lectern. The thud breaks the silence. He strides to the blackboard and writes his name: Professor Drago Lucian. He is dressed in the same black leather coat tied in the middle with thick string and heavy black boots.

He turns to The Special-Special One. "Please take your place, Mr. Bollsinger."

As Bollsinger moves to the back of the class, Professor Drago Lucian dangles over the lectern, pointing to each of us as he calls out our names.

It's him! The alley, the desert, now here? Why?

When he comes to me, he leans forward, glowering down with his one dark red eye as the yellow spot crosses my body. He flashes his yellow teeth in a grimace. "We've met before," he hisses. "In the alley. Alone in the desert. You are her son. Now you're here."

His head jerks away, surveying the room. He taps the blackboard. "Professor Drago Lucian," he scowls. As he speaks, he creeps up behind Dazmonique as she watches Dani's signing hands and screams his name in her ear. She doesn't respond. Dani is about to speak when Professor Lucian lurches his head around to face her. "No need to tell me. The mumbo-jumbo voodoo girl is deaf."

He turns and flashes his hand in front of Leonel's face, the Professor' long fingernails inches from Leonel's eyes. Leonel doesn't react.

"He's blind, Professor Lucian," I point out.

"Did I ask you to speak, boy? Did I?" he roars. "Did anyone in this room hear me ask this boy to speak? No!" He leans forward, his face inches from mine. The stench is overpowering. "Don't think your uncle or any of the others can protect you from me, boy," he snarls.

"Where is my uncle?" I ask.

Professor Lucian rears up. The yellow glowing dot in the middle of his eye patch blazes. His arm pull back as if about to strike me. He stands still, panting and hissing. "He has left you to me. Why did he do that? You'll have to ask him when…if you ever see him again."

A wave of his arm dismisses any further conversation with me.

He stands, addressing the whole class stretching to his full height, towering above us, his dark red eye staring down his hooked nose. "I have a task for all of you. One that will determine if you are worthy of joining me, or not. Outside, all of you. The task involves a long walk. A very long walk."

As we exit the building, The Special-Special One slides up alongside me. “Still time to join me, Howell. I can tell you all the things I learnt from Professor Drago. If you heard them, perhaps you’d doubt what your Uncle Tal says. Maybe together, you and I can find your mother. Think about it.”

As he joins his friends, I am left wondering. *He called me Howell, not Howl or Howling Boy. And he knows I’m looking for my mother. He even offered to help me find her. Maybe he has changed.*

36. The Unhappy Wanderer

"Two groups," Professor Drago Lucian growls as we stand outside in the desert heat. A butler quickly pushes Leonel, Dazmonique, Dani, the twins and me into one group. The rest into the other.

As he passes me, The Special-Special One whispers, "Always with the same group. Don't you get sick of them?"

Dani dark brown eyes stare into mine. "Don't let him get in your head." Dazmonique joins Dani, her pale blue eyes meeting mine. "*Danje! Gran danje! Batay*! Fight!"

"That team has nine members. Ours only has six," I protest. Professor Drago Lucian strides across the room and stares down at me. A pause before his face spreads in a sickly smile, revealing his yellow teeth. "Maybe I should take some from that group, add them to yours, or maybe you should join that group," he growls.

Dani takes my arm. "We don't need any more in our group."

Professor Drago Lucian hands a rolled-up scroll to Bollsinger's group. He tosses our scroll at my feet on the desert floor. "Here are your instructions. If you're not back in time for dinner, you can stay in the desert and rot." And with that, he leaves.

The Special-Special One opens his instructions, reads them silently to himself and gathers his group. "Follow me. I know exactly where to go and what to do."

Dani picks up our sheet of paper and thrusts it in my hand. "You're supposed to be our leader, Howell. So lead."

Dani, Dazmonique, the two Jimis and Leonel huddle around me, waiting for instructions.

"It says here: Find four apache tears and bring them back to the professor." I pause. "What are apache tears?"

"Small black, red and brown stones," Dani answers. "The tears of apache women crying for their fathers, sons and husbands who died in battle."

"The Jimis don't like that story. It sounds scary." They pull faces.

"It says these stones are near an oak tree." I burst out laughing. "An oak tree in the desert? This is ridiculous?"

Dani faces me. "Don't be so negative, Howell. Haven't you heard of Gambrel Oak? It grows around here."

"Here's what we do. We find this Gambrel Oak," Leonel asserts, "then we divide the area around it into squares. Each one of us will search a square."

"Would a real leader trust a blind boy, Howl?" I spin around. It's Professor Drago Lucian's voice. But he's not here.

"I know exactly what will happen," the voice continues. *"The blind boy will wander off and get lost. And the twins will fight each other and eventually get lost."*

"The Jimis will be good," the identicals promise, their fingers placed beneath their chins as they smile sweetly. "Loveable emoji. They promise not to fight."

Do they hear Professor Lucian's voice in their heads too?

"Unless my brother hits me," adds Jimi One or Two.

"Or he hits me," replies Jimi Two or One.

"Can you trust them not to fight?" The voice hisses in my ear.

Dazmonique grabs the Jimis. "Peye atansyon! Pay attention!"

All five look at me. "Which way should we go, Howell?" A long pause. I look around, not know which way to travel.

"I'll lead," Leonel suddenly responds.

Professor Lucian's voice resounds in my head. *"A blind boy as leader. I thought you were the leader. Maybe the deaf girl should lead, or the twins. Be honest. Your group couldn't find an oak tree if it sprung up in front of them. Still time to join The Special-Special One's group. He's a real leader."*

I look across the valley to the other group. The Special-Special One strides out in front. The voice is right. Bollsinger knows exactly where he's going. He's a real leader.

Maybe he could help find my mother.

Dani follows my gaze. "Would you rather be with them, Howell?"

I shake my head. I don't convince her or myself.

We walk about fifty yards when Leonel suddenly veers to the left. A wash leads up to a mesa top.

"Stop lagging behind," Dani calls to me.

Again Professor Lucian's voice hisses in my ear. *"Time for a decision, Bollsinger's group is still in sight. Look, they're all singing and waving to you. Still time to join them."*

I bump into Dani who stands still, deliberately blocking my way. "Are you with us or not?"

I shrug my shoulders and follow my group. My head is down. My boots kick the red dust of the wash. I bump into the Jimis. Both scowl at me, fists raised.

Suddenly everyone stops.

Dazmonique stands before me, tracing her hands around my face. Then she rubs her fingers in the dirt and draws two parallel lines across my forehead.

"What are you doing?" I ask.

"Dazmonique not like what you think. Bad thoughts. Listening to voices in your head."

"That's ridiculous!" I snap back.

"Is it?" Dani responds. "You're slouching behind, holding us back. You keep looking back at the other group. You don't to be here with us, do you? You want to be with them."

In the distance, I hear Bollsinger's group singing, whooping and hollering. *Have they found something already?*

Dani pushes her face into mine. "My people say: Those who have one foot in the canoe, and one foot in the boat are going to fall into the river. Where are your feet? With them or with us?"

"Go on," Professor Lucian's voice urges. *"Tell them what you really think."*

The words burst out of my mouth. I can't stop them. "Leonel couldn't see an oak tree unless he walked into it. And what will the twins do if they find apache tears? Fight over them. And do you or Dazmonique have any idea what you're doing or where we're going? No!"

Dazmonique grabs a dead branch lying on the ground and draws a line separating me from the others.

"What are you doing?" I scream. "I don't want to be the leader of this group. I'd prefer to be on my own." A dull roar grows steadily louder in my ears. Sand whirls around me forcing me to close my eyes. Although I can no longer see the members of my group, I hear their voices, "You do us with be to want don't you?"

"You're not making sense," I shriek in the direction of the voices.

"Unkind really is saying you're what," the voices continue.

"Why are you talking backward?" I bellow.

The roar of the hot desert wind swirling around me is deafening. I dare not open my mouth for fear it will fill with sand.

And that's when it happens.

37. Backwards in Time and Space

A gust of hot wind hurls me down the wash and into the canyon. It forces me backwards, arms and legs straight out behind me, wind screaming in my ears, past the huts and out into the open desert.

I slam backward into the front seat of the school bus. It races in reverses at breakneck speed. No driver is at the wheel, nobody else is on the bus. A thud and I'm sitting in the passenger seat of Uncle Tal's van. Again, breakneck speed in reverse. Again, no driver. Cornfields, sunflower stalks, grapevines, white church, trailer, forest, talking tree—all flash past me. Finally, I am hurled from the van and crash through the front door of my home and into where I am plopped in a chair at the table in the dining room.

Alongside me sits Tommy Foxglove smirking. He pushes his face toward mine. "Wake up, Howell. Welcome back," he whispers.

"And close your mouth," Sister Sarah snorts. "Are you catching flies?"

"Leave him alone," my father orders. "Are you all right, Howell? You fell asleep at the table."

"Daydreaming again," Sister Sarah giggles. "Probably thinking of his girlfriend, Erin Powell. Howell loves Powell. Howell loves Powell." She sings, sucking her hand and making sickening kissy-kissy sounds.

My father places his hand on my forehead. "You have a temperature."

"Uncle Tal…" I begin.

"We haven't seen or heard from your uncle in months," Tommy Foxglove sneers. "For all we know, he might be dead."

"That's not nice, Tommy," my father says.

"Sorry, Mr. Evans," Tommy responds.

He's not the slightest bit sorry.

"You need an early night," my father continues.

That's the excuse I need. I run from the table and bound up the stairs to my bedroom.

Why home? Why didn't my body shake when Tommy Foxglove pushed his face into mine? Why didn't I see a shadow surrounding him? My Doeth power is leaving me.

I put my hand to my neck. The necklace Dani gave me is no longer there. "Help me to overcome my greatest enemy," I whisper. "Myself.'"

I failed. My friends are lost.

My bedroom is not the same. The painting of the woman riding a horse has gone. In its place, hanging over my bed, is a poster of a rock group, Dead Men's

Bells. Two men and a woman, dressed as groom, bride and preacher. It's the group I saw standing in front of the church in the cornfields.

"Would you recognise them if you met them again?" Uncle Tal had asked.

Yes.

Someone knocks at my bedroom door. "Who's there?" I snap. My chest tightens. My fists curl. I pant with fear.

"I brought you some ice cream, Howell," my father says, entering. "You mustn't take notice of Sister Sarah. She may act unkind, but she loves you."

But she's inhabited and controlled by Tommy Foxglove, I think to myself.

"Do you remember Uncle Tal rushing me off in the middle of a stormy night, father?"

"Of course, Howell." My father gives me a pitying look. "Uncle Tal rushed you off in the middle of a stormy night just like you say."

He doesn't believe a word I am saying.

"You have a temperature, son. Get some sleep, and we'll talk more in the morning."

I want to tell my father about the camp in the desert and my new friends. Are they still my friends?

"Get some rest," my father calls out as he leaves.

"Where's the painting of the lady on the horse?" I shout. "Where is it?"

"Tommy told Sister Sarah you'd like this new poster much better. Those two look just like Sister Sarah and Tommy, don't they? I don't recognise the one in the middle, though, the one with a patch over his eye. Sleep, Howell," my father mutters as he exits.

Sleep? With the faces of the bridal group staring down at me? The bride's face frozen in fear. The other two with manic grins on their faces.

I look up. Tommy Foxglove stands at the end of my bed, eyes glowing. "Back home where I can keep an eye on you, Howell," he smirks. "You didn't want to search for apache tears with that bunch of losers, did you? You should have gone with The Special-Special One. He knows the way."

How does he know about Bollsinger? Unless... My body shakes. Chills run up and down my spine. *That's it! The Special-Special One hadn't changed. He pretended to be my friend. Promised he'd help me rescue my mother. And I abandoned my friends.*

Tommy Foxglove backs slowly out of my bedroom. "Do you like the poster?" he sneers. "Dead Man's Bells." He walks slowly to the door. "Your room looks so much tidier, so much safer now." He giggles softly as he leaves.

I dive under my blanket. My brain is racing. I punch myself hard in the thigh. *Dazmonique was right: the* Drygoni *voices were in my head. The Special-Special One was in my head. And I listened. I failed my friends.*

I lie there, a huge lump in my throat, tears welling up in my eyes. The eyes of the two male members of Dead Man's Bells glow redder and redder. They anchor me in place, tying me to the bed. I want to yell for my father, but my throat tightens. No sound leaves my mouth. With a sudden lurch, I swing my left leg over and grip the bed frame with my hand. I strain until I drag myself across the bed and crash onto the floor.

My father rushes into my room. "Are you all right, Howell? You fell out of bed. You're sweating. Come on; let me help you get back into bed."

"No. Not here."

My father puts his arm around my shoulder. "Would you like to sleep on the couch in front of the TV?"

I nod vigorously. Anywhere but in my bed. Anywhere but here, beneath Dead Man's Bells.

38. An Old Photograph

I lie on the sofa in front of the television, my head resting on my father's thigh, my arms clinging to his leg.

His job done, Tommy Foxglove has left, leaving Sister Sarah to spend time alone, playing with the computer in her bedroom.

I look up at my father. *Should I tell him about Professor Drago Lucian? About how I let The Special-Special One and the* Drygoni *into my thoughts and abandoned my friends? About how I failed to find and rescue my mother? And what about Tommy Foxglove? Will my father understand any of this?*

"Have search and rescue found mother yet?" I ask.

I know they haven't. They don't know where to look.

My father stifles a tear. "They expect some information in a day or two," my father replies. "They've brought in some excellent trackers with dogs. People who know the Sierra Nevadas."

Even they won't find her, I think to myself. *Uncle Tal knows where she is, why she was taken, and why I am needed if she is to be rescued. But what use am I now?*

An old photo album lies beneath the coffee table. "I haven't seen this before, Dad," I mumble, picking it up.

"I thought we'd lost it," he responds. "Where did you find it?"

"Under the coffee table."

"Odd. I clean there every day. I don't remember seeing it there."

As Dad watches television, I flip through the photo album. Very old photos. Some black-and-white, some going brown. Everyone standing absolutely still.

Suddenly I stop. My chest tightens.

It's her. The girl dressed all in black—black sweater, black skirt, black, stockings and black shoes—with red bangs in the front and red hair, red bangs covering her forehead, long red hair flowing down her back. She stares back at me from the photograph through those large glasses that magnified her eyes. She stands next to a tall, thin young boy dressed in a patchwork of strange clothes. His hair pokes here, there and everywhere.

The words of the two Jimis echo in my head. *"Our grandfather, Elder Jimi One and Elder Jimi Two, see her. They ask, 'Who is it you don't know now who one day you'll know?' That's what Elder Jimi One and Elder Jimi Two ask."*

I turn to my father. "Who are these two?" I stammer, pointing to the photograph.

The edges of Dad's mouth twitches. He holds back tears. "Your mother and her brother, Taliesin. Your mother was about your age when that photograph was taken. Taliesin two years older. She has such beautiful green eyes." He turns back to the television, but I can hear him sniffing. He really misses my mother.

What do I tell my father? That I saw this same girl at the camp in the desert? That she twice saved me from the Drygoni *butlers?*

I peer closely at the photo. Behind my mother and uncle is the painting of the woman on the white horse, the one that hung above my bed.

"There's that painting, Dad. Where is it? I want it back, hanging above my bed."

"Sister Sarah wrapped it in a black garbage bag and gave it to Tommy."

At that moment Sister Sarah comes down the stairs and enters the room. "Tommy phoned me, Dad. He said he's going out with friends to celebrate."

"Celebrate what?" I snap.

"I don't know, and even if I did, do you think I'd tell my stupid brother?"

"Where does Tommy Foxglove live?" I ask.

"What's that to you?" Sister Sarah retorts.

"Have you ever been to his house?"

"Maybe I have. Stop asking questions."

She hasn't.

My father breaks the tension. "Howell was asking about that painting? The one that hung above his bed?"

"Tommy put it in storage," my sister answers.

"I want to find it," I blurt out. "Help me look for it, please."

Sister Sarah pinches my cheek. "Does the little boy miss his painting? You told Tommy you were sick of it."

"I never said that," I snap. Now I definitely want it back.

Sister Sarah locks her arm around my head and raps her knuckles on my head keeping rhythm with her words. "If Tommy said you were sick of that painting, then you were sick of that painting. Got it, dweeb?"

"I never said I was sick of the painting." Sister Sarah is still under Tommy Foxglove's spell.

"I think I heard you say you were ready to put a different poster above your bed, Howell," my father adds.

Oh, no! Father too? I have to find that painting!

That night I beg Dad to let me sleep in the living room. Sofa or floor, I don't care. "All right, Howell, but only for one night."

I am not going to spend one more night beneath the red, glowing eyes of Dead Man's Bells.

39. Sweetikins? Yuck!

I try sleeping on the sofa but toss and turn all night. At 5:00 am the next morning, I rattle around in the garage searching for the painting. My father staggers in, still in his pyjamas. "It's Saturday morning, Howell. Can't you watch cartoons on television? You'll wake the neighbours."

"I'm looking for that painting." My father groans and crawls back to the house. *Watch cartoons! Hah! That's what Safonal kids do.* I look at myself in a dusty mirror. "*Doeth*," I murmur. "You are not Safonal. You are potential Doeth."

After an hour, I've searched the garage, the living room, the kitchen, and the dining room. I've even put scarves across my eyes, protecting myself from the gaze of Dead Man's Bells, and searched my bedroom. Nothing. I sit in the kitchen drumming my fingers, trying to figure out a way to wake Sister Sarah. On Saturdays she never wakes before noon.

While Dad quietly prepares breakfast, I *accidentally* turn the television up full volume. As planned, Sister Sarah stomps down the staircase in her fluffy bunny slippers and pink pyjamas, teeth bared in a snarl, eyes glaring. Any fool who considers Sister Sarah pretty never saw her before noon on a Saturday morning.

"Sorry, Sarah," my father says. "Howell won't sleep until he finds that painting."

She screams, telling the world exactly what she thinks of her stupid brother and his stupid painting. Finally she calms down and agrees to phone Tommy Foxglove. And that is the moment she changes from raging monster to a cuddly kitty cat.

"Tommy, I know it's early on Saturday morning, but my stupid stupid stupid brother is annoying us." She glowers at me. "Remember that painting above his bed? The one with the woman on the horse? You said you'd put it somewhere safe. He wants to know where." I hear a few "yeses" before she ends the conversation. "See you later, sweetikins."

Sweetikins? Yuck!

She spins to face me. "He says it's safe, and that's all you need to know," she snarls.

"Do you know where it is?" I ask.

"Maybe I do, maybe I don't. Do you think I'd tell you, dweeb?"

She doesn't know where the painting is.

She storms back upstairs. The air is filled with threats of what she'll do if I dare wake her again.

Tommy Foxglove lied. He knows exactly where it is. And its powers are not safe as long as it's in his possession.

40. An Old, Broken Compass

No way am I going to sleep in my bed one more night. But what excuse can I give? *"Dad, that Dead Man's Bells' poster is evil. I feel the eyes locking me in place, draining any small amount of power I might have."* No. And now I have another problem: Tommy Foxglove knows I'm looking for the painting. He knows I want to rip down the Dead Man's Bells and replace it with the woman on the white horse. He knows I want to return to my friends in the desert, to continue my journey to the transfer, to rescue my mother.

I creep into my bedroom, covering my eyes with a scarf so I won't see the poster. I feel the stare of Dead Man's Bells burning into my scarf, wanting to rip it from my head, wanting to lock me in place. Their place.

I rummage around but find nothing. Clothed head in my hands, tears welling up in my eyes, I collapse on the bed. I've failed. I abandoned my friends, believing they were losers, giving into my doubts. And now it might be too late.

And that is when I hear this faint buzz. What is it, and where's it coming from? A bottom drawer. I drop to my knees and scuttle across the floor, one hand holding the protective scarf to my eyes. I open the drawer and rummage through the contents: socks, underwear, and knick-knacks. Nothing special. I close the drawer. Buzzing. Again, I open the drawer. What's making that noise?

Buried beneath everything, tucked in the corner lies the broken compass Uncle Tal gave me as a birthday present two or three years ago. As I grab the compass, its rusty needle flickers. The needle revolves, pointing…where? That's not north. I follow the pointer. South. Straight into the bedroom wall. I put it back in the drawer. Useless.

The buzzing continues.

What if the compass is pointing through the wall? To something outside?

I stand, compass in hand. The red eyes of Dead Man's Bells burn into my hands as if wanting me to drop the compass. I force myself forward. The eyes shift, now focusing on the bedroom door, holding it shut. I pull with all my might. Finally the door opens a slither, enough for me to slide through, broken compass in hand.

I run down the stairs, walk into the yard and stand beneath my bedroom window. The compass points to the greenhouse where my father grows tomatoes. I move forward. Suddenly the compass jerks, now pointing at Dad's small tool shed.

I walk toward the shed. A noise behind me. I whirl around.

"Going somewhere, Howell?" Tommy Foxglove hisses. His outline flickers. "Following an old broken compass? Useless. Throw it in the trash." He digs his clawed hand into my shoulder. "Let's take a walk."

"What are you doing out here, Howell?" I whirl around, freeing myself from Tommy Foxglove's iron grip. My father approaches us.

"Howell and I are checking out this broken compass, Mr. Evans," Tommy Foxglove mutters. "We think it should be thrown away, don't we, Howell?"

The claw digs into my shoulder. I have to think quickly. "Look, Dad, this compass points to your tool shed. Why would it do that?"

It works. My father is intrigued. "So it does. That's odd. My tool shed lies due south from where we stand, not north."

The iron claw digs harder. "I'll take Howell to the hardware store, Mr. Evans, and buy him a new compass. One that's not pointing in the wrong direction."

My father takes the compass from me and shifts to various places in the garden. "It doesn't make sense. Wherever I stand, it always points to the old shed."

I grab the compass from my father and hold it out to Tommy Foxglove. "Here, why don't you try it, Tommy?"

Tommy backs away, shaking his head. His face grimaces as I push the compass toward him. He doesn't want to touch Uncle Tal's compass. "I'll believe you."

My father smiles. "Perhaps you should let Tommy buy you a new compass, Howell."

The iron claw digs again. I pull away. It's time to throw one of those stubborn fits. "I want to look in the tool shed now," I insist.

"There's nothing there," my father responds, a little shaken at my insistence. "Just tools and bags of manure and things. What do you think is in there?"

"I won't know until I look, will I?" I snap. I don't usually talk to my father like that, but I'm getting desperate.

"Well go ahead and look and, if you find nothing, then you can go downtown with Tommy. I'll pay for a new compass for you."

Before the claw can reach out to me again, I dive into the tool shed.

Rakes, shovels, hatchets, various other garden equipment, and bags of fertiliser are thrown out as I search frantically.

"I don't know what's the matter with you, Howell," my father exclaims, dodging a hand trowel that comes flying out the door.

"You're making a terrible mess," growls Tommy Foxglove. "Are you sure it's worth all this effort?"

I stop, panting in the dust that swirls around me. My eyes meet Tommy Foxglove's. "I know it is."

I redouble my effort, digging deep to where black widow and brown recluse spiders live.

My father places his hand gently on my shoulder. "Give up, Howell. You go rest. I'll clean up."

"Very generous of you, Mr. Evans." Tommy Foxglove's voice is oily. "Come, Howell. I'll take you to the hardware store."

I slap Tommy Foxglove's outstretched hand aside. "It's in here, isn't it?"

The compass buzzes, forcing my hand down. A floorboard, recently moved, wobbles beneath my weight.

I grab a hammer and begin wrenching up the floorboard.

My father tries to grab me. "What are you doing, Howell? I've never seen you like this."

"We should stop him before he hurts himself, Mr. Evans." But, before anyone can reach me, the floorboard comes loose, hurling me backward.

I thrust my hand in the darkness and pull out a large black plastic bag.

"Is that what you're looking for? A useless plastic garbage bag," snarls Tommy Foxglove, grabbing at the bag. "Let me dump it in the trash for you."

I push his hand away and open the bag a fraction, just enough to see the corner of the painting. "Here, Tommy Foxglove." I spit out his name. "Why don't you pull out the painting that's inside?"

He backs away, hissing and snarling. "Why would I want to do that?" He tries to lock a smile to his face but, as I pull out the painting, he leaps back hissing through clenched teeth.

My father stares in amazement at the two of us, both covered in dust and fertiliser. Me thrusting the painting; Tommy Foxglove retreating. "What's got into the pair of you?" my father demands.

He helps pull the large painting out of the black plastic bag. "You're right, Howell. It's the painting your mother gave you. Why is it hidden under the floorboards in the tool shed? Is that where you put it for safe keeping, Tommy?"

"Is it, Tommy?" I say, glaring at the retreating Tommy Foxglove.

Tommy Foxglove, eyes glaring, slinks away before turning and running.

"What is the matter with him?" my father asks, shaking his head in disbelief.

I hug my dad and promise to return and clean up the mess I've made. I run to my bedroom, holding the painting before me as I rip down the Dead Man's Bells' poster. The painting of Rhiannon, Princess of Faery, dressed in a long white dress and riding a white horse is restored to its rightful place. As I do this, I hear a low whistling sound followed by a screech. The ripped poster of Dead Man's Bells dissolves slowly on the bedroom floor until all that remains is blackened ash.

I clean up the tool shed as promised, planning to go to bed early that night. Tommy Foxglove hasn't been seen all day. Sister Sarah blames me. "What did you say to him?" she grunts as we sit down for dinner.

"Howell said nothing," my father replies. "He found the painting hidden under the floorboards in the tool shed. Tommy ran away. That's it. I was there."

Sister Sarah pinches me on the arm and whispers, "Do you expect me to believe that? You're in serious trouble."

The dishes washed and dried, I tell Father I'm going to bed.

"So early?" he questions. "It's only five o'clock."

But I'm already bounding up the stairs. I lie beneath my beloved painting, fully clothed, waiting.

A gust of wind circles my bedroom. Slowly at first, then faster and faster. A tornado. Suddenly I feel myself sucked up inside it. I pass through the window into Uncle Tal's driverless waiting van. We move forward at breakneck speed. Forest, talking tree, trailer, white church, grapevines, sunflower stalks, cornfields, desert. The van stops and I am hurled forward into the front seat of the now vacant school bus. Racing forward until it stops. A hot desert wind pulls me up the canyon and…

41. What's There to Hear?

"Tug on the roots of the sagebrush to pull yourselves up the gully," Dani yells.

I grab a piece of tattered sagebrush. As I do, Dazmonique smiles at me before spitting on her fingers and rubbing the dirt from my forehead.

"Elder Jimi One and Elder Jimi Two ask," she says. "'Who is it you don't know now that you will soon know?' You have answer, right?"

I nod. "I have an answer. She's been here all the time."

Dazmonique giggles and put her finger first to her lips then to mine. "Howell confused," she whispers. "Not trust friends. Not trust himself. He go back home. Learn. Come back to us." She holds out her hand. "*Mwen ba ou men mwen, ou ban m 'pou ou. Zanmitay dire,*" she whispers. "Proverb: I give you my hand, you give me yours. Friendship lasts."

I squeeze her hand in mine before looking ahead to where Dani leads Leonel. The two Jimis stumble along behind. Jimi One shoves Jimi Two, who falls down, leaps to his feet and shoves Jimi One. And vice versa.

"Stop it, both of you!" Dani shouts. "And stop hanging behind, Howell."

"I'm coming." I grab Dazmonique's hand and pull us both up, soon overtaking Dani and Leonel.

Dani pauses and looks over the desert below. "*La dama blanca de* White Sands," she pants. "The desert has so many stories."

"The Jimis want to know what you just said. *La dama* something."

"The white lady of White Sands," Dani translates.

"Is it a scary story? Will the Jimis be frightened?"

"A little," Dani giggles.

"The Jimis could put their fingers in their ears, but then they'll fall flat on their backs and slither down the gully."

"A soldier sets out with a battalion to fight Indians at White Sands," Dani begins.

"Will there be ghosts or vampires or zombies in the story? Ghosts and vampires and zombies really frighten the Jimis." They put their hands to their cheeks, pull down their mouths and open their eyes wide. "Scared emoji."

Ignoring them, Dani continues. "This soldier was only engaged to his fiancée for one week. They planned to marry as soon as the soldier's battalion returned from seeking marauding Indians."

"But he was killed by the Indians, and the ghost of his fiancée now walks the White Sands looking for his bones," the twins blurt out.

"Well, *muchas gracias* for spoiling the story," Leonel growls. "You forgot to mention that she wears her white wedding dress and bridal veil. Dani."

"The Jimis didn't like your story."

"How do you know it's a story?" Dani replies. "Maybe she'll appear at any moment."

That disturbs the twins. Any strange noise and they whirl around, hands to the side of their faces, mouths open, terrified.

"And then there's the story of *La Llorona*, the Weeping Woman," Leonel chimes in.

The twins pull their faces again. "No. The twins don't know that story."

"*La Llorona* is a ghost-woman caught between the spirit world and the living world. At night you can hear her wailing across the desert as she searches for her lost children," Leonel continues. "If she finds a child, like one of you, wandering alone at night, she snatches them up and claims them as her own." He grabs for the twins who scream and jump back almost slipping down the gully. "Her children are never seen again. They say that those who hear her…"

Dani suddenly holds up her arms, calls for silence and points to a large black cloud perched on the mesa top.

The twins clutch Dani's legs, terrified. "Is it the ghost woman? "Those who hear her what, Leonel?" It's her, isn't it? Don't let her take us!" they wail.

"Listen," Dani insists.

We all listen. Nothing. Dani stamps her feet in frustration. "You're not listening hard enough!"

"I hear it," jokes one of the Jimis. He leans toward his brother. "My brother's giving birth to an alien." He grabs his nose and pretends to run. "Run for your lives!"

Dani grabs the identicals. "Listen."

"It's her, isn't it?" the twins ask, their voices quivering.

Dani holds up her arm, demanding silence again.

I can't hear a thing—except the whistle of an occasional hot gust of wind. I look at the others. They all shrug their shoulders. Whatever it is, only Dani can hear it. She looks up to the sky. A single dark black cloud over the mesa top in an otherwise blue sky. "Quick," she calls. "Follow me." She scrambles higher and higher up the side of the gully.

We finally stop, sweat dripping down our faces and soaking our clothing.

I'm about to ask Dani what she hears when she calls out, "Where are the Jimis?"

"Perhaps *La Llorona* has…" Leonel jokes. Dani gently places her finger on his mouth, demanding silence.

42. "Look into My Eyes"

I look around. Dazmonique, Leonel, Dani and me. No twins.

"Where are they?" Dani calls out.

"There," I answer. "Down in the gully." I notice a stream of water from the mesa top now swirls around the twins' feet.

"Get them up here before it's too late," Dani screams.

"I'll go get them."

Leonel grabs my arm. "Wait. Tell me exactly what you see."

"The twins are standing still in the gully. Their backs are to us. They're staring at the base of a huge boulder. Water streams down the gully. It's over their ankles now."

Dani grasps my shoulder. "It's coming. A flash flood. Sudden and deadly. That's what I heard. We must get the twins."

"I'll get the twins, not you," Leonel says.

"But you can't see where they are," I protest.

Dazmonique joins in. "If Howell go, he get trapped too."

What are they both talking about? Get trapped? Don't they want to save the twins?

Dazmonique draws some letters in the red dust.

"Dazmonique is writing something," I tell Leonel. "It looked like '*adron*'."

I spell out the complete word. "*Adroanzi*. What is that?"

Dazmonique signs. "Dangerous snake," Dani translates.

"Nothing more dangerous than rattlesnakes around here," I say, shouting over the sound of steadily rushing water. "And they're not really dangerous. As long as you don't sneak up and surprise them. I'll get the twins."

"*Non*! Howell *pa ale. Danjere*!" Dazmonique screams, grabbing my arm. "Howell not go. Danger. *Pa krotal!* Not snake!"

"I've heard stories about the *Adroanzi*," Leonel adds. "My people talk of a huge snake that hypnotises people before dragging them under water and drowning them."

"But that's not a real snake," I interrupt. "It's a story. Made-up. A fiction."

Dazmonique stabs her finger into my chest. "We here now, not there. This not Safonal place. Between here and there. Crossingway. Leonel get twins. Not Howell!"

I look at Dani. "Dazmonique is right. Leonel should get the twins."

Before I can protest, I hear a voice, that of Professor Lucian Drago, *"She's challenging your leadership. Tell them you are the leader, not them!"*

"No!" I shout, gritting my teeth. "I listen to them."

Dazmonique looks at me and smiles, as she places her two fingers on her lips and kisses them.

I watch Leonel scramble down the side of the gully toward the twins as Dani yells directions to him. He wades into the water—now knee-deep—sliding until he stands close to the identicals.

"Grab them by the shoulders and tug them hard," Dani screams.

Leonel pulls. He cannot move the brothers. "I can only bring one at a time."

"We don't have time," Dani insists. "You must bring both. It's coming."

I hear the thunderous roar of water farther up the gully, heading downward.

I grab Dazmonique by the shoulder and turn her to face me. "I must go down and help Leonel before they're all swept away." Dazmonique glances from Dani to the two Jimis then back to me.

She grips me by the shoulder. "Pa koute vwa. Pa gade je. Do not listen to voice. Do not look into eyes."

"Look at us at all times," Dani adds. "Reach out for Jimis and drag them back. The snake lies under the boulder. One look into its eyes and you're lost.'"

The roar of the raging water pounds in my ears as I scramble down the gully, all the time repeating Dani's words, "Look at us. One look into its eyes are you're lost."

My foot slips. As I steady myself, I hear his voice.

"You're a leader, boy," Professor Lucian whispers in my ear. *"Leaders are not afraid of snakes. A real leader would strangle it with his bare hands."*

My hands grasp for the rocks and shrubs as I slither down the gully. Bang! My shoulder cracks into the side of the boulder, halting me. The stench of stale, rancid gym socks combines with that of dead animals. My stomach heaves.

I lean against the boulder. My fingers and knees bleed. I hear Dani's cry, "Don't look at it, Howell. Look at us."

At the same time, Leonel shouts, "Look at me, Howell."

"Look at me! Look into my eyes," comes the voice of Professor Lucian from beneath the boulder.

The contradictory commands pulsate in my brain. *"Don't look! Look! Don't look! Look!"* My head throbs.

The roar of water tumbling down the gully from the mesa top grows louder. I keep my eyelids tightly closed.

A hand grabs my shoulder. "Look at me!"

"Leonel?"

"Yes. Look at me!"

I squint through my eyelids, not knowing what will happen.

"Look into my eyes," Leonel shouts.

I open my eyes. The thing I was told not to look at is before me—reflected in Leonel's sunglasses. Beneath the heavy boulder behind me, the glaring white eyes of a huge coiled snake holding the identicals in place. Slowly its hypnotic eyes fix on me.

"You're safe as long as you don't look at it directly, Leonel shouts above the roar of the rushing water. "See its reflection in my glasses."

"Grab the twins," Dani shouts.

"Don't listen to her," snaps the voice of Professor Lucian. "*Leaders face their opponents. A leader is never scared. Face the snake. Stare into its eyes. Challenge it! Defeat it!"*

The water now roars around our waists. Broken tree branches crack against our legs, and large lumps of saltbush and tumbleweed wrap themselves around our knees, threatening to pull us into the current. Leonel's nails dug into my shoulder. "Keep looking at its reflection in my glasses. Guide my hand to one of the Jimis. You grab the other." I place Leonel's hand on the shoulder of one Jimi and my hand on the other.

"Ready?" Leonel shrieks above the roar of the floodwaters. "Pull!"

We tug, digging our feet into the red soil as we drag the Jimis up the side of the gully away from the monstrous snake and rushing water.

All the time, the Professor's voice slithers into my ears. *"Come back, boy. Turn and face me. Be a true leader, not a coward."*

By the time we reach the girls, the roar of floodwater ripping down the gully is deafening. We scramble higher, hiding behind a boulder as the thunderous water rushes by, only inches below us, pushing and dragging dirt, vegetation, stones and boulders in its path.

The flood subsides as quickly as it appeared.

"Why are you holding the Jimis' shoulders so tightly?" the twins ask, slapping our hands away.

"Did that thing drown in the flood?" I ask.

Dazmonique shakes her head. "*Li pa janm mouri*. It never die."

"What was it? A zombie? That ghost woman?" the Jimis ask together.

"Dazmonique will not say its name," Dani responds. "Saying its name will bring it back. Even thinking about it is dangerous."

"Oh no," cries the voice of The Special-Special One. *"That freaky girl's been reading too many books. She expects us to believe her mumbo-jumbo voodoo crap. Beware the snake! Say its name and it will come slithering up the slope and swallow us all. Me so scared!"*

"It's him," I think to myself. *"Bollsinger being what he always was: a potential* Drygoni*!"*

I shrug off the voice. What I saw in Leonel's glasses was real, not made up. I'd never seen anything like it before, and I don't want to ever see it again.

We continue dragging ourselves up the steep side of the gully until we stand on the top of the mesa. The black cloud has gone, replaced by a blazing sun that shines down, heating the stones and baking the wet earth. The air is moist, suffocating.

In the distance, we see The Special-Special's group, like little ants, scurrying along the canyon floor. Even though we trace our path carefully, we can't find the huts.

"No huts," Dazmonique murmurs. "*Mondyal kochma*. Nightmare world. *Mond yo*. Their world."

We tramp across the mesa. The stifling humidity and thin air makes my chest heave as I suck in as much oxygen as I can with each step. My head is light, dizzy, and my clothes cling to the sweat on my body. I need water.

Soon none of us walks straight under the boiling hot desert sun. We stagger left and right, forward and backward. My skin burns and my lips blacken. It feels like my parched mouth and throat are aflame with fire. I need water. A metal band tightens around my head giving me a blazing headache. My legs feel like iron rods as the muscles tighten. The heat of the stones burns through my tennis shoes. I am walking on flaming hot coals.

Flickering forms dance before my eyes. Hunting dogs, pure white except for red tips on their ears.

What does Uncle Tal call them? The Hounds of Annwn. Why here? Why now?

"Howl's seeing those dogs again, Biggie Pug."

I jerk around, expecting to see The Special-Special One and his gang.

"He's going crazy," Jack Rabbit giggles.

"The hounds of death," Biggie Pug snorts.

"If you don't boil in the sun, you'll freeze on the mesa tonight," Professor Lucian adds.

The voices grow louder, rolling over one another. I can't tell one from the other.

"Tomorrow, what's left of Team Reject will roast in the desert sun."

"All dried up like shrivelled worms on hot concrete."

The voices grow to a crescendo, racing around my brain. I grit my teeth and clench my fists. *I'm not going to let the voices win. I won't return home to Tommy Foxglove and Dead Man's Bells.*

The six of us stagger about, bumping into each other, falling down, getting up and stumbling on, not knowing where or which way we're going.

I barely feel any pain as my body crashes down, flattened against the scorched earth.

Is this the end? Is this the end? I can't stop the question by repeating itself in my brain.

43. Front Back, Forward Backward —Which Is Which?

Burning dust fills my parched throat. My tongue is an oversized woollen sock stuffed in my mouth.

I hear the snort of a horse and wait for the voice of Bully Harold Bully, The Special-Special One or Professor Drago Lucian tell me I'm going crazy, hearing things.

No voices.

Something paws the ground in front of me. My hand reaches out. I feel a horse's hoof. My fingers move higher. A thin, bony horse's leg. I push myself up, staring into the face of a horse with a gold coat, white mane and tail.

"A golden palomino," Dani croaks. We all lie on the ground gazing up at the horse. Sitting on the horse is a man facing backward, his face toward the horse's tail. The man's long black hair is braided at the neck and flows down to his waist. Three long eagle feathers stick out of its hair. He is dressed in heavy furs.

"The Jimis think the rider must be boiling hot dressed like that."

"Maybe it's a witch," warns Jimi One or Two.

"Or a werewolf," replies Jimi Two or One.

"Werewolves don't ride horses," mocks Jimi One or Two.

"How do you know werewolves don't ride horses?"

"I just do. Anyway, why would werewolves ride horses? They're wolves. They don't need horses."

"But what if they wanted to travel extra special fast? As fast as a horse?"

"Wolves can run as fast as horses."

"Maybe it's a zombie on a horse."

Dazmonique grabs both the Jimis and shakes them.

"Sometimes I glad I deaf," she says. "Your lips always flapping. Flap, flap, flap."

Dani pushes herself to her feet and moves slowly toward the man on horseback. As she does, the rider guides its horse so that his back always faces Dani.

"It's an *Heyoka*," Dani croaks, the words forcing themselves through her dry mouth.

"Does the whatever-it-is have water?" Leonel begs, as we all haul ourselves to of feet.

The rider dismounts and, keeping its back to us, kneels down and throws dust into its face, pretending to drink it. Then it leaps onto its horse again—backward.

"What's an *Heyoka*?" I ask.

"Is it a type of werewolf?" inquires Jimi One or Two.

"Stop it with the werewolves," Dani commands. "An Heyoka is a man. He's like a clown."

"He doesn't look like a clown. The Jimis know clowns. They wear baggy clothes, paint their faces, blow up balloons and twist them into animal shapes."

"Not that type of clown," Dani insists. "An *Heyoka* is a holy man. A keeper of sacred knowledge. To keep his power, he has to perform tasks, and until he's finished, he has to do everything backward."

"Crazy that is."

"No," the other twin corrects his brother "Crazy is that if you're speaking backward."

"Listen," Dani orders. "He's speaking."

I can't hear a thing. Nor the others. Just Dani.

"He said, 'Me follow,'" Dani says. "So backward that's Follow me."

"Right that's think Jimis the," the twins chuckle as they hop from foot to foot, giggling.

"Why don't you try, 'water need we?" Leonel asks.

Again, the man dismounts and, with his back turned to us, hands Dani a brightly coloured blue feather and a flute. He then pulls six empty pots from beneath the rugs on the horse's back and places one before each of us. I grab my pot, eagerly looking for the water inside. Nothing.

"Why," asked one of the twins,

"do we get empty pots,

"and that whatever-you-call-it gives Dani

"a feather and a flute?"

Instead of answering, Dani puts the flute to her lips and begins playing a slow tune.

"Great! The Jimis are dying of thirst and Dani's playing music," the twins groan.

"Quiet, both of you!" Leonel yells.

Dani stops playing. She holds a blue feather up and mumbles a prayer.

"Dani ask heavens for rain," Dazmonique responds. "I read her lips."

"Are there any clouds in the sky?" Leonel murmurs. "Black rain clouds?"

"No," I reply. "Just white clouds. I see an eagle circling overhead."

We all stare up at the eagle, watching it disappear into a white cloud.

Dazmonique stares at Dani's lips as she chants the prayer. "She tell rain gods pots thirsty. They need water."

"The Jimis are thirsty. Not the pots."

Dazmonique glares at the twins. "*Si ou bwè dlo nan po, remèsye po yo*," she cries before turning to us and smiling, flashing her white teeth. "Haitian proverb. 'If you drink water in pots, thank the pots.' Dani pray for water for pots."

Dani stops her prayer poem and touches each of the pots with the blue feather.

Dazmonique picks up her pot and drinks. "Dlo," she smiles. "Water."

"What if there's poison in there?" Jimi One or Two mumbles.

"She'll die

"and we'll have to carry her back to camp."

"Stop it, both of you!" I yell.

The twins, Leonel and I wait.

I half-expect Dazmonique to keel over, fall to the ground, and grab her throat. She doesn't.

Leonel takes my arm. "Is Dazmonique all right?"

"She's seems fine," I respond. I pick up Leonel's pot and place it in his hands. Deciding they aren't going to die, the twins grasp their pots and guzzle down the water.

"Don't rush!" I warn. "You'll get…"

Too late! Both twins hiccough loudly. They stare at each other, waiting for the next hiccough before bursting out laughing, jumping up and down with each hiccough, then rolling around on the ground, getting red dust all over their face, hair and clothes.

"Now we're whatever-you-called-it. Clowns," they giggle.

Dani and I are the last to drink. The cool water glides slowly over my swollen lips, soaking into that dried-up old sock, my tongue, and slithering down my parched throat, putting out the fire.

I tap Dani on the shoulder. "That's not an eagle feather, is it?"

"No. Feathers like this are from the macaw bird," she replies. "Probably from Mexico. My people consider them sacred. The feathers speak to the eagle which circles higher and higher asking for help from the kachinas, the spirits who bring us rain and water."

None of us want to argue. Not while happily drinking cool, fresh water.

Between gulps, we all thank Dani for bringing us water. "Thank the pots," she replies. "They'll stay full as long as you thank them."

The man dressed in heavy furs raises his spear.

"Quiet," Dani calls, "he's speaking again." Except for Dani, none of us hear a word.

"He says, 'Tree oak a beneath waiting lady old an to you lead will I,'" Dani call out.

We all mumble the sentence aloud—backward.

"He says he's going to lead us to an old lady waiting beneath an oak tree," I answer.

"What if it's a trick?" asks one Jimi.

"Trick a it's if what?" the other giggles.

"Funny so is that," replies the first one.

"What do you think, Howell?" Leonel asks.

"It must be midday, and we really don't know where we're going. I say we follow the *Heyoka* for about an hour and then turn back. Otherwise it'll get dark, and we won't find our way back to the huts."

"And the Jimis will get eaten by werewolves."

"Stop with the werewolves!" Dani snaps.

"Zombies!" they whisper.

"And zombies."

Everyone agrees to my plan.

"Wait," Dani says. "Since everything backward. We go in front of horse to be led."

"I don't know which is the horse's face or its backside," Leonel laughs.

"The horse faces forward," cries Jimi One or Two, leading Leonel to the front of the horse. "And the rider faces backward."

"That way the rider can look for werewolves or zombies sneaking up behind us," Jimi Two or One joins in.

We all glare at them, cutting short their laughter.

"Will you ever see his face?" Leonel asks.

"No," Dani responds. "Not if it's a true *Heyoka*."

"The Jimis wonder if it's one of those *Drygoni* things all dressed up."

Dani glowers and shakes her head. "We can trust the *Heyoka*," she responds. "It's guided by the gods."

And so we march across the mesa top, leading the man on the horse that is really leading us. We try to avoid the rocks that threaten to twist our ankles and send us crashing to the ground, breaking our water pots.

We walk for about thirty minutes when Dani stops, listening to the silent *Heyoka*. Then she runs ahead, turns and signals. "Oak tree!" she yells. "I see an oak tree!"

44. Apache Tears

"The Jimis think Dani had too much sun." They both lean their heads to the side with one eye winking and their tongues drooping out of their mouths. "Crazy emoji." Before they can laugh, the *Heyoka's* horse knocks them both forward with its nose.

Leonel tugs on my arm. "Tell me what you see."

"It's a gully," I reply. "That's why we couldn't see the tree from the mesa top. About halfway down the gully, there is an old building shaded by an oak tree."

Dani corrects me. "It's a mud hut."

"How do the Jimis get in? There's no door."

Dani points to a ladder poking out of the smoke hole. "Climb down that."

"Won't the Jimis get burned?"

They leap around putting out the supposed flames on their backsides—until the horse nudges them forward again.

I help Leonel slide down the narrow gully.

"What if that snake thing is in there?" the Jimis ask, remaining on the mesa top with horse and rider.

"If it's in there," responds Leonel, laughing, "it can stare at me until it collapses exhausted. I'll never see its eyes. Where's that ladder?"

Dani glowers at the twins. "If you like, you two can stay with the *Heyoka* and his horse."

The horse gives a huge snort and shifts its weight from one foot to another. That scares the twins who quickly slide down the gully to the hut.

Dani clambers down the smoke-hole ladder. I peer inside, using my hand to fan away puffs of smoke that burn my eyes and nose. Nothing but darkness.

I follow Leonel and Dazmonique down into the mud hut. Above us, the Jimis fight over who should go first.

A hand reaches out from the darkness and grabs my arm. "Sit here," Dani whispers.

In the quiet between the commotions from the two Jimis above, I hear heavy breathing. Someone wheezes loudly, struggling for each breath. Before me, lying on the earth floor next to the small fire is a figure, covered from head to toe in a long white cloth.

"It's a woman," Dani murmurs.

"How do you know?" I ask.

"The old woman against the wall sings a wailing song for the sick. For a sick woman," Dani answers.

I peer into the darkness to where an old woman crouches against the wall, staring at the sick person as she chants. The old woman is hunched over, tattered rags falling around her thin body. Threads of white hair dangle from the scarf that covers her head. Every so often, a skinny arm appears from beneath her rags, and long scrawny fingers draw figures in the air.

"Do you know who the sick woman is?" I ask.

"No," Dani responds. She points to a small hole in the ground near the figure. "My people call it a *sipapu*, a hole from which the spirits of the underworld emerge. The sick woman needs their help if she is to get well."

A sudden grunting and scuffling as the Jimis tumble down the ladder, both determined to be first to the ground.

"Shhh!" we all say together.

The two boys creep forward, dusting off their clothing. They sit beside us.

"Wow! The Jimis think this is real creepy," they whisper, pointing to the woman lying on the ground. "Look at that."

"Look at what?" Leonel growls. "Have you forgotten? I'm blind!"

"The Jimis see stones lying next to that figure lying on the ground. Are they apache tears?" the twins whisper.

"Yes," Dani replies.

"They're the ones we must take back to Professor Leather Coat," the twins blurt out gleefully.

As they say this, the woman on the ground groans louder and breathes deeper.

"The Jimis say, let's grab those stones, stuff our pockets and get out of here quickly."

They move toward the woman but quickly return as the old woman sitting against the wall stands. Her knees and back groan and crack. She shuffles across to the fire and drops something that looks like dust into it, causing spitting sounds. A sweet smell slides up my nose and whirls inside my head.

Dark shapes slide back and forth in the shadows at the edges of the mud hut, muttering deep-throated growls and hisses. As soon as one shape gains one form, it instantly dissolves and becomes another form.

The shapes kick the stones toward me. As they do so, the woman in the thin white cloth moans, her body writhing in pain from head to toe.

"Stop!" I call to the shapes. "Whatever you're doing is hurting her."

I grab at the moving shapes, wanting to stop them from kicking the stones, but they dissolve in my hands.

More shapes shuffle around me, giggling as they thrust the stones toward me.

I pant heavily. I want Uncle Tal or that young girl, my future mother, to be here. To talk to me. Tell me what to do. But they're not. The only sounds are the giggles and screams of the shapes.

I grit my teeth and spit out the words. "I will not take the stones. Not if they bring this woman more pain."

The sounds echoing around me grow quieter. The shapes dissolve before me, shimmering downward. In their place stand small round figures, each with two glaring red eyes, a head, arms and legs. They drop the stones and scuttle across the floor, disappearing into the walls.

"Are you all right, Howell?" Dani cries. "You're drenched in sweat, and you looked as if you were screaming something, but no sound came out of your mouth."

I look down at the woman suffering under the cloth. The stones are still in place, untouched.

"Do not touch the stones," I order.

"But what about Professor Leather Coat? He scares the Jimis."

"Do not touch the stones," I repeat. "Let the woman lie in peace." A pause, and then the old woman shuffles across to me. Her skinny arm reaches out and pins a broach on my shirt. Two silver birds face each other, their long beaks, wings and legs intertwined. The old woman leans closer and mutters "swim," pointing to the birds.

Swim? What does that mean? Swim?

A horn, about two inches long, dangles beneath the birds. The old woman points to the hunting horn and mumbles another word "key."

A key? To what?

The old woman shuffles back to the wall.

The Jimis stamp their feet and whine. "Can't we just take one or two stones? The professor will do horrible things to the Jimis if they don't take some stones."

I don't know why the woman cries in agony when the stones are moved. What I do know is that we must not take the stones. We must not inflict more pain.

I glower at the twins. "I said, do not take the stones."

"Trust Howell. He our leader. No take stones," Dazmonique announces, standing beside me.

Dani and Leonel join us. "We obey Howell. Our leader"

The twins stare at the four of us, then at each other. They quickly bend down, each grabbing an apache tear.

As they do so, I see the woman on the floor twisting back and forth in agony.

"Look!" the twins say. "Nothing happens to the Jimis when they took the stones. We only took a few. Most are still there on the ground. We don't want Professor Eye Patch to cane us, or be laughed at by the others. Let's just each take one each, please."

"Put them down, now!" I roar, my voice booming as it echoes around the walls.

The twins drop the apache tears and hold each other, terrified.

Questions race through my head.

Did the others see the changing shapes and the woman twisting in agony when the Jimis picked up the stones? And why didn't anything happen to the Jimis when they grabbed stones?

Dazmonique takes my hands. "*Kè ou pale pou ou.* Your heart speak to you." She points to the broach attached to my shirt, then to the figure on the ground. "*Majik kado*. Magic gift."

Dani looks up at the smoke hole. "We must leave now. Quickly." She drags me toward the ladder, pushing the twins before her. Dazmonique and Leonel race ahead, climbing the ladder rapidly. I glance up. The smoke hole is closing slowly. As it does, I hear that same low hollow whistling growing louder.

Dazmonique, Leonel and Dani all escape through the smoke hole. The twins follow, screaming about witches, zombies and snakes grabbing at their legs.

The hole in the roof is almost closed. I struggle to crawl up the rungs of the ladder, my head bursting with the low hollow whistling. Something is pulling at me, trying to drag me back down.

"Hold my hand, Howell!" Leonel shouts. I grab it. Then it's a tug-of-war between Leonel and whatever is dragging me down.

The hole narrows, squeezing around my body, threatening to cut me in two at the waist. "Pull!" I scream. I inch higher until there is a loud pop and I'm dragged out of the mud hut. Hole and ladder disappear.

I collapse on the ground and breathe in the cold, night air. A hand touches my shoulder. Dazmonique holds my face close to hers. "*Toujou anpil danje, men nou sekle gen lidè*! Still much danger, but we now have leader!"

45. Prickly Pear

We all lie in the gully, exhausted. Suddenly Dazmonique staggers to her feet and shouts, "We leave this place now."

A huge thunderclap explodes over our heads and forks of lightning flash in a circle around us, illuminating the *Heyoka* at the top of the mesa. His horse rears up, front legs and hooves pawing and kicking at the red, yellow and black thunderclouds that roil overhead.

We grunt and groan, slipping and sliding as we struggle up the gully, collapsing onto our knees and faces from the slick mud. Finally, we lie on the mesa top, our clothes and bodies soaked.

"This is not just rain," Dani gasps.

"The Jimis don't understand. Rain is rain."

"No, this is not the rain of the *shivana*," Dani asserts. "The rain of the *shivana*, the rain cloud people, helps corn and crops grow. This is hard rain, a killer of crops."

"Listen!" Leonel shouts.

"The Jimis hear nothing."

"Exactly!"

"So you tell the Jimis to listen to nothing?"

"It's quiet," Leonel adds. "Too quiet."

It is true. The roar of the rain, explosions of thunder and flashes of lightning abruptly cease. In their place a terrifying silence, so quiet you can feel it slithering around, blocking the slightest of noises from entering.

I watch as a grey mist slowly slides across the mesa, gliding between and around us until I can't see the *Heyoka*, his horse, or any of my friends.

"Are you all still out there?" I call out. "I can't see a thing!"

"Nor can the Jimis."

"I'm still here," Dani responds.

"What about Dazmonique?" I ask.

"She can't hear us, and I don't know where she is," Dani replies.

Suddenly laughter rips through the silence. "So none of you can see a thing." It is Leonel. "Now you're all in my world. You'll need to rely on me for a change. Who can guess where I am?"

As I search for Leonel, arms outstretched before me, the low, hollow whistling sound echoes in the darkness. Hunched dark-grey shapes, sometimes balls, sometimes tall and skeletal, hurl themselves toward me, turning away inches from my face. Fireballs, accompanying the shadowy shapes, explode before my eyes. That same pungent smell slides up my nose and into my mouth and throat, choking me. I close my hand around the silver broach as I feel fingernails as sharp as razors slice at my arms and legs.

The others scream. The razor-edged fingernails must be ripping at them too.

"We've got to find each other," Dani yells.

I stagger forward, arms outstretched, not knowing if I'll fall off the edge of the mesa at any moment.

My foot strikes something.

"Ouch," cries Leonel. "Here, hold my hand." My arms swing wildly, trying to grab Leonel. Our arms crack into each other's. I slide my hand down his arm and hold his hand firmly.

"Shout out your names," Leonel calls.

"Over here. It's me! Jimi One!"

"No, I'm Jimi One and I'm over here! And something with razor-fingers is slashing my arms and legs."

As Leonel leads, I grab another hand.

"I'm not holding my brother's hand, am I?" Jimi One or Two whines.

"You're holding my hand," I reply. "Where's your brother?"

"I'm not holding anyone's hand," says the other Jimi's voice followed by a sudden cry. "Whose hand is this? Not my brother's, I hope."

"It's mine," replies Leonel. "And if you're pulling one of your faces, it's no use. None of us can see you. Where are Dani and Dazmonique?"

"I think I'm behind you," Dani shouts.

Bang! Something hits me in the back. "Is that you, Dani?"

"Yes, it's me. I'll move to the end of the line and grab a free hand."

Leonel leans closer to me. "Do you notice something? Those things that were cutting us with their long fingernails have stopped."

"It's because we're holding hands," Dani says. "We're safer together."

"What about Dazmonique?" I cry.

We all yell her name. "It's no use!" Leonel notes. "She can't hear us!"

"What if she's fallen over the edge?" one of the Jimis groans.

"Or those things are eating her."

"Or werewolves and zombies…"

"Would you two shut up!" Dani yells. "Let's move forward."

"The Jimis don't know which way is forward. What if they fall over the edge like Dazmonique? They wouldn't like that."

A pull from Leonel. "This way."

A tug and I stumble sideways. I want to put out my hands in case something is in front of me. But Leonel and Jimi One or Two grip me tightly. We edge forward slowly.

How does Leonel know which way to go?

Another bump, but this time to my face and body. Somehow Leonel had led us to the *Heyoka*.

"Hey, it's the horse!" one of the twins shouts. "I hope that is its face and not its rear end."

"Quiet!" Dani shouts. "The *Heyoka* is telling how to find Dazmonique. He's saying, Move left. There! I'm holding Dazmonique's hand. We're all together."

We give a small cheer. We're together, but the dark grey fog filled with shapes slithering back and forth still surrounds us.

"Remember," Leonel calls, "we go to the front of the horse to be led by it."

"I'm touching the horse's head," Dani calls out.

We shuffle to our left, following Dani's voice.

Suddenly both Jimis cry out. The horse's head has butted them in the back, pushing them forward.

On we stumble in the thick grey fog, led by the blind Leonel and the horse with its backward-facing rider. Every so often the horse snorts and thumps one of us in the back, as if complaining that we move too slowly.

We've gone about twenty paces when Jimi One or Two releases my hand and lets out a terrible shriek. At the same time, his brother roars in pain.

I grope with my free hand, trying to find one of the twins.

Leonel tugs my arm. "Stop! You're going the wrong way. Catch hold of Dani's hand and follow me."

The four of us stumble through the fog, led by Leonel, searching for the twins, whose screams come from all directions.

"Jimi One feels razors cutting his arms. And he has a large nail stuck in his hand."

No sooner do we shuffle in the direction of one voice than the other Jimi's voice comes from somewhere else.

"No, I'm Jimi One and I feel razors cutting my arms, and I have an even bigger nail stuck in my hand."

Back and forth we go, following the Jimis' voices as they spin around us.

"Stand still," Dani shouts.

"The Jimis are standing still. They have balls of fire flying at them, and they can't see you!"

At that moment, Leonel gives an almighty grunt as the *Heyoka's* horse hits him squarely in the back. He is hurled forward, dragging the two girls and me with him. We crash to the ground, tripping over something.

The Jimis scream beneath us as we fall on top of them.

"Grab my hand," Dani yells.

"The Jimis can't hold hands. They have sharp things sticking in their hands."

Leonel jerks on my arm. "Look at their hands!"

I stretch forward in the fog. My hand touches a leg.

"You're touching me, Jimi One."

"I'm Jimi One and…"

"No time for arguing," I shout. "Reach for my hand."

"The Jimis can't move. You'll have to come to them."

"I'm going to have to let go of your hand, Dani, so I can reach the Jimis."

Dani doesn't have time to object. I reach for the Jimis. As I do, the ghostly shapes rushed forward, slashing at me. Overhead fireballs whistle back and forth bouncing on the mesa top.

I grab Jimi One's hand and pull him closer. As a fireball flies past our heads, I move closer, peering at the hand. It's red and swollen, double its normal size. Stuck deep in the middle of his palm is a prickly pear thorn. I try pulling it out, but it won't budge.

"What's happening?" Leonel cries.

"He has a large thorn stuck into his palm," I answer. "His hand is twice its normal size and is infected. I tried pulling the thorn out, but I can't."

"Witchery," Dani yells.

Witchery?

I'm about to ask Dani what she means when she adds, "It's the right hand, right? The hand he used to grab the apache tear."

"Yes," I reply. "It is the right hand."

The horse snorts. As it does, a dim light glows overhead. I look up. The *Heyoka* has raised a wooden staff. A circle of light glows around us. In the encircling darkness, the dark-grey shapes screech back and forth, enraged that they cannot come within the circle of light. We have enough light to see the twins' swollen hands. Again, I try pulling out the thorn with my thumb and index finger. No luck.

"The Jimis are in real pain. Are they going to die?"

"I told you not the pickup the stones," one Jimi calls to his brother.

"No, I told you."

"Stop!" Dani calls. "You're not going to die. I'm going to use the feather!"

"What use is a feather?" the twins cry out. "The Jimis need a pair of pliers or a claw hammer,"

Dani takes the blue macaw feather from where it is tucked in her skirt. As Dani circles the macaw feather around the thorn on the palm of one of the Jimis, Dazmonique mutters, "*Nou toujou nan plas yo. Kote maji.* We still in their place. Place of witchery."

"Why his hand first and not mine?" cries Jimi One or Two.

"*Silencio*!" Leonel shouts. "Dani is asking the feather to remove the thorn."

"Please, pretty please, Mister Feather," the Jimis plead. "Do it quickly."

We all, including the blind Leonel, focus our eyes on the feather.

Slowly the swollen palm gets smaller, deflating like a balloon, until the thorn no longer sticks in the skin. Dani brushes it to the ground with the feather. Dazmonique leans forward and kisses Jimi One or Two's now healthy palm.

Dani repeats the circling of the thorn with the macaw feather and the other twin's thorn falls to the ground. Again, Dazmonique leans forward and kisses the healthy palm. She then digs into the pouch she wears around her waist and pulls out some long, hairy roots she carries in her pouch. She rips off some strands and rubs them together, crushing them into a powder.

"Beardtongue," she murmurs. "*Manje.* Jimis eat."

She carefully divides the crushed roots in two and offers them to the Jimis. They touch the crushed root with the tip of their tongues.

"Yuck!" they both yell. "This stuff will make the Jimis throw up."

"Eat," Dazmonique insists. "Poison still inside you. Beardtongue move it through body."

The Jimis hold their noses and lick the powder from Dazmonique's palm. Finished, they turn to each other and compete to see who can make the most grotesque face. We laugh.

For a short time.

Suddenly both Jimis whirl around, throwing up on the mesa.

"*Sa se bon.* That good," Dazmonique notes.

"Sa se not bon. That not good," comes the reply. "The Jimis don't like."

"We must go," I order. "Everyone hold hands and stay close."

We edge forward, holding each other tightly within the circle of light. As we shuffle along, I look at the arms and legs of my friends. The cuts are healing themselves.

With the horse's snout pushing us along, we soon reach the edge of the gully leading to the valley floor and the huts. Somehow a couple of hours walk to the mud hut is reduced to thirty minutes shuffling forward in darkness and fog.

"What about that snake thing? The Jimis don't want to meet that again."

"The *Heyoka* won't let it hurt us," Dani replies.

"You're telling us the clown will protect the Jimis from the big snake?" They don't sound convinced.

Dazmonique turns in the direction of the huts, a look of horror on her face. "Loud shouts."

"I see a black cloud, like a swarm," Leonel adds.

"The Jimis are exhausted. They want to slide into their warm beds and sleep."

We all groan. Whatever waits for us, bed and sleep sound like a great idea.

We slide down the gully, the fog growing clearer as we near the valley floor. In the distance I see a dim light and the fuzzy outlines of the huts.

We crawl back along the canyon floor toward the camp.

I look back. The *Heyoka* and its horse are no longer behind us. The two have stopped farther up the canyon. I wave and shout "thank you," but the figure doesn't wave back.

We all edge forward slowly toward the huts. Their huts. Their evil place.

46. *Sa Ki Mal Plas Yo*: Their Evil Place

I wake from a restless sleep to see The Special-Special One standing over my bed. "Your group didn't get any apache stones, did it, Howl? What sort of leader are you?"

The ugly sneer on his face tells me that the old Bollsinger is back.

"No stones," Biggie Pug yells, "but he got a pretty broach. Did you steal it? It looks so girly."

"You'd better pretend to be sick so you losers can get out of class," adds Jack Rabbit. "No apache tears? Professor Lucian will rip you to shreds."

I rise from my bed and face the three. "I have no stones, and I have no fear of Professor Lucian."

The three back away, laughing uncomfortably and quickly turn their attention to Leonel and the twins, taunting them. "Were the stones too heavy for you to carry? Or maybe you didn't want to get your nice clean hands dirty."

"Tell me if I'm guessing right," growls The Special-Special One. "Your group found the apache tears, but your leader, H-h-o-o-w-w-l-l, told you not to take them. He felt sorry for the woman wrapped in bandages, right? Feeling sorry is so Safonal."

I push myself between The Special-Special One and the twins. "But you felt no pity for the woman, did you? You had a choice and you chose to inflict pain. 'Why worry?' you thought. 'She's almost dead anyway.' Is that how a Doeth would think? Is it?" I ram my face into Bollsinger's face. "No!" I answer. "You are so full of yourself, so determined to please, so drunk with power that you don't think of how your actions can cause pain and grief to someone else."

A pause before Biggie Pug breaks the tension, bouncing up and down in front of the twins, shadow boxing. "You wanted to bring the stones, didn't you?"

"My brother wanted to.

"Not me. Him."

Their argument is cut short as Leonel sneezes. "It's cold in here."

"You'll be hot enough when Professor Lucian gets his hands on you," snorts Jack Rabbit. "Maybe you've caught the reject virus." High fives.

The Special-Special One struts up and down before us. "You half-wits didn't have a real leader. Nobody disagreed with me. I knew exactly where to go and what to do."

"Nobody disagrees with a real leader," Biggie Pug and Jack Rabbit echo.

I move toward them. "Get away from us now!" I growl.

Biggie Pug bounces around in front of me, shadow boxing again. He dances backward quickly when I step toward him.

Not the Biggie Pug of yesterday, I think. *Something has changed. I have changed. Dazmonique's words: 'Still much danger, but we now have leader!'"*

"Breakfast in the grey hut in five minutes," Bollsinger shouts. "And after that, Professor Lucian is waiting to see our stones—which you losers don't have."

They stomp out of the hut, chanting, "Rejects, losers."

I place the broach the old woman gave me in my pocket. It should be safe there.

Immediately we exit the washed-out green hut, we are knocked sideways by a gale-force wind battering our camp. All four of us crash to the ground as tumbleweeds smash into us. The desert sand stings our bare faces, arms, hands, and legs like a million tiny needles.

I close my mouth, not wanting it to fill with dust. My eyelids become narrow slits. Dark grey shapes dance in front of my eyes.

Leonel is first on his feet, digging his shoes into the ground so as not to be blown away, and pulling the twins and me up. We hold each other tight. Leonel stabs his index finger in the direction we should go. We shuffle forward, like Arctic explorers in a freezing snowstorm. Except it isn't the Arctic, and it isn't a freezing snowstorm. It's a howling, fiery desert sandstorm in New Mexico.

We finally stand in front of the dining hut.

Not even a grain of sand follows us into the grey hut, blocked at the door by some invisible shield. Same for the heat. Inside, the dining room is freezing, chilling us to the bone as if standing in a refrigerated meat locker.

Dani and Dazmonique sit at the table, hunched over, teeth chattering with the cold.

"I don't remember this room being so cold yesterday," Dani groans, her words panting little clouds.

"The Jimis don't see any adults. Why?"

Leonel leans across to us. "Remember what Elder Jimi One and Elder Jimi Two asked, 'What is not here but still here?'"

"The adults are here but not here? The Jimis don't understand."

"What don't you two runts understand?" sneers Jack Rabbit.

I leap in. "The Jimis are worried about the storm outside." It's my way of finding out if The Special-Special One and his gang experienced the storm too.

Jack Rabbit laughs and runs to the door where he cowers and whimpers as if scared to open it. "Help, help! There's a desert storm outside." He opens the door. Before us is the bright, sunny desert.

"Anything else you fools don't understand?" Biggie Pug adds. "Maybe you think this room is freezing, like a refrigerator."

The Special-Special One leaps in. "Or that there's some strange smells in the room. The stench of losers."

Storm, cold, rotten smell—somehow they don't experience any of these. To them, this is not "their evil place: Kote sa ki mal yo."

The Jimis point to three large steaming-hot tin pots on the table and hold their noses. Large, fat blue flies fly over the tin pots, buzzing loudly.

Dani wraps her arms around Dazmonique, trying to keep her warm. "She says she can't feel vibrations when it's this cold," Dani whispers. "Everything—people, plants and things—gives off vibrations. Dazmonique feels them. But not when it's this cold."

My mother is like that. She'll know something bad is about to happen before it happens. She is never wrong. Where is she now?

Dani grasps my arm. She points to Leonel who has collapsed in a chair, gasping for breath.

"The smell blocks his nose," I whisper.

"Well that's two of our group," she mutters.

Before I can ask what she means, the twins rush to the table, swat the flies aside and stare into the large tin pots. "Yuck! The Jimis don't like what they see."

"I see an egg floating around. I think it's an egg!"

"That's not an egg! It's blue!"

"Now it's green."

"What's that? A lump of fat? A frog?"

"And the water is oily and black."

The Jimis poke at the contents of the boiling pots. They recite a list of what they see: ants, chicken legs, fish heads, bare roots with globs of earth still clinging to them, hair balls, fur, and on and on. I look in the pots. The twins are not making this up. All sorts of unnameable things float inside the steaming liquid.

"Are we supposed to eat this?"

"The Jimis see something that's looking back at them. It's an eyeball! Yuck! The Jimis feel sick."

Dani and I agree. As for Dazmonique and Leonel, they sit still, heads in their hands. They're not going to eat.

Meantime, The Special-Special One and his gang dip a ladle into the tin pot and pour the stinking slop into their bowls. They slurp it down before returning for seconds, thirds and fourths. My stomach heaves as I watch them. They can't see, smell or taste this garbage.

While they eat, Bollsinger's group chatter loudly about how they found the apache tears. How the sick woman had screamed when they took the stones. And how they laughed and danced with delight around the figure. Now and again, they pointed at us and call out, "Losers!"

A question dances around in my head. *Are all of these strange happenings—the desert storm, freezing rooms, and stomach-wrenching breakfast—punishment because we didn't bring back the apache tears? I don't care. Even if I knew this before we descended into the mud hut, I still would not have collected the stones.*

Suddenly the words of the Jimis' grandfathers come to me: "Success is failure. Failure is success. Lessons learned. Lessons not learned. Who learns what? That's the question."

Was our failure to bring the apache tears, to leave the woman in peace, success? If so, what's next?

Professor Lucian enters and sits at the top table, staring at us through his one eye as the yellow dot moves across our bodies. A butler pours some slop into the Professor's bowl. He eats, and then has seconds.

"My mother helps cook in this camp," Dani whispers to me. "She'd never serve this pig swill."

Professor Lucian glares down at us, "Why are you not eating?"

The English butlers stand over us, pour the potion into our bowls and wait, ladles ready, to refill our bowls.

We don't eat.

Finally, Professor Lucian stands, bangs a spoon on the table, and announces that breakfast is finished. "Class begins in the muddy brown hut in two minutes."

I lead Leonel outside. Dani supports Dazmonique. The twins stagger behind us. All of us are weak.

As we stumble toward the muddy brown hut, Dazmonique murmurs, "*Pa bon! Pa bon! Drygoni mond lan*. Not good! *Drygoni* world."

Dani and I look at each other.

How do we get out of here?

47. *Drygoni* World

I enter the muddy brown hut and stop. "Tell me what you see," Leonel demands, tugging at my sleeve before releasing another mighty sneeze.

The classroom has changed. We are now in an old-fashioned schoolroom: gloomy, tiny, high-up windows, and heavy wooden desks in lines facing the teacher's huge, imposing desk upfront.

Leonel doubles over and puts his hand to his mouth. "Furniture polish and disinfectant," he blurts out. "Gallons of it left to dry. It really stinks in here."

As expected, Bollsinger and his gang don't notice any changes. They push past and rush to the desks at the back of the room. I lead Leonel to a two-seater desk at the front and sit next to him.

No offers from The Special-Special One to join him. Not now. He knows I am no longer that Howell. The Howell of yesterday.

Dani and Dazmonique sit at the desk alongside ours. The two Jimis, after much scuffling and fighting, finally settle at a nearby desk, each dangling off their side of the seat, pretending not to be with one another.

"The Jimis are cold."

"I'm colder than you."

"No, you're not. I'm the most frozen person in the whole wide world."

"I'm the most frozen in the whole entire wide universe."

Their argument is cut short when a voice booms. "Face the front, all of you." Professor Lucian slides into class unnoticed and writes something on the blackboard. He strides toward us and slams his hand on my and Leonel's desk.

"Tell the class what I wrote on the board, boy." Professor Lucian snarls, his face inches from Leonel's.

"I've told you before, sir," I say testily. "Leonel is blind."

"Again, you speak when I do not ask you to," Professor Lucian thunders, his face scarlet with rage. His one eye glows black and red as the pupil enlarges. I hold my breath, trying not to inhale the stench of his foul-smelling breath.

"You're in my world now, boy," he hisses. "Not your uncle's or your mother's. I stare at his blood-red eye as the yellow dot traverses my body. I stand, determined not to be intimidated, "I tell you, Leonel is blind. He cannot see the board."

A split second, face to face, before the Professor lurches back and points to The Special-Special One who leaps to his feet. "What did I write on the board, boy?"

"You wrote the words 'Oaktree and apache tears' clearly, sir," Bollsinger replies smugly.

"Well done, boy! Did you hear that, blind boy?" Professor Lucian raises his hand as if to strike Leonel.

I hold up my arm, prepared to block the blow. "Leonel is not well, sir," I declare. "He's been sneezing all morning, and the stench in here is overwhelming."

"Again, you speak," Professor Lucian roars. "You talk, you think—without my permission. Are you a medical doctor able to diagnose this boy? He's not sick. He's not cold. None of us is cold, right? And none of us smells anything unusual, right?"

"Absolutely right, sir," Bollsinger's group chants.

Professor Lucian whirls around, his face inches from mine. I stare back unblinking. Stare for stare. He lurches up to face the class.

"I assigned you all a task," he continues. "A stupidly simple task. Do you have the stones?"

Bollsinger opens both hands, each with two apache tears. "We have ours, Professor Lucian." He marches to the front and places the four stones on the desk.

"Excellent!" Professor Lucian announces after examining the stones.

"And who accompanied you on your highly successful quest, Mister Bollsinger?"

"My friends Jack Rabbit and Biggie Pug, sir."

Brenda coughs. "And Brenda and her two friends, Professor Lucian. And those three boys in the back. Nine of us all together, sir."

"Stand up, those whom Mister Bollsinger named. You have all done extremely well. You may be seated. Tell me what happened, Mister Bollsinger."

"The stones surrounded a figure lying on the ground. It was a woman, wrapped in a white cloth, sir."

Just like ours.

"Did you know this woman?"

"Didn't matter, sir. She groaned, wailed and screamed in agony as we grabbed for the stones, but that didn't stop us. We completed the task as demanded."

"Excellent. You completed your task as demanded. Show no sympathy. Sympathy is for Safonals." He whirls to face me. "And what about you and your crew?"

"We don't have any stones, sir," I state, my words making little clouds in the freezing cold air.

"Repeat what you just said, boy," he growls, leaning closer me. "Tell the whole class."

"My group has no stones, sir."

The room rumbles as Professor Lucian roars. "Did you even bother to look, boy? Or did you all lie in your beds and do nothing all day?"

Dani stands beside me. "We found the stones, Professor Lucian."

"Who asked this girl to stand up? Who asked you to interrupt my interrogation of this fool? He was your leader, not you. Sit down, silly girl." I take Dani's hand as we both face Professor Drago Lucian.

The professor, his face now white with rage, screams out, "I'm waiting for your answer, imbecile. You found the stones, but you did not bring them to me. Why?"

Bollsinger's group laugh and howl.

Something has changed. Tommy Foxglove, Dead Man's Bells, the directionless compass, the hut, the figure and on and on. Something has changed—in me.

I slowly turn to face Bollsinger's group, who all sit, before thrusting my face into Professor Lucian's. "Do not call me by any name but my own. As for your question: yes, we found the apache tears but left them in place."

The room shakes as the professor confronts Dani and myself. "You what? Left them where you found them? Was that the assigned task? No!"

"I hear there was disagreement in the group, Professor Lucian," Bollsinger announces from the back of the room. "The twins wanted to bring the stones back."

Professor Lucian whirls around leaning over the twins. "You two agreed that the task needed completion, but your leader said no. Am I correct?"

The identicals slide closer to each other, hypnotised by Professor Lucian's stare.

"The Jimis picked up the stones, sir. They wanted to bring them to you."

Professor Lucian leans even closer, transfixing the twins with his eye. "But you didn't, did you? Because he told you not to. He's not a real leader, is he? You'd like to follow a real leader like that boy, wouldn't you?"

I flash a glance at Dani.

Would we lose the twins? Something needed to be done—and quickly.

"Correction, sir," Dani blurts out, pointing to one or other of the Jimis. "Jimi One wanted to bring the stones, but not Jimi Two."

That's it!

In no time, the twins are screaming at each other. "Why are you pointing at Jimi Two? I'm Jimi One, not him."

"No, I'm Jimi One."

"You've always been Jimi Two."

"Never!"

The hypnotic one-eyed stare of the Professor breaks as the twin's growl, punch and push each other.

Professor Lucian leans forward, his hooknose almost touching Dani's. "Your group was guided by compassion, by pity, by sympathy. Sickly Safonal emotions. You reject those if you want to be one of us."

Again, I confront Professor Lucian. "'Us' meaning *Drygoni*, correct?"

Professor Lucian's clawed fingers grasp for my throat but stop at the last moment. "I will break you, boy!"

And that is when Dazmonique stands, her hands tracing Professor Lucian's face. As she does, he backs away slowly, heaving and panting before marching out of the room.

"You've done it now, Howl! You're in real trouble. Where's your invisible girlfriend? Do you think she'll help you," Bollsinger sniggers? "I think not."

Biggie Pug grabs his stomach as if to throw up. "Oh, I see his invisible girlfriend. She has dirty, stringy blond hair and buck teeth."

They can't see her—but neither can I.

"And she stinks," Jack Rabbit giggles, holding his nose. "Probably hasn't changed her underwear in weeks."

Dani faces Bollsinger's gang, hands-on-hips. "You are all so cruel."

Brenda rises slowly, her hands on the desk, her eyes fixed on Dani. "What are you going to do about it, Pocahontas?"

Brenda seems taller, wider. Her form shimmers. Her pupils redden as she continues to stare at Dani.

Brenda saunters down the aisle toward Dani, The Special-Special One and his gang close behind her. I immediately stand up and confront them. I feel strong, powerful. I could fight them all—and win! No one hurts my friends. Not now.

Again, Biggie Pug shadowboxes as if preparing to knock me to the floor, but none of them dares come any closer. Finally, they all sit down, bragging about what they will do—later.

The door swings open, an English butler enters and stands in place us like a sentry. He points to Bollsinger and his gang. "You outside. Play games."

The Special-Special One and his gang whoop and holler as they rush outside.

"You wash pots and pans in the kitchen," the butler commands. "Follow me."

As we leave the room, Dani turns to us. "We must stay together."

I look around the group. "And we must find our way back to the other adults."

Dazmonique takes my hand. "We find them. They find us," she whispers.

"How and when?"

48. A Mountain of Pots and Pans

In a matter of minutes, the six of us travel from the North Pole to Equatorial Africa, from refrigerated meat locker to steaming sauna. As we enter the kitchen, the moist heat licks on and around us, clinging to our bodies, blocking the flow of air to our lungs. Rivers of sweat trickle from the top of our heads to the spaces between our toes. Within seconds my clothes are wringing wet.

Before us, pots and pans are stacked, challenging and defiant, as high as Mount Kilimanjaro.

"The Jimis have never seen that many pots and pans in their lives."

"Too many for a small school," Dani gasps.

"Maybe the Army, Navy and Air Force bases in New Mexico, the Carolinas, Arizona, Colorado, Utah, Texas and California have dumped their pots and pans in our school's kitchen. Glad I can't see them," Leonel laughs.

We all hug Leonel. He's well again. "I'll have to get sick more often," he announces. "I enjoy hugs."

As expected, the English butler doesn't have a drop of sweat on him. He stands, pale and stiff, clicking his head to the right, then left, then back again, awaiting his unheard orders from an unseen command headquarters.

Suddenly he snaps into motion, producing six buckets of soapy water and six dishcloths from nowhere.

Soapy water? Dishcloths? What good are these? We need scrubbers, coarse-hair brushes, chisels, and electric sanders.

Outside, those playing games squeal with delight.

"Jimi One, Jimi Two want to splay outside?" the butler queries in his monotone, robotic voice. His head jerks from one twin to the other. The butler opens the door. The sunlight and cool dry air drift in. Outside the others run around, playing soccer. The twins look tempted.

Who wouldn't be?

Dani dashes any temptation the twins might have. "Jimi One wants to go, but not Jimi Two."

That leads to an argument between the two. Who's Jimi One? Who is the better soccer player? Who is better at a host of other sports?

Dani and I smile. The twins argue. They're safe.

"Scrub pots and pans," the butler orders, slamming the door shut and locking us inside.

"Argh!" Dani screams. "There's a huge cockroach in the bottom of this pan."

"The Jimis don't want to look."

The butler grabs two pots and thrusts them into the twins' hands. "You clean," he announces as he dumps pots, pans and soapy dishcloths in our laps.

We try, unsuccessfully, to remove the baked-on food. Every thirty seconds or so, the butler takes an unfinished pot from us and dumps another in our laps. Cockroaches, huge spiders, rats, rancid food, and encrusted mold—all lurk, waiting for us in the pots and pans.

Dani and I glance at Dazmonique. What does she know about the adults? When will they return?

Every ten minutes or so, the butler leads us, in pairs, to the front door for a glimpse of the cooler, drier outside where the others play.

Always the same question. "You want to join others?"

The "nos" gradually grow weaker. We're all tempted. Who wouldn't be? We slouch back to the pots, heads down, not wanting to look at each other. Will one of us give in soon? And when one does, will all of us rush outside into the fresh air? How much longer can any of us hold out? My stomach heaves as the butler presents me with another pot containing its surprise gifts.

And then it happens.

Without warning, Dazmonique stands. Her hands stretch before her as she walks toward the wall. She stops about six feet from the wall, moving her hands back and forth before her. All, including the butler, watch, wondering what she's doing.

"*Yon rad pral pwoteje ou*," she shouts, her voice booming around the walls. "A cloak will protect you."

What does she mean?

Dazmonique's arms glide in front of her as she shouts the same words. Then she adds two more sentences, "*Pa fè dezespwa. Prepare aswè sa a.*"

"The Jimis don't understand what she's saying."

"None of us do," I reply.

Whatever it is, Dazmonique's words really upset the English butler. He jerks back and forth as if he doesn't know what to do.

"The Jimis think she's reading an invisible message on the wall."

"I agree," Dani responds, "but I don't see any words."

"Nor me," Leonel adds, giggling.

"Do not despair. Be ready this evening," Dazmonique continues.

She suddenly turns to face the butler. A long, unbroken rattlesnake skin dangles across her hands. I have no idea where she found it among the mountain of pots and pans. She holds it before her and repeats the words, "*Pa fè dezespwa.* Be ready. *Aswè sa a.* This evening."

The snakeskin and the words really disturb the butler. After a few agitated clicks of the head, he marches to the door and throws it open. "All return to the green hut now. One line," he announces, his eyes fixed on the rattlesnake skin that Dazmonique now wraps around her waist.

We march out of the humid kitchen into the cooler, bright sunlight. When they see us, The Special-Special One and his gang rush across, forming lines on each side. "Did you clean the pots, losers?" and "What was in the pots?" they yell. None of us care. We're trying to figure out what Dazmonique's words mean, and why the butler reacted so quickly.

As Dani and Dazmonique enter their half of the red hut, Dazmonique shouts those same words again, "*Pa fè dezespwa. Prepare aswè sa a.* Do not despair. Be ready this evening."

49. Passing Through You

We stumble into the dirty green hut, exhausted. The Special-Special One and his gang follow, threatening us. I stand near my friends, hands on hips, defiant. Despite all their threats, none of Bollsinger's gang touches us. Biggie Pug bounces around in front of me, shadow boxing but afraid to strike. The Special-Special One screams in my face. I push my face forward, challenging him. He doesn't accept the challenge. Instead he backs away.

After about half an hour, the bullies stop their taunting and rush outside to continue their game. Six English butler replace them, their pasty faces jerking back and forth as they watch our every move.

"Put me near the bookshelf," Leonel says. "I have an idea what Dazmonique is saying."

The twins and I watch as Leonel, with an English butler on his heels, takes down a book. The butler grabs it immediately and flicks through the pages before handing it back to Leonel.

"Nothing on the page," Leonel laughs, opening the book and showing us and the other butlers the blank pages. "Or is there?" Leonel whispers, staring down at the book. "Can anyone remember what Dazmonique said?"

"*Yon*

"*rad*

"*pral*

"*pwoteje*

"*ou*," the twins reply.

"How did you remember that?" I ask.

"The Jimis each remember every other word."

Leonel's fingers dance across the blank page of the book, quietly mouthing the words of Dazmonique. All four butlers shuffle forward, crouched over Leonel, peering at the blank page.

Leonel sighs. "It's no good. It's still a blank page." The butlers shuffle back to their places next to our beds.

"The twins don't see anything on the page."

"Nor me," I add.

"Look again," Leonel whispers.

We watch as little bumps appear on the page. Braille. Leonel slowly strokes the fingers of his left hand across the Braille. Dazmonique's words "*Yon rad pral pwoteje ou*" appear below the bumps as if written in invisible ink.

"The twins see..."

I put my finger to my lips, silencing the twins. "But what does it mean," I whisper.

We watch as the bumps on the page reform themselves. Leonel draws his fingers across the page. He whispers, "*Una capa te protegerá*. A cloak will protect you.'"

"The Jimis still don't understand."

Leonel strokes his fingers across the page again. Dazmonique's other words appear. "Do not despair. Be ready this evening," Leonel whispers.

The Special-Special One suddenly appears. He grabs the book from Leonel's hand. "What did he say?"

"Leonel is telling the Jimis a bedtime story," the twins say. "About a boy who thought he could walk through quick sands filled with rattlesnakes." The twins stare at The Special-Special One before pushing past him and his gang and leaping into bed. "But he couldn't." They put their fingers up to their mouths, pretending to nibble at their fingernails. "Emoji fearful. Good night."

The Special-Special One flicks through the blank pages. "The four of you are up to something," he growls. "I'm going to find out what it is and report to Professor Lucian. There are plenty more pots and pans to wash."

"In the meantime," Biggie Pug hisses, "we're going to watch you every single minute. Even when you're asleep."

I lie on my bed, my hand grasping the silver broach given me by the old woman.

My mind races as I repeat Dazmonique's words, "Do not despair. Be ready this evening." I add those words Leonel found in the book, "A cloak will protect you"

What does all this mean?

The Special-Special One stands over me, staring without blinking. I feel I'm lying under that Dead Man's Bells poster again. Bollsinger's eyes glow red and his face contorts from a sickening smile to a frightening scowl and back again.

I leap out of bed. "I'm going to the bathroom."

"You go when and if I tell you."

"Wrong," I spit back in his face. "I go when I want to go."

Bollsinger backs away. "We go with you."

I walk to the bathroom in the centre of the hut. Bollsinger, his bullies and two English butlers follow me.

I duck under the black plastic and look around. Bathrooms, shower. Nothing unusual.

My hand slides into my pocket, closing around the broach.

And that's when I see them! Four large rainbow-coloured ponchos covered with strange symbols hang from towel hooks next to the showers. I move toward them.

A scuffle of feet as Biggie Pug, Jack Rabbit, The Special-Special One and the English butlers rush to me. "Where are you going?" Jack Rabbit sneers.

I hold up the broach, pointing it at each of them. They're fixed in place, unable to stop me from moving toward the ponchos. I remove one from the hook and slowly pull it over my head.

The bullies and two butlers remain frozen in place, panting heavily, their eyes fixed on the ponchos. The butlers' heads click back and forth, waiting instructions. None comes. I grasp the other three ponchos and return to the bedroom. All five back away before me, matching each step I take.

I hand the twins two of the ponchos. "Put them on. One each. No arguments." I then help Leonel put on the fourth.

The butlers and Bollsinger's gang stand, protecting the door. The Jimis clamber up on a chair and push open the window between their beds. They leap through the window. Correction: they both try to go through the window at the same time—and get stuck. Jammed in the window, each blames the other for not going second. Biggie Pug grabs two feet—one belonging to Jimi One or Two, the other to his brother—and holds on.

Meantime, Leonel and I walk slowly to the door.

What should we do? Just push past The Special-Special One and the remainder of his gang?

"Throw down that broach, take off the ponchos and return to your beds," The Special-Special One commands. "We won't hurt you."

And that is when two hands from the outside push through the solid wooden door. Two sleeves, one purple and one green, follow them. The whole multi-coloured shirt, a head, large thin body and legs appear. Uncle Tal walks forward, passing right through the group of boys and butlers clustered at the door. "Time to leave," he announces, grasping our wrists. He pulls us through the others' bodies as they scream, yell and try grabbing at us. I don't feel a thing. Not even when we march straight through the closed wooden door.

In seconds we're standing outside the red hut. The full moon shines down, bathing us in its light.

"Good to see you again," Uncle Tal murmurs, smiling. "Now wait here," he orders. He moves to the window where the twins dangle, kicking furiously as they try desperately not to be dragged back inside by The Special-Special One and his gang.

Again, Uncle Tal walks through the wall. After some scuffling, yelling and blows from inside, the twins suddenly shoot out through the window, pushed by something or someone inside. Then Uncle Tal walks back through the wall. He turns to me, stretches out his arm and touches the silver broach I've pinned back on my shirt. "Well done, Howell. You earned this. Don't lose it. Let's go."

And that's it. No explanation. Nothing.

Ahead, in the darkness, I hear the jangling of necklaces and bracelets. Esther Evening Star waits for us with Dani and Dazmonique, both with multi-coloured ponchos.

"Brenda and some other girls tried to stop us at the door," Dani pants excitedly. "But we held my mother's hand and walked right through them."

"Hurry!" Uncle Tal orders. "Professor Lucian will soon find out we've escaped. The time for the transfer is getting nearer."

That word again.

The Jimis' complaining halts any further questions. "The Jimis don't have shoes. They left them in the hut, and they don't want to go back."

I look down at my feet. Before I can add that I don't have shoes, a pair of woven sandals appear at my feet.

"Step into them," Esther Evening Star commands.

"But they're too big for the Jimis' little feet."

"Are you sure?" she asks with a smile.

The six of us slip into our much-too-big sandals.

"They're shaping themselves to my feet," Leonel giggles.

I watch, fascinated, as the woven sandals curl and tighten, fitting themselves exactly to my feet. A moment later I lurch ahead, as the sandals leap forward—with me in them.

On I rush, all the time imagining I can hear the squeak of Professor Lucian's leather coat behind me. What I do hear, in the distance, are the yelps of hunting dogs.

"Can you hear those dogs?" I pant as I run alongside Dani.

"No. But they must be important."

No more time for questions. Red streaks of dawn light the distant mesas. Soon the whole camp will be awake, following us.

Although Esther Evening Star is a large lady, she runs, followed closely by Uncle Tal, as if both are Olympic marathon runners.

"As fast as you can," Uncle Tal yells to us.

"Why do the twins have to run so fast?"

"If you don't," Leonel replies, "Professor Drago Lucian will catch you and roll you in prickly pear cactus."

"Then feed you to the huge snake," adds Dani.

"That makes the Jimis run fast," the twins reply.

And we run.

50. Racing Ahead

Never once do I feel tired as we speed along the canyon floor. I dodge and leap over sagebrush and boulders like a gazelle.

"When I return to school," I say to Leonel. "I'll use these shoes to run the marathon and steeplechase. Erin Powell will cheer me on."

"Who's Erin Powell?" Leonel asks.

"A girl in my school," I whisper, embarrassed that I said her name.

"Is she as pretty as Dani or Dazmonique?"

"I hope we stop soon," I say, trying to change the subject.

Too late.

"Answer him, Howell. Is this Erin Powell as pretty as us?" Dani asks, smiling.

"Although I can't see him, I think Howell is shaking his head," Leonel chuckles. "No girl is as pretty as Dani and Dazmonique, right?"

I nod.

Thankfully, Esther Evening Star signals for us to stop and rest ending the conversation about girls.

I'm about to sit when Dani taps me on the shoulders and points at the two Jimis. They stand holding hands, eyes glazed. "Elder Jimi One and Elder Jimi Two speak. 'What are he and she when not him and her?' they ask."

Dani and I look at each other and smile. We now know that it's no good trying to guess at the answer. That's like trying to catch a hawk in total darkness. The answer will come to us when we're ready to hear it. Not before. The Jimis' trance ends. They grumble menacingly at each other as they cleanse the hand that touched the other twin's.

Leonel and I sit against a big rock. "Tell me what you see," he says.

"We're in a valley. Sagebrush, rocks and boulders. Sun climbing. Late morning. A blue sky with puffy white clouds. A black cloud in the distance. It looks like it's raining over there."

"Not rain," Dani corrects, "Virga. The rain that falls from a cloud but doesn't hit the ground."

"Isn't there any gravity over there?" interrupts Jimi One or Two.

"Do you think the rain falls up?" his brother mocks.

"The rain evaporates before hitting the ground because of the desert heat," Dani clarifies.

"Maybe my brother will evaporate if we're lucky," giggles Jimi One or Two.

"Maybe a werewolf or zombie will eat you," comes the reply.

Dani sits between the two Jimis. "No more werewolves or zombies."

Leonel leans closer to me, "Any fast-food restaurants nearby?"

"I see a McDonald's, a Taco Bell, and a drive-through Sonic," I giggle. "Today's special is grilled rattlesnake on a prickly pear bun."

"No thanks," Leonel replies. "Just lost my appetite."

Esther Evening Star takes a large brown root from the small leather pouch around her waist. She cuts the brown skin from the root. It looks like a potato.

"Not hamburger," she exclaims, handing slices of this root to us, "but very good for you. And it has a lot of water, so you won't dry out. Eat."

Leonel, Dazmonique, Dani and I bite into the potato thing and munch happily. The twins stare at the root. "Is that really food?"

Esther Evening Star pulls another root from her small pouch. Somehow, they all fit in there.

"This will make you strong," Esther Evening Star continues. "You'll need it. We have a long way to go."

"It's called Queen of the Night," Dani adds. "The root of a cactus. Delicious."

"The Jimis need something to drink."

Esther Evening Star smiles at me. "Maybe Howell will get us all some water."

"Why don't you jog over to the local 7-11, Howell," Leonel giggles, "and get a couple of Cokes and Seven-ups."

"You know where to find water in the desert, don't you?" Uncle Tal chimes up.

I surprise myself. "The bushes with the orange and greenish-yellow flowers over there. They're cholla cacti. Their stems store water."

Uncle Tal smiles. "Well done, Howell."

Soon we're all drinking water from the stems of the cholla cacti.

"Eat and drink," Esther Evening Star encourages. "Need strength to climb the cliff wall."

"The Jimis want to know if they're being chased?"

Uncle Tal scours the horizon. "We must arrive at the cliff dwellings before the Drygoni reach us."

"And what happens if we don't get there in time and the *Drygoni* catch us?" the twins ask.

"Not want to know answer," Dazmonique joins in.

No, we don't.

51. Lessons Learned, Lessons Not Learned

We eat and drink until we are full.

"Have Professor Lucian and the other kids all become *Drygoni*?" I ask.

Uncle Tal passes a live lizard from hand to hand, while Esther Evening Star scratches strange symbols in the desert floor.

"And what about the one who calls himself Special-Special?" the twins interrupt. "Why was he in our school?"

"He came from a family of *Doeths*," Esther Evening Star offers. "But family, money, education is not enough."

I recall Dazmonique challenging Bollsinger when he set down his rules on our first meeting. "Boasting not good for Doeths," she said.

"All of you have some power," Uncle Tal continues. "His family hoped that his power would become Doeth power. But he wasn't like them. Instead the Drygoni found him—and that's how they found you."

"And that Professor Leather Coat made us look for those stones," the twins say. They look down at their hands and shudder.

"Apache tears," Uncle Tal responds. "Finding them was not the task. It was what you did when you found them that was the real test. Removing the stones caused extreme pain to the sleeping figure. So you had a choice: show pity or inflict pain. Sadly, the other children didn't care who they hurt as long as they won."

I thought back to Shirley Reese, the girl who was mercilessly teased in school and on Facebook. The girl who one day disappeared.

Suddenly Dani blurts out, "That's the answer to Elder Jimi One and Elder Jimi Two's third question."

"What is the question? The Jimis forget."

Dani speaks slowly, wanting to remember exactly what Elder Jimi One and Elder Jimi Two asked. "'When is success failure…

"'… and failure success?'" I add.

"'Lessons learned. Lessons not learned. Who learns what?'" Dani says, clapping her hands with excitement.

Leonel leaps forward, his body shaking with excitement. "So by failing Professor Drago Lucian's test, we succeeded."

Uncle Tal grasps Leonel and Dani's hands. "Exactly. You could have picked up those stones. It would have been easy. And some of you did."

"My brother made me do it," says Jimi One or Two.

"No, you made me do it," replies the other twin.

"It was easy to pick them up, do what the professor asked," Uncle Tal continues. "You feared him. Feared what he would do if you failed. Fear of others can make us do what we do not want to do. What we should not do. The easy way and the way of fear is not the Doeth way. Often you need to struggle and fight against yourself. These are things we must teach the Safonals."

A silence follows as we all think about Uncle Tal's words.

"*Señor* Quit and *Madame* Bouzius are not here," I note, breaking the silence. "Where are they?"

"They've gone ahead to the place," Uncle Tal replies.

"What place? The Jimis want to know."

Uncle Tal stares at me. "The place where the transfer will happen."

We all look down at our feet, frightened by Uncle Tal's words.

The silence is broken when Esther Evening Star stands, pointing in the direction from where we came. "They're getting closer. I will find out how close. Everyone close your eyes."

"Even me?" Leonel asks.

"Everyone," Uncle Tal commands. I shut mine.

I hear Esther Evening Star pant as she runs a few steps. *Will she make it*, I wonder. *Maybe I should volunteer to go. But what if Professor Drago Lucian catches me?*

My question is interrupted by a deep growl. I squint through my eyelids. I see a large grey wolf, white from tip to tail, bounding away.

The same wolf on Main Street and at the breakfast trailer. It's Dani's mother.

A sudden chill wind slides across the desert floor.

"Open your eyes, everyone," Uncle Tal shouts. "We must get to the cliff face before dark."

I look around. "But what about Esther...?"

"We must get to the cliff face before dark," Uncle Tal repeats, glancing at each of us in turn. "No more questions."

52. "Call Them to You"

I sprint, avoiding sagebrush clumps and rocks, while making certain that Leonel doesn't fall. The sun gradually edges closer to the western hills on the horizon. In the distance I see the cliff face.

"The Jimis don't think the cliff is getting any closer."

"If we don't reach that cliff before dark," Uncle Tal growls, "we'll have to spend the night out here in the sagebrush."

"And the *Drygoni* will find the Jimis, right?"

No need for Uncle Tal to answer.

"Maybe the *Drygoni* are making us believe the cliff isn't getting closer," Dani pants. "That makes us more discouraged and tired, slowing us down."

"Excellent," Uncle Tal responds. "Now you're thinking like a Doeth."

The sun is close to the horizon when I hear the galloping of a large animal behind us.

"Don't look back," Uncle Tal cautions. "Focus on the cliff ahead."

The animal roars up behind us, howling.

The growling stops, and Esther Evening Star jogs alongside me. "We must run faster," she shouts. "They will overtake us before dark if we don't."

Leonel struggles on, periodically stumbling against sagebrush. Soon the others are far ahead of us.

Dani looks back. "Hurry! I see dust clouds in the distance. *Drygoni*. We must reach the cliff face."

A gleam from the setting sun reveals a huge cave chiselled into the cliff face. Inside the cave stands the wall of a ruined building, two stories high. "How are we going to get up to the cave?" I shout. "It's about fifty feet up from the canyon floor." Dani points to a ladder laced with rope leaning against the reddish-brown cliff face.

The *Drygonis'* shrieking and screaming grows louder. They're close. Too close.

Crash! Leonel stumbles on a rock. He lies on the desert floor, a large bloodstain spreading across one knee.

"We must get to the cave, Leonel."

Leonel tries to stand but collapses immediately. I jam my shoulder under his arm. "Let me take your weight."

We stagger forward, Leonel leaning against me. "How far to the cliff face?"

"About forty yards," I reply. "The others are climbing the ladder."

Leonel drops from my arm, hacking and coughing. "The stench is sickening. The *Drygoni* are almost upon us."

It's true. The high-pitched screeching of the *Drygoni* is deafening.

Something hits me in the middle of my back. I lurch forward, almost dropping Leonel. More rocks whistle past our ears.

Leonel collapses. "Leave me here," he pants. "I'm slowing you down."

"I'm not leaving you."

"But it's you they want, not me."

"We stay together," I insist.

Professor Lucian stops about twenty feet from me, flanked by The Special-Special One and his gang. All shimmer before my eyes. Surrounding them are a group of English butlers, snarling, snapping and growling. The ghostly shapes we saw on the mesa circle us and strike at our faces.

"Leave me," Leonel begs.

"No!"

The others scream at us to join them in the cave. I lift Leonel and back slowly toward the cliff face.

"Join us," Professor Lucian hisses. "We won't hurt you."

"Never," I scream.

A stone thuds into my shoulder. Biggie Pub snarls, "Next one will be between your eyes."

"You didn't bring me the apache tears," Professor Lucian growls. "You felt sorry for that wretched figure. Feeling sorry is so sickening, so Safonal." Another stone smacks into my thigh. I cry out in pain.

"I have a huge rock in my hand," The Special-Special One hisses. "It's begging me to crush your head with it."

He pulls his arm back, preparing to throw.

And that's when I hear Uncle Tal's voice whispering in my ear. "Call them."

"Call who? Call what?" I scream. "*Drygoni* surround us."

Again the voice of Uncle Tal. "Raise the horn to your lips. Call them."

What horn?

Then I remember. I grasp the broach pinned to my shirt. As I do, the horn beneath the two birds slips loose, falling into my hand. It quickly pushes outward and upward, growing in size. My arm jerks upward as the horn attaches itself to my lips. I blow. The hunting horn roars louder and louder, its echo bouncing off canyon walls.

At first, the yipping sound is distant. But it grows louder by the second. Bollsinger and the others hear it too. The rock drops from The Special-Special One's arm as he and the others spin around, staring back across the desert.

"Call them," Uncle Tal yells. "Call them to you."

Again, the hunting horn fills the valley with its blare.

"The Jimis see a dust cloud racing this way," the twins call from the safety of the cave.

I see them against the gathering darkness. Hunting dogs, pure white except for red tips on their ears. They bound across the desert, heading straight for Professor Lucian and the others.

“The old woman pointed to the hunting horn and said the word ‘key,’” I shout. “But it wasn’t a ‘key’ for a lock she was saying, it was ‘ci,’ the Welsh word for dog. She was telling me the hunting horn would call the Hounds of Annwn.”

I lift Leonel and together we stagger toward the cliff face. Behind us we hear the screaming, snarling and tearing as the hounds rip into the *Drygoni*.

We reach the cliff face and climb the ladder. When we are both inside, Uncle Tal reaches down and hoists the ladder up into the cave.

We are safe—for now.

53. Shifting Petroglyphs

I lie in the darkness, cold stones and jagged rocks digging deep into my back. My fingers are jammed in my ears, trying to block out the shrieks and screams of the battle raging below on the valley floor.

A light flares in the darkness. Uncle Tal holds a clump of lighted sagebrush. He pokes his hand into his tiny pouch and produces twigs and branches.

"The Jimis want to know if Esther Evening Star has a gun in her pouch to shoot the *Drygoni.*"

Uncle Tal smiles. "Weapons are no use against the Drygoni."

"What about an AK47?" the twins insist.

"What about a zombie with an AK47?" Jimi One or Two suggests.

"Or a battalion of werewolves with missile launchers?" the other Jimi says.

"Or…"

"No more!" Uncle Tal interrupts. "All useless."

We huddle around the fire behind the wall of the ruined house. The wall is a barrier against the cold night wind of the desert.

Esther Evening Star holds up her hand. We listen. The fighting has ended. No sound. Just an eerie silence.

Lightning strikes flash over the distant mesas providing an instant of light. Not enough to see what—if anything—remains below.

"The Jimis think zombies might live in a cave like this. They'll come back in the middle of the night and…"

"Enough with the zombies," Leonel snaps.

Esther Evening Star waves her hands back and forth, pointing to the walls of the cave. Figures and symbols line the roof.

"Petroglyphs," Dani explains. "Drawings scratched into the walls by the ancients. They tell stories."

I stare at the carvings. "I see a bent-over figure playing a flute."

"That's a *kokopelli,*" Dani responds. "A storyteller."

Esther Evening Star and Uncle Tal move to the back of the cave, chanting as they wave their hands back and forth in front of the petroglyphs.

What are they doing?

Before I can ask, the two lay down asleep, in opposite corners of the cave.

The cold wind is blowing across the desert slicing through the holes in the walls of the buildings, forcing us to huddle closer to the fire. We sit in the darkness, each of us full of questions. Now and again we look across at the two sleeping adults, hoping they'll wake so we can get answers.

Dani nudges me and points to the Jimis. "They're holding hands and staring into space again."

"Elder Jim One and Elder Jimi Two ask, 'When does one minus one leave one?'"

I look around the group. "'Does anyone have the answer?"

Before any of us can think of an answer, the Jimis leap apart, screeching and cleaning their hands. They march up and down the cave before hitting a pose. "The Jimis are bored."

"Climb down the ladder and see if the *Drygoni* are still there," Leonel suggests.

The twins glance at each other and rapidly change the shape of their faces. "Emoji not bored."

A few minutes of silence before the Jimis rush to the back of the cave, giggling as they mimic the adults swaying back and forth in front of the petroglyphs. Suddenly they stop, their mouths dropping open as they back away from the wall.

Dani crosses to the twins. "What's the matter with you two now?"

"That koko thing. The Jimis saw it move."

Leonel laughs, "It can't move. It was engraved into the wall by long-ago ancestors."

Dazmonique holds out her hands and stands before the petroglyphs.

"It move," she says. "One leg down before. Now other leg down."

We all stare at the *kokopelli* in the flickering light of the fire.

Leonel runs his fingers over the figure. "No way. You told me his right leg was back and his left leg forward, right?"

Dazmonique touches Leonel's shoulder. "Leonel try again."

"Right leg back and… Where is it?"

"It move," Dazmonique responds. "Left leg now back."

Our fascination with the *kokopelli* is suddenly cut short as we hear voices calling out, "Help us. We're stuck down here. It's so cold. Let the ladder down so we can climb up." It's The Special-Special One, Biggie Pug, Jack Rabbit and Brenda.

The Jimis move to where the ladder lay on the floor.

"No," Dani shouts. "Don't let the ladder down."

"We're cold," the voices whine. "Let us join you sitting around the fire."

"Look at koko," Dazmonique cries.

The *kokopelli* has moved. It now stands above two arrows, the tips of which point at each other. Some small circles surrounding a larger one lie between the arrows.

Dazmonique turns to Dani. "What that mean?"

Dani studies the figure. "Arrows pointing at each other means danger."

The voices from below grow louder. "It's freezing cold. Let us near the fire. We need warmth. We want to be your friends. We were wrong to listen to Professor Lucian. He tricked us. Forgive us. Help!"

Contradictory thoughts jostle back and forth in my head. *Think like a Doeth. Forgive them. Help those in need. But a Doeth must also be careful and know when someone is telling the truth and when lying.*

Dazmonique, Dani and Leonel stand facing me, waiting for me to say something. I blurt out, "One of Elder Jimi One and Elder Jimi Two's questions: 'What are he and she when not him and her?' Bollsinger and the others might speak like the ones we knew, but they are not the ones we knew. They are *Drygoni*!"

I glance over at the *kokopelli*. The small circles surrounding the larger one lying between the arrows glow brighter. Danger!

I grab the two Jimis who stand on the edge of the cave, staring out into the night. "If we let them into the cave, we are the ones in danger." Dazmonique, Dani and Leonel join me, all wrapping our arms around the twins, pulling them away from the cave's edge. They seem rooted to the spot. I look to Dazmonique. She takes a deep breath before uttering some mystical, whispered words as she traces the outlines of the Jimis' faces. Her arms shake as she moves away from the twins. She's dragging something unseen from them. With a final pull, she lurches back. Her hands hold two squirming objects, like large black moccasin snakes. She walks to the edge of the cave and hurls them down. "*Tounen nan fènwa*!" she screams. "Return to darkness!"

The twins drop from my arms, collapsing on the floor, coughing violently.

"Was my brother a zombie?" cries Jimi One or Two.

"No! It was you who was the zombie," answers Jimi One or Two thrusting out his arms and walking stiff-legged. "You were walking around like this."

Dani shakes them. "You were *both* acting like zombies."

54. Shapeshifting

I pull the twins back from the edge as the hissing and screaming from below grows louder. The sounds bounce around the walls of the cave.

"What of Esther Evening Star?" the voice of Professor Lucian whispers in my ear. *"She wasn't herself when she was a shape-shifter. Maybe she is a* Drygoni *too."*

Dani grabs me as I shudder. "What is the voice saying?"

"That your mother, Esther Evening Star, is a shape-shifter."

Dani hugs me tightly and kisses me on the forehead. "My mother is a very powerful Doeth. Nerth Doeth. Whatever she does, whatever she becomes, she uses for good."

The twins suddenly rush to the back wall. "The koko thing," they shout. "It's changed again."

Leonel's fingers tighten around my arm. "What is it doing?"

"The flute player is pointing to two huge hands cradling a sun," I reply. "And there are two normal-sized hands below each of the huge ones."

"Hands wait to catch the sun," Dani explains. "But this hand is not open. It's a clenched fist."

Dazmonique leans closer. "Open hand catch sun. Light, knowledge, kindness. Closed hand crush sun."

"A gift of kindness offered," Dani continues. "We can accept, open-hand, or reject, closed fist."

"The choice is ours," Leonel blurts out. "That's what Tal told us earlier. We are offered power gifts."

Dani whispers in my ear. "One of my mother's gifts is shape-shifting. Maybe soon you'll have that gift. Use it only for good, like my mother."

My Uncle Tal, I think to myself, *became a dragon to drive off Bully Harold Bully and his friends outside my bedroom window.*

"Your gift was getting a great brother like me," says Jimi One or Two, punching his brother.

"No way. I'm the gift, and I'm a greater greater brother than you ever will be. Cat, dog, infinity," replies Jimi Two or One, returning the punch.

Esther Evening Star stands, raises her arms and gazes into the night sky. Wisps of black cloud race across the face of the moon. Again, I hear the low hollow whistling sound, the one I'd heard in the cornfield.

"They're coming," Esther Evening Star murmurs. "Tomorrow is the end of the harvest."

"When the Sun begins its journey to its winter home," Dani adds. "Powerful time of the year."

Uncle Tal joins Esther Evening Star. "*Calan Gaeaf*," he murmurs.

A Welsh word my mother used for November first, my birthday.

"The sun begins its journey to the darker half of year," Uncle Tal adds.

He and Esther Evening Star stare out into the night sky. "Time for the meeting," Esther Evening Star murmurs.

"Time for the opening," my Uncle Tal adds. "Transfer or wedding."

"The Jimis don't understand any of this."

Nor do I. Meeting? Opening? Transfer or wedding?

"Sleep now," Esther Evening Star says, turning to us. "Tomorrow is a very important day."

Esther Evening Star gives us each a plant to chew.

No way I'm going to sleep, I think to myself. *My heads is filled with questions.* And then I hear my mother's gentle singing my favourite Welsh lullaby Suo Gan.

Huna blentyn yn fy mynwes, / Clud a chynnes ydyw hon./

Breichiau mam sy'n dyn am danat, / Cariad mam sy dan fy mron;

Sleep my darling on my bosom, / Warm and cosy, will be true, /

Round thee mother's arms are folding, /In her heart a mother's love.

The questions bouncing around in my head move slower and slower keeping time with the melody.

Until the questions stop.

And I sleep.

55. Apache Stones, Circles and Crossing Places

In my dream, I am again in the darkness of the mud hut standing over the woman covered in a long white cloth held in place by apache tears. The old woman stands nearby. Only now there is something new. The gentle voice of my mother singing the Welsh lullaby continues into my dream.

As the melody floats through the darkness, the old woman pulls back the long white cloth. Beneath it lies my mother.

She sits up and hands me four apache tears, two in each hand. "*Bendithion i ti, fy mab, Howell, ar eich penblwydd*! Blessing to you, my son, Howell, on your birthday! *Byddwn yn cwrdd eto yn fuan.* We'll meet again soon."

As she lies back down, the sound changes. The sweet singing is drowned beneath low hollow whistling. Dark-grey, hunchbacked figures whirl around the inside of the mud hut. Before me stands Tommy Foxglove, his form expanding and contracting. An evil sneer covers his face. He raises his arm and The Special-Special One and his gang leap upon the figure on the floor, grabbing at the apache tears, which they ram into their pockets before disappearing through the smoke hole, screaming with delight. I watch as the torn white cloth, now rags, slowly disintegrates. The figure beneath the sheet has disappeared.

Someone shakes my shoulder. "Breathe deeply," Uncle Tal whispers. "*Penblwydd hapus, nai.* Happy birthday, nephew. Today is your thirteenth birthday. It's time."

My birthday. Time for pizza, soda, ice cream, friends and a trip to Waterworks in Redding. But not this birthday.

Uncle Tal points to a distant mountain. A series of flashing lights. "Signals from *Señor* Quit and *Madame* Bouzius," Uncle Tal whispers. "They warn of the gathering. It's time."

Uncle Tal puts his arm around my shoulder and walks me to the back wall of the cave, stepping carefully over my sleeping friends. "What do you see?"

The full moon shines on the petroglyphs. "A series of circles within circles," I answer.

Uncle Tal points to an opening on the outer circle. "If you begin here, how do you get to the middle?"

Five minutes later and I'm still stuck in the outer circle.

Uncle Tal pats me on the shoulder. "Don't give up. You were given something in your dream. Look in your pocket. It was a gift from the Crossingway, the thin veil between here and there."

I reach into the pocket of my shorts. Four apache tears.

"Hold up one of them," Uncle Tal commands.

The moonlight traces a pattern through the stone. When I hold it to the petroglyph a connection appears joining the outer circle to the next. I take a second stone from my pocket. One circle connects to the next. The pattern continues stone by stone, circle by circle, gradually guiding me to the centre.

"What if there is no moonlight?"

Uncle Tal moves, blocking out the moonlight. Even in the darkness, the stones reveal the pattern.

Uncle Tal pats my shoulder. "The stones will lead you. But only you can see the patterns. The others will rely on you. Look carefully. When you hold up the stone, the end of the first pattern doesn't attach to the beginning of the second. There's a gap. You'll need to find a way to cross that gap."

Dazmonique joins us. She points to the gaps. "These called crossing places."

Uncle Tal nods.

"How do we pass through these crossing places?" I ask, speaking slowly so that Dazmonique can read my lips.

"Howell know answer when time come," Dazmonique interrupts.

"Yes, he will," asserts Uncle Tal. "Now let's try the fourth stone."

I hold it up to the moonlight. Dazmonique stares at the pattern. "*Gwo ouvèti, travèse plas, nan sant sèk. Danjere.* Large opening, crossing place, into centre circle. Dangerous."

Uncle Tal stares out into the darkness. "Yes, dangerous," he announces. "This day will be demanding—and very dangerous."

Esther Evening Star hands us a plant. "Passionflower help you sleep more. Need energy."

My eyelids flutter as I watch two ravens land, one on each of Uncle Tal's shoulders. He nods, listening to the birds.

The passionflower does its work. Troubling questions about circles, crossing places and talking ravens slowly drift away.

Again, I sleep.

56. A Birthday and a Wedding

A loud sneeze. I shudder from head to toe, waking myself. The Jimis kneel, one on each side of me, tickling the inside of my nose with blades of grass. "The Jimis think it's time for the birthday boy to wake," they giggle. They pull the sides of their mouths up. "Happy birthday emoji."

"November the First, Howell. *Baa hózhǫ́ǫgo ni'dizhchį́,*" Dani squeals with delight, kissing me on both checks.

"What did you say?" I ask.

"I gave you Birthday greetings in Navajo," Dani replies.

"*Felix cumpleaños*," Leonel calls out.

"*Jodi a se bon anivèsè nesans ou, zanmi m'. Jou espesyal ou.* Today is your best birthday, my friend. Your special day," Dazmonique adds as they all leap on me, pinching my arms and legs.

Uncle Tal and Esther Evening Star stand at the mouth of the cave, gazing across the vast expanse of desert, dimly lit by the early morning sun. The ravens sit on Uncle Tal's shoulders, periodically swooping down into the desert floor below, then returning.

"Birds tell when safe to move," Dazmonique whispers in my ear.

The Jimis suddenly squeal. "That koko thing. It's moved again."

Leonel stands against the back wall, running his fingers over the petroglyphs. "The *kokopelli* points to two figures."

"Dazmonique see dark spot between the two. It grows bigger." She puts her hands over her ears. "Hear screaming as two spots pulled apart."

Esther Evening Star faces us. "All of you has a Doeth figure in your past or present. Someone who will, either now or at a future time, pass their power to you—unless the Drygoni prevent it."

Now is the time for the transfer. The time for my mother to pass some Doeth power to me—if the Drygoni *don't prevent the transfer.*

The two ravens return, cawing loudly. Uncle Tal claps his hands. "We have far to go before nightfall." He then places his hands on Dazmonique and Leonel's heads. "What do you hear and see?"

"Dazmonique hear screams and yells. Snarls and shrieks. Groans and shouts of triumph."

"Leonel sees many gathering. Fighting, flying, eyes flashing. Evil."

Uncle Tal signals to us. "Down the ladder. No wasting time."

Before I move, Esther Evening Star catches my arm, "Birthday or wedding. Winter solstice. This night. Be ready."

Yes, it's my birthday. Yes it's the winter solstice. But birthday or wedding? Who's getting married? Not me. I'm only thirteen.

57. Wrapped Inside a Boulder

I run fast. Almost too fast. Not because of the sandals. Esther Evening Star took those and stuffed them in her little sack. She gathers us together and mutters some strange words. And I fall forward on all fours.

My feet and hands are large pads, beating hard on the hot dry desert. Behind us thunders the *heyoka's* horse, driving us onward. The ravens fly ahead, watching the canyon for any movement.

Our muscular back legs hurl us onward, and our front pads stretch forward pounding the desert floor. We are powerful mountain lions racing down canyons, bounding up gullies, and speeding across mesa tops, driven on by the galloping horse and its backward rider.

Where are the voices? I expect them to ask: 'You became what? A mountain lion? Speeding at thirty miles an hour?' Laughter.

But no voices, no laughter. Just myself asking, *"Will anyone believe me? Do I care if they do or don't?"*

An eagle hurtles down, landing on the *heyoka's* shoulder. It leans forward, its beak close to the man's ear. I glance back and see the galloping horse swerve to the right heading for the base of a mesa. We all swerve right, guided by the *heyoka's* horse, headed in the same direction.

We gather at the base of the cliff in an area surrounded by large boulders.

"Wow. The Jimis have never run that fast in their whole lives."

"I couldn't see where I was going," Leonel chimes in, "but I felt the wind rushing through my hair as I swung to left and right."

Esther Evening Star smiles. "All power like that you use only for a short time. Too long," she warns, "and you remain in that shape."

A clatter of hooves as horse and *heyoka* gallop away. They scramble up a nearby gully, headed for the mesa top. Uncle Tal gestures for us all to gather into a tight circle. "We are close to our destination," he whispers.

"Dazmonique hear Drygoni voices. Very close."

"I see Professor Lucian," Leonel adds. "And Bollsinger and his gang."

Uncle Tal signals to us. "Do what I do," he calls out. He shifts backward slowly until he leans against a huge boulder. He stretches out her arms and flattens himself, back against the boulder behind him.

We all back into one of the large boulders surrounding us and flatten ourselves against it, arms outstretched. Uncle Tal looks around at each of us. "Whatever happens, do not be afraid."

He leans back against his boulder and begins chanting quietly.

I feel myself moving slowly backward, sinking into the boulder behind me as if it is foam. My legs, arms, body and head are soon locked in place. My eyes are the last to stop moving, fixed straight ahead.

And not a moment too soon.

Professor Lucian, in his long leather coat, leaps into the centre of the ring of boulders, followed by The Special-Special One, Biggie Pug, Jack Rabbit and Brenda. All hiss and growl, their faces sunken and pinched, their eyes flashing bright red. They move from boulder to boulder, poking them with the spears and knives they hold in their hands.

The Special-Special One whacks me hard in the stomach with a club, but I feel nothing. "When I catch Howl, I'll squeeze his neck until his eyeballs pop out," he snarls.

"Remember," Professor Lucian growls, "we need to stop that boy, stop the transfer. When the ceremony is complete, you can do whatever you like with him and his friends."

This remark brings much whooping and hollering, and tales of the tortures planned for my friends and me.

"Silence," Professor Lucian roars. He moves slowly from boulder to boulder, staring and sniffing at each.

Has he figured out Uncle Tal's strategy to hide us?

He stands before me, his one eye fixed on my unseen eyes. He moves closer. His stench is almost overpowering. Slowly he raises the patch on his other eye. Beneath the yellow spot, the eye is a blazing white. No pupil or iris. He leans closer. Spirals whirl in the centre of the white ball searching out what lies beneath the surface of the boulder. A sudden flick of his hand and he holds a small lizard. The X-ray eye focuses on his prey, scouring the length of its body. Satisfied it's just a lizard, he hurls it to the ground. It scuttles away.

Professor Lucian hisses and his teeth flash as he surveys the circle of boulders. "We wait here," he commands.

"Why here?" Biggie Pug asks. "Why not some place in the shade?"

Professor Lucian spins around, his long fingernails digging into Biggie Pug's neck. "I said, we wait. An hour. Two hours. Maybe three. We wait. Here."

A chill runs through me. Esther Evening Star warned us about only using *Doeth* transformation power for a short time. "Too long and you remain in that shape," she cautioned.

How long is too long? Too long and I will stay imprisoned in my boulder-tomb forever.

The midday sun begins its descent toward the western horizon. The Special-Special One and his bullies shift restlessly, bored with sitting still so long.

Suddenly Jack Rabbit stands. "I hear sounds, Professor Lucian. Permission to check them out."

Without taking his eyes off the boulders before him, the professor signals his assent. Jack Rabbit scrambles up the gully. He's back in minutes, standing before Professor Lucian who leans forward, his good eye inches from Jack Rabbit's face.

"Voices. I heard their voices," Jack Rabbit shouts. "They're on the mesa top." The Special-Special One and the others leap to their feet, shaking their spears and whooping. "The hunt is on," Bollsinger screams, thrusting his spear into an invisible opponent cowering before him.

Voices call from the top of the mesa. "Is this the way? The Jimis are tired."

"We'll soon be there," replies the voice of Uncle Tal.

"What if there are werewolves or zombies nearby?" cry the Jimis.

"Stop with the werewolves and zombies," comes another voice. Dani's voice.

Did the others escape from their boulders and leave me stuck here? I struggle to move but can't.

Professor Lucian and the others rush away in pursuit of the voices.

I wait—and wait. I can't feel my legs, arms, or body. Nothing moves. Even my breathing has stopped.

I'm trapped in this boulder forever.

After fifteen minutes, an African wild dog and jaguar bound into the circle of boulders. I watch fascinated as the two wild animals sniff at the large boulders. Then they move close to each other before turning in ever-faster circles until they become just a blur. And then…

Standing before me are *Madame* Bouzius and *Señor* Quit. The former removes some necklaces and bracelets and collects them in her hands. She blows upon them, muttering an incantation. I fall forward, released from the boulder, landing face down on the desert floor. Around me, the others collapse forward and slowly stretch their aching muscles.

"My brother has no nose," Jimi One or Two whispers.

"And you have no ears," Jimi Two or One replies.

Leonel laughs, "Maybe you both should have left your tongues behind."

The twins look at *Señor* Quit and *Madame* Bouzius. "Your voices sounded just like my stupid brother," they giggle.

"It was not us," *Señor* Quit responds.

"It was the *heyoka,*" adds *Madame* Bouzius.

"And my brother's voice was his horse," joins in Jimi One or Two.

I look around. The others are as happy as I am that we're no longer trapped inside the boulders.

I dig deep into my pockets. The four apache tears and brooch are still there.

'Swim,' the old woman said. What did she mean? Swim in the desert?

58. Power Shifts

We run, entering a wide sandy valley with steep grey cliffs on both sides. Uncle Tal points to a cave ripped into the cliff face. "We'll rest in that cave and regain our strength, in preparation," he declares.

Preparation. I shiver at the word.

Leonel grabs my hand and asks me to describe where we are. Dani replies for me, "We are in a canyon. The home of the ancient Puebloan peoples."

"The place they abandoned?" Leonel whispers.

"What are you two talking about?" I ask. "And why whisper?"

Dani pauses before continuing. "This place was once a gathering place. The centre of religious life, filled with huge multi-storied buildings joined by dark tunnels."

"The Jimis don't like dark tunnels."

Leonel joins in. "Priests performed religious ceremonies in the huge kivas, spiritual gathering places. Suddenly, the place was abandoned."

"Why?"

"Werewolves?" the twins cry out.

"Not werewolves," Dani snaps.

"Zombies?" the twins add.

Dani takes a deep breath before speaking, "Some say drought. Others…" Her head drops. Silence.

"The Jimis don't like you not speaking."

Dazmonique's voice breaks the quiet. "Religious men and women bring good power to people. But some priests not happy with only good power. *Vle tout pouvwa. Tankou bondye.* Want all power. Be like gods. *Men, prèt yo fè move pouvwa.* But priests make bad power."

We all tremble as a dark thundercloud explodes overhead.

"*Pa pale de move pouvwa.* No talk of bad power. *Pa plis.* No more," Dazmonique demanded. "*Ou pale, li vini.* You talk, it come. Silence now."

We run to the cave in the cliff face. Esther Evening Star passes out large slices of jicama, which I devour, enjoying the liquid sliding down my throat as I crunch the root. As we eat, *Madame* Bouzius stops before each of us, holds out the ponchos taken from us earlier, turns them inside out and slides them over our heads. She then presses her thumbs into our chests, tracing a line under our ribs up to our hearts. As she does this, she mumbles, "*Pirifye yon sèl sa a.* Purify this one." *Señor* Quit follows her, seeking our protection, in Spanish, "*Protege éste.* Protect this one." Meantime Esther Evening Star moves through the cave with lit sagebrush, tracing the outline of each of our bodies' shapes.

"The twins are frightened. Why do they need all this protection? They're scared."

Before they pull their faces into their "Scared Emoji," I take their hands. "Do not be afraid."

"Will the…

"…twins be…

"…invisible…

"…with these…

"…ponchos?"

Madame Bouzius smiles. "*Totalman envizib*."

"Just like in that book the Jimis read." The twins pull at their faces. "Happy Emoji."

Uncle Tal raises his arms. "Soon the sun will sink, and the full moon will rise, lighting the doorway and tunnel to the great kiva. The six of you will enter. You are all needed to journey through the tunnels to the large, central kiva where the transfer will occur. The adults will not be with you in the tunnels. As you see, a huge army of *Drygoni* gather for this ceremony. All wish to enter the tunnels, to be present for the transfer. We adults will prevent many from entering the tunnels. However, there are too many, and some will pass successfully and join the gathering in the large kiva." He pauses and look at each us in turn, "One final thing: you will not be invisible once inside the tunnels."

We look at each other and hold hands. We must face *Drygoni* inside the tunnels alone, and they'll be able to see us!

"What happens or does not happen this night," Uncle Tal continues, "will affect each of you. *Mae ein bendithion yn mynd gyda chi.* Our blessings go with you."

"All these foreign words. Now the twins are really scared."

Before we can protest, Uncle Tal waves his hand and murmurs a few mysterious words. I slip into a deep sleep free of dreams.

Uncle Tal taps me on the shoulder. "It's time," he whispers. His green eyes stare into mine. "No more doubts, nephew. No more voices. Trust your Doeth voice. It alone will guide you." He hugs me tightly and cups his hands over my head. *"Y bachgen hwn yw gwir heres i fy chwaer, pŵer Rhiannon. Gadewch i daioni a gwirionedd ei arwain.* This boy is the true heir to my sister, Rhiannon's power. Let goodness and truth guide him." He kisses me on the forehead before removing his hands. "Now you must wake the others, Howell. You'll need their help."

When we're all awake, Uncle Tal faces us. "I'll whisper a power word in each of your ears. Do not share this word. Not even with your friends. And do not use it until you absolutely need to." He pauses, looking at each of us in turn. "Misusing a power word can be terrifying."

By now the roars are deafening. I peek outside. My chest tightens and my fists tighten. Before me is an open carriage drawn by a white horse. Long grey veils droop down the sides of the carriage, hiding the occupants. A slight gust of wind and I see them: Sister Sarah and Tommy Foxglove sit side by side in the carriage. Surrounding the carriage are not one but many Professor Drago Lucians Bollsingers, Biggie Pugs, Jack Rabbits and Brendas. Hundreds of them, all identical and all clashing their spears against their shields. Over their heads, dark grey shifting shapes dart to and fro, throwing fireballs, which explode as they crash into the ground and against the walls of the canyon.

Sister Sarah sits frozen, staring straight ahead, covered in a white wedding dress. A white veil cascades from her head down over her shoulders. Tommy Foxglove, sporting a tuxedo, a top hat on his head, stands, laughing and waving to those surrounding the carriage.

I want to ask Uncle Tal what this means, but he has gone, as have the others, except for Leonel. We're alone.

"Where is everyone?" Leonel whispers.

My eyes open. "I see them. They're outside, walking among the *Drygoni*!"

Leonel grabs my arm. "Let's follow them. Say your word."

I mumble the word quietly and, holding Leonel's hand, cautiously step out of the cave, wondering if we will be attacked and ripped to shreds by the Drygoni horde.

Nothing happens. The ponchos and magic words make us invisible. Yet I can still see Uncle Tal, the other adults and my friends. They're not invisible to me.

"Be careful," I whisper to Leonel. "We don't want to bump into…"

Too late. Leonel bumps into one of the Bollsingers—and moves straight through him! I follow, walking through Jack Rabbit. The *Drygoni* can't hear, see or feel us.

Beyond this first group of *Drygoni* I see a larger crowd being dragged along by chains.

"The *Drygoni* dig deeper and deeper into the Safonals until they are possessed," Uncle Tal whispers to me. "Painless and unnoticed, the *Drygoni* now have their shades. They still have time to resist—if they want to, if they'll listen. Only then will they change."

I recognise many from my town: bullies, young and old; gossips who say hurtful things about others when gathered in grocery stores, churches, street corners, schoolyards or on Facebook; children who hurt animals and others; some who play with their parents' guns, bringing them to school and threatening others; and, so many more. The slumped shades of Bully Harold Bully and his family, Pug the Pyro, Sloppy Jack and Brenda Blackstone crawl along, dragged by chains. They stand, hunched over, before falling forward on all fours and scuttling along like animals. They pass through me and are gone.

Uncle Tal points to the rock face. "Look! The opening to the tunnels, which lead to the central kiva. Years ago, it was bricked up. But, when the moon shines on this night, the bricks fall, revealing the breach. You'll have one hour."

"What happens after an hour?"

"The bricks close the opening. You'll be locked inside."

Leonel grabs my hand as we run through the *Drygoni*, unseen. As I pass the carriage, I glance at Sister Sarah. Through the thin veil I see her eyes. They're dull, fixed straight ahead, filled with tears. She doesn't know where she is or what's happening. I reach out and touch her hand. She looks down for an instant as if she feels something. Tommy Foxglove whirls around, his teeth bared and his red eyes glaring. Seeing nothing, he turns back.

Sister Sarah's head rises. She stares straight ahead. Blankly.

Why is she here?

59. The First Crossing Places

Guided by Uncle Tal and the other three adults, we creep closer to the bricked-in tunnels.

Finally, Uncle Tal stops and whispers his final instructions. "Follow the light of the moon along the wall until you find the doorway. All of you must enter. As I told you, the adults will stay here to prevent too many of the *Drygoni* from following you. We'll be here when—if—you return."

And with those chilling words, Uncle Tal waves his hand, points us in the direction of the doorway. "Go!"

We creep forward, our hands scraping along the moonlit wall. We walk about twenty yards when the Jimis point to a doorway from which bricks had recently fallen.

"I saw it first," responds Jimi Two or One.

"Didn't!"

I separate the pair and put my finger on my lips. Time for silence.

The six of us dive through the opening.

"It's dark," Dani murmurs. "Really dark."

"No problem for me," giggles Leonel. "Follow me."

"Who's holding my hand?" Jimi One or Two asks. "It's not my brother, is it?"

A scuffle of feet in the darkness as the twins race in different directions. A few paces later, we hear a solid thump.

"My brother made me run into a wall," wails Jimi One or Two.

"No way. You made *me* run into a wall!" Jimi Two or One cries.

"If you don't hold hands," Dani warns, "you'll get lost and never see each other again. And," Dani adds before the two can respond, "you'd miss each other. And don't say you wouldn't."

Dazmonique taps me on the shoulder. "Dazmonique hear."

Hearing without hearing, I think to myself.

"Professor Lucian and others behind us. Enter opening with young man and woman I don't know."

I do.

"One has a top hat and tuxedo," I mutter. "The other a wedding dress. A veil covers her face."

"They see us if we not hide," Dazmonique adds.

"The Jimis could say their special words again."

"Don't," Dani replies. "Power words must only be used when you're in real danger."

"But the Jimis are in real danger. All of us are in real danger."

I see a nearby hollow in the wall.

"Quickly," I call out. "Follow me."

We press ourselves together in the darkened hollow, hiding from the procession of *Drygoni.*

"I'm pressed up against my brother," whispers Jimi One or Two, "and he smells."

"Do you want us to be caught?" Dani whispers.

The Jimis are silent as Professor Lucian, chanting in an unknown language, marches down the tunnel. Behind him, Tommy Foxglove and Sister Sarah. Bollsinger's group and some English butlers follow. All chant and beat drums. I put my hand over my mouth and pinch my nose, trying to block the smell. After the whole procession has passed, we step back into the main passageway.

"Dazmonique hear Professor. He chant, 'I bring the bridegroom and bride. Prepare for ceremony.'"

So the wedding is for Sister Sarah and Tommy Foxglove, bride and bridegroom!

"The Jimis say, 'Let's rush after them.' They went that way."

Leonel grabs them. "I see two guards ahead. Hiding. Waiting for us."

Dani chimes in. "They pretended not to see us because they wanted to lure us deeper into the passageway."

"So we'd get lost," Leonel adds, "and the guards could capture us easily."

Dazmonique turns to me. "What stone say?"

I take an apache tear from my right pocket. It shines a blue laser light down the darkened passageway veering to the left. I signal for my friends to follow.

The light from the stone leads us down one passageway and into another. We arrive at the end of the light from the first stone.

I place the first stone in my left pocket and take a second from my right pocket.

The Jimis stumble past me and crash straight into an invisible barrier.

"Something stopped the Jimis. It hurt them," they whimper, rubbing their heads.

"The first crossing place," I murmur.

"Dazmonique hears sounds. The Jimis scream."

"We're not screaming. The Jimis are whispering."

Dazmonique stamps her foot and repeats, "The Jimis scream."

"Think of a time when you both scream," Dani demands. "I know," she responds, answering her own question. "When you hold hands,"

Leonel interrupts. "And there was that time they had those thorns in their hands. Do you still have them?"

"Of course the Jimis still have their hands."

"Not your hands," Leonel snaps. "The thorns."

The twins reached into their pockets, produced the two thorns and stab at the invisible barrier, trying to break through.

"Adults tell Dazmonique forty-five minutes."

"It's going to take the Jimis forty-five minutes to break this barrier with these thorns?"

"No," she replies. "Only forty-five minutes left, voices of adults say."

"The Jimis never understand her. She makes no more sense than Elder Jimi One and Elder Jimi Two's questions."

"That's when the outside door closes," Dani explains. "When we'll be trapped inside."

"I see the adults holding off hordes of *Drygoni* at the entrance," Leonel whispers. "Dragon, jaguar, wild dog, grey wolf—all fight."

"Dazmonique hear growls, snarls, screams."

The twins slash wildly at the invisible wall with their prickly pear thorns.

"It's breaking," Dani calls out. "When you hit together, at the same time, the wall breaks. Hold hands."

"Never. The Jimis…"

"Hold hands now," Dani demands.

With the twins holding hands and working together, grumbling all the time, the wall collapses. As it does, I pull the second stone from my pocket.

We edge forward, step-by-step, down the darkened passageway.

60. The Jimis Will Guard the Stones

Leonel grips my arm. "I see a large circular room. Fire in the centre. Iron stands support a huge iron pot. Three large blocks of stone. Dark green smoke gushes from a hole in floor."

"It's a kiva," Dani murmurs. "These passageways end in the large kiva. The huge iron pot boils ceremonial liquid. The hole in the floor is a sipapu, a hole through which spirits from the underworld pass into this world."

"Why dark green smoke?" I ask.

"I don't know," Dani continues. "It doesn't sound good."

"The evil ones, Drygoni," I murmur.

We are all silent, fearful of what we're saying.

When we enter the second invisible barrier, the Jimis try breaking it with their prickly pear thorns. No luck.

"Dazmonique hears adults tell us to hurry. Must arrive before it is too late."

"Too late for what?" I ask. "The ceremony?"

Dazmonique doesn't answer. She stands still, staring at the second invisible barrier. The words she says were barely audible. "*Sèvi ak objè a ak pouvwa majik.*"

"Dazmonique's talking in that language the Jimis don't understand."

"The last bit sounds like a 'power' and 'magic object'." Dani offers.

"That's it," Leonel responds. "In Spanish you'd say, *'Usa el objeto con poder mágico'*, or 'use an object with magical power'."

"It's your rattlesnake skin," Dani tells Dazmonique.

Dazmonique carefully unwraps the rattlesnake skin that scared the butler. She lays it on the ground, walks along its length and continues straight through the invisible wall. We all follow, being careful not to break the snakeskin.

I remove the third stone from my right pocket.

We hurry, all following the blue light of the third apache tear. The ground beneath us now throbs.

"Earthquake!" the Jimis call out. Dani corrects them. "Drums."

"Drums…and…earthquake?"

"No. People scream and chant to the pounding of drums," Dani adds.

"Not people, Jimis think. It's…"

"Don't say it!" Leonel warns.

The light from the third stone ends. We reach the third invisible barrier.

"It's one of those crossing places again. The Jimis don't like them."

"What other tokens did we pick up?" Dani asks.

"The Jimis can't remember anything else." None of us can.

"This can't be the end of our journey," Leonel mutters. "What happens if we don't get to the kiva at the centre of the passageways? Maybe none of us will become Doeths. And then what? Life as Safonals? Tormented by Drygoni?"

"The twins solved crossing place one," I murmur. "Dazmonique number two. So, it's Dani, Leonel or me who has the answer for the third crossing place."

We look at each other in the dim light.

A pause. And then I remember.

"It's you, Leonel. The book," I say, grabbing him by the shoulder. "Remember the book. Bollsinger and the others laughed at you," I add. "They said you couldn't read because you were blind. But you read something."

"*La mano derecha y el pie izquierdo primero, si quieren pasar*,'" Leonel recalls. "Right hand and left foot first, if you want to pass."

I place Leonel before the barrier. He stretches out his right hand and left foot. We watch as he squeezes through what looks like a sheet of liquid glass. When halfway through, he drags his left hand and right foot behind him.

"Me next," says Jimi One or Two.

"No, me."

While the Jimis argue, I slide through the glass, followed by Dani and Dazmonique.

"Hurry," I call to the twins, who continue to argue about who should go first.

Finally, we can wait no longer.

"Both of you wait here," I call out. "We'll find you on the way back."

"Promise?" they both cry. "A Doeth would never leave his friends behind. Especially in an earthquake and surrounded by zombies with AK47s and…"

"I promise I will find you and lead you out," I interrupt.

I take the three stones from my left pocket, slide my hand through the invisible barrier and place them on the ground.

"Guard these for me. If we don't have them, we won't find our way out."

The twins smile and give me a thumbs-up. "The Jimis will guard the stones even if they're attacked by…"

Their words fade.

61. The Final Crossing Place

I take the final stone out of my pocket and rush down the passageway with my three friends, turning left and right as the stone's light changes direction.

The pounding of drums, chanting and shrieking echo around the walls and shake the ground beneath us.

We reach the final invisible barrier. Before us lies a short tunnel opening into a huge kiva. We see The Special-Special One and his friends, arms and legs flung about wildly, in a wild ceremonial dance.

Dani grips the turquoise and silver necklace that hangs around her neck. Holding it before her, she passes through the final crossing place.

Dani has the necklace, but she's on the other side. What about the rest of us?

Then I see him. A huge man with tattoos all over his body, dressed in a loincloth and wearing a feathered hat towers over Dani. The three of us run to help, but the invisible barrier prevents us.

The tattooed man swoops Dani up in his arms, throws her over his shoulder and carries her, screaming and kicking, into the lighted kiva. The shrieks and screams in the kiva grow even louder as the guard enters carrying Dani.

My brain reels. *What can I do? How can I cross the final crossing place and rescue Dani?* I keep repeating to myself, *Think like a* Doeth.

The old woman said, "swim." But swim where? Then I thought, *"Key" was the Welsh word* "ci," *so what could "swim" be?* A Welsh word?

I remembered. My mother once gave me a bracelet, which she called a '*swyn*,' the Welsh word for a charm or talisman. Maybe the word the old woman said '*swyn*,' not swim? But what use is that? The talisman bracelet is home in Mount Shasta.

Then I remember the broach the old woman pinned on my shirt. That's the talisman! My fingers close around it. Two silver birds with long beaks face each other, their wings and legs intertwined. My mother showed me this image in a book of Celtic images. "These birds are the messengers between the worlds of the living and the dead," she informed me.

Holding the broach before me, I walk through the final crossing place.

62. The Wedding and the Transfer

I am alone in the tunnel.

Leonel and Dazmonique remain behind, unable to cross. Dani alone passed through the final crossing place, only to be grabbed by huge guard and hauled down the darkened tunnel to the large kiva.

Shall I rush in to rescue Dani?

The drums beat louder and faster, accompanying the ear-splitting shrieks. My body stiffens, tingling with icy fear.

"Stop," I think to myself. *"Don't rush in. Don't think, feel or act like a Safonal."*

Two huge guards appear. I flatten myself against the wall. It's no use they will find me.

"Only use your power word when you're in danger," Uncle Tal had said.

I am in danger. Terrible danger.

I whisper the word and step away from the wall. If the power word doesn't work, the guards will drag me into the kiva and throw me into the pot of boiling oil.

The two guards move slowly down the tunnel, their spears thrusting into the darkness. I stand still, bracing myself, waiting to be skewered by their spears. Their razor-sharp points thrust into and out of my stomach and chest as if I don't exist.

My power word works. I step through the two guards and move toward the huge kiva.

My eyes burn. Thick green smoke pours out of the sipapu and slides around the walls of the kiva. I squint through the haze.

Before me is an oblong pit with six English butlers sitting cross-legged beating six huge drums. The Special-Special One, Biggie Pug, Jack Rabbit and Brenda dance wildly, flinging their arms and legs in all directions as they circle the huge iron pot in the centre. Professor Drago Lucian stands, arms raised, chanting before three stone slabs, each about three feet high.

I stagger back, steadying myself against the wall of the kiva. On the far slab lies Dani, held down by two guards. On the near slab Sister Sarah, her body held in place by Tommy Foxglove. And, on the centre slab, the one Professor Lucian stands behind lies the figure draped with a white cloth. The veil is pulled back from her face: it is my mother.

Professor Lucian raises his arms summoning someone or something from the sipapu directly behind the iron pot. Each time he calls, the dancers flail around frantically, bumping into and falling over each other as the drums beat louder.

Even though Professor Lucian speaks in a strange tongue, I understand him. He is calling upon *Meistr Drygoni*—the Grand Master of the *Drygoni*—to appear. Professor Lucian's arms and fingers gesture from Sister Sarah to Tommy Foxglove to my mother saying all is ready.

Ready for what? Is this the wedding?

"Come," Professor Lucian shrieks. "It is the appointed time for some of the power of this *Nerth Doeth* to transfer to the living."

Is Sister Sarah to inherit some of my mother's Doeth *power? But if so, why is Tommy Foxglove holding her down and why does she look so terrified?*

And then I answer my own questions. *Sister Sarah is the unwilling vehicle for some Doeth power to transfer to Tommy Foxglove—and be used for* Drygoni *evil.*

Unconsciously my head shakes back and forth. My fists clench and my body tightens. This must not happen. But how can I stop it?

Professor Lucian voice drops to a low mumble, gradually growing louder as the pitch of his voice becomes higher and higher, speaking words that send shivers down my spine. Pointing to the figure draped in a white sheet he screams, "To you, *Meistr Drygoni*, I bring this woman, a recently captured *Nerth Doeth*." The earth rumbles and an explosion of green fumes pours from the *sipapu* engulfing the whole kiva.

Professor Lucian slides across to Sister Sarah and Tommy Foxglove. "To you, *Meistr Drygoni*, I bring this young woman, a Safonal, blood-daughter of the powerful *Nerth Doeth*. And I bring this young man, a devoted and trusted *Drygoni*. It is time to marry him to the Safonal, to transfer the *Nerth Doeth's* power to him, your faithful servant."

Images flash before me: Sister Sarah dressed in bridal clothes before the church in the cornfields; the wedding in Dead Man's Bells poster; and, Sister Sarah in the open carriage.

63. "Do You Know What You've Done?"

Another explosion and blast of green fumes from the *sipapu*.

I watch in horror as hunched dark-grey shifting shapes pour out of the *sipapu* and race around the kiva. Low hollow whistles now mix with the pounding of the drums. The sickening stench sticks in my nose and throat. Fireballs fly out of the *sipapu*, whistling and flashing around me.

A large, dark form engulfed in green fumes rises from the sipapu. Professor Lucian, a manic grin on his face, greets the emerging figure. "Come, *Meistr Drygoni*, you who challenged the gods and learned to control the natural and human world. You who taught us weak humans how to gain and use power for your purposes. Come to us."

The form continues to rise out of the *sipapu*, constantly forming and reforming itself. It now stands about fifteen feet tall. Its face has three large eyes, two on the sides and a blood-red one in the centre of its forehead. Its mouth is open, the fleshy tongue surrounded by long, pointed teeth. Huge horns protrude through the writhing snake-hair that dances on its head. The skin on its chest is drawn tight, revealing the skeletal bones beneath.

Its blood-red eye widens as it fixes on the figure beneath the white sheet, my captured mother. Its arms rise, a gesture that brings silence to the kiva. As his hands open, I see a bulging eye in the centre of each hand. The hands glide forward and hover over my mother. After a pause, it throws back its head and roars with laughter, an action that brings even louder shrieks and the pounding of drums.

Again, its arms rise, silencing the noise. His hand-eyes jerk to face Sister Sarah, who stared blankly ahead, and Tommy Foxglove, who snickers with delight. He has served his master well.

Professor Lucian walks to the Grand Master, offering him a cup filled with the iron pot's bubbling brew, before turning to face Sister Sarah and Tommy Foxglove.

The form's voice is a low growl. "By the power invested in me and by me, I give this young Safonal woman, daughter of a *Nerth Doeth*, to this young man, my faithful servant. As he takes her hand in marriage, some of the power of this *Nerth-Doeth*-mother will transfer through the *Safonal*-daughter to this young man, her *Drygoni*-husband. And the son of the *Doeth*-mother will be denied his inheritance."

The thing is talking about me. Denied my mother's Doeth *power. I have to do something. And quick. But what? I'm invisible. All I have is the word. The word I'd used against Bully Harold Bully in the schoolyard. What if I use it now?*

I scream the word.

Suddenly I become visible to all. The guards turn and leap toward me. But, before they can grab me, I run to the centre of the kiva, knocking aside The Special-Special One and his bullies.

What now? The only thing I have left is the broach given to me by the old woman.

The *Meistr Drygoni* faces me, rising higher and higher. Without thinking, I hurl the broach into the bubbling iron pot.

The huge pot explodes, showering everyone with the boiling liquid. People and figures run wildly, bumping into one another, screaming in pain as the liquid from the iron pot splatters on them.

The red, laser eye of the *Meistr Drygoni* fixes on me. He towers high above, rising still higher. Suddenly he lunges downward, his huge eye-hands with their sharpened fingernails grabbing for me. I slip under his arms and run to the slab containing my mother. As Professor Lucian staggers back in horror, I place my hands on the sides of her face and stare into her eyes. Immediately a rush of electricity surges through my body, shaking me violently from head to toe. The gentle voice of my mother speaks, "*Longyfarchiadau, fy mab*, Howell. Congratulations, my son Howell. Take some of my *Doeth* power. Use it wisely. It will grow in you in the years to come."

And with that my mother's arms rise upwards, and her body rises off the slab, floating higher and higher. The *Meistr* lunges at her form, slashing and grasping, but his hands and arms pass through her, unable to grab the floating body, which finally passes through the roof of the kiva in a blaze of light.

A scream of rage rips around the kiva, battering the walls, as the *Meistr Drygoni* slides back into the *sipapu*, followed by the slithering hunched dark-grey shapes and the green fumes. The body of Sister Sarah, now released, fades until there is only a wedding dress and veil on the stone slab. Mother and daughter are both free!

Dani, freed from the guard, grabs my hand. "Follow me."

We run, hurling aside any of the Bollsingers and his bullies that stand in our way, and head for the short tunnel leading to the passageways.

Tommy Foxglove stands before us, blocking our way. "Do you know what you've done?" he screams. "You've destroyed me. Take this spear and plunge it in my heart. Kill me."

A spear appears in my hand. I look at it then at Tommy Foxglove. "Hurry, Howell," Dani shouts. "Do what you must!"

Tommy Foxglove grins and spreads his arms wide. He wants me to stab him with the spear. Chants of "Do it! Do it!" echo throughout the kiva.

I lie the spear down and push my way past Tommy Foxglove, who roars with fury. "Stab me! Kill me! Show us your anger! Release your rage."

"No!" I scream.

Dani and I rush down the short tunnel to the fourth crossing place. We need no talisman to cross this time. Dazmonique and Leonel join us as we follow the path from the light of the fourth apache tear.

"Let's hope the twins are still there," Dani pants as we run. "You gave them the other three stones. We need them to guide us to the exit."

64. Never-Ending Passageways

Leaving three stones with the twins was not a good idea. The Jimis took one stone each, which left a third one. They argued over that stone, finally throwing the stones at each other. Now all of the stones are lost.

"What did you expect, Howl?"

We spin around. There, barely visible in the darkened passageway, stands The Special-Special One and his bullies, holding lighted torches.

"Be careful," Leonel warns as the six of us huddle together for protection.

"Don't be afraid," The Special-Special One calls out.

Even though they position themselves directly in front of us, their voices swirl around, bouncing off the walls. "We can still be friends. It's the professor who came between us. We wanted to be friends, but he made us enemies. It's all his fault. If it weren't for him, we'd be the best of friends, helping each other at all times."

"The Jimis think maybe that's true."

"Dani knows it is a lie," she says, grabbing the twins.

"We can guide you out of these passageways," The Special-Special One continue. "We don't want to stay here with that professor and his creepy friends. We'd all be stuck here. That doorway won't open for six more months, the summer solstice. You wouldn't want that, would you? We help you, and you help us."

By now The Special-Special One and his gang stand very close. In the firelight their outlines shimmer.

"Don't listen to them," I shout. "Get out before the door closes.

We back away from the advancing gang, their voices deepening into growls.

A scream of rage echoes from deep within the central kiva. "Where are they? Bring them to me now," Professor Drago Lucian roars.

We turn and run.

"This way," the Jimis call, running down a passageway.

"No," cautions Dazmonique. "Madame Bouzius tells Dazmonique that wrong way. Hers good voice."

But it's too late. The twins had already rushed down the wrong passageway.

"We have to find the twins," I announce, "before the others do."

Dani peers into the passageway. "It's really dark down there."

"I'll lead you," Leonel announces.

After about twenty yards, Leonel stops. "The twins are nearby," he whispers, pointing to a passageway to the right dimly lit by flickering torches, "but so are Bollsinger and his gang."

Without a second thought, I march down the tunnel. Leonel is right.

Before us are the hunched forms of Bollsinger, Biggie Pug and Brenda, circling their prey, the twins, and growling. Periodically they fall forward on all fours, lurching sideways like hyenas. Jack Rabbit emerges from the shadows, a twin in each hand.

Bollsinger shifts toward me, snarling through his teeth. "If you were a real leader, Howl, you'd leave these two pipsqueaks behind," he scowls. "But you're weak and stupid."

"Howell wouldn't leave any of us behind," Leonel shouts. "He is a real Doeth."

"Oh, I'm so afraid of the blind boy," Brenda mocks.

"Howell good," Dazmonique adds. "One day he very powerful."

Jack Rabbit bursts out laughing. "That freaky deaf girl is trying to frighten us."

Bollsinger gestures to his friends, "Grab them. Take them to Professor Lucian. Leave Howl for me."

Brenda grabs Dazmonique and Dani, as Biggie Pug grips Leonel's wrist.

"The Jimis are sorry," the twins whimper.

Jack Rabbit, who still holds the twins, roars with laughter. "And you two runts thought you'd be *Doeths* one day."

"Who becomes a Doeth is not for any of us to decide," I reply.

The gang shrieks with laughter. "You're powerless—all of you."

"Are you sure?" My question stops their fun—for a minute or two.

Jack Rabbit can't resist. "I'm so frightened," he giggles, shaking the twins. "Idiot Tweedle Dumb One and idiot Tweedle Dumb Two."

We wait. Has Jack Rabbit forgotten his lesson from last time? However much the twins argue, never criticise one in front of the other.

But the twins remain motionless.

"The fools are powerless," Jack Rabbit hisses. "This is our place, not yours."

At that moment, a tingling sensation races from my shoulders to my fingers. I reach out and grab the twins by the shoulders as I stare at Jack Rabbit. "Did you hear what he said? He insulted your brother."

The Jimis heads snap around to face Jack Rabbit. "Did you call my brother an idiot?"

Before Jack Rabbit can reply, the twins crouch down. One hand covers their forehead, the other their mouths. Only their eyes can be seen. "Ninja emoji," they both cry. Then, with a blood-curling yell, they put their arms before them, hands open and leap forward. One twin grabs Jack Rabbit's head, the other his feet. Then, holding him above their heads, the twins spin him around, passing his head and feet from one to the other. He rotates like a helicopter blade above their heads, rising into the air until he stops at the roof of the passageway, still spinning furiously.

I turn and reach out to Leonel. One touch of my hand and he removes his glasses, focusing his blazing white eyes on Biggie Pug. A force, like a bolt of lightning, hurls Biggie Pug against the wall.

By now Brenda is shaking. Above her Jack Rabbit rotated rapidly, while Biggie Pug, after crashing into the wall, crouches on all fours, squealing like a pig. He scuttles past Brenda, headed back to the central kiva.

Dani grabs Brenda's hand, then reaches out to Dazmonique. With no effort, Dani and Dazmonique lift Brenda off the ground and catapult her down the tunnel after the fleeing Biggie Pug. As she flies past them, the twins gesture down the tunnel as if a jet plane is departing an aircraft carrier, complete with sound effects. In a flash Jack Rabbit, still rotating at a dizzying pace, disappears down the tunnel, crashing into the fleeing Brenda and Biggie Pug.

I walk slowly toward The Special-Special One, holding out my hands. I feel the power pulsating down to my outstretched hands. The Special-Special One shudders from head to foot, shrieking as I grip his shoulder. Without effort, I raise him slowly in the air. When I release my grip, he drops to the ground with a sickening thud. He scuttles away on all fours, squealing as he runs.

65. "Take Your Revenge"

"*Madame* Bouzius tell Dazmonique which way to go. We listen to her."

No disagreement. We rush back down the passageway.

Guided by Dazmonique, we soon see the opening ahead of us.

"The opening is closing, brick by brick," Dani shouts. "Hurry! We'll be bricked inside."

I help my friends leave through the narrowing gap and out into the moonlight.

I'm about to crawl through the opening myself when a voice calls out. "Don't go, Howell," Professor Lucian Drago scowls. "You still don't have the answer. Your mother drove slower, preparing for the dangerous curve ahead. Suddenly the car lurched, hit from behind."

Outside Dani and the others shout for me to get out before the opening closed.

But I can't move.

"She panics," Professor Lucian continues, "slamming her foot on the brake and ripping down through the gears. But still the speedometer leaps. Sixty, seventy miles per hour. She tries to steer the car to the side of road. But the steering wheel is locked. Nothing to prevent her headlong rush forward. Ninety miles an hour and still climbing. The car spins out of control, flipped up and over, crashing through the barrier, and plunging into the canyon below."

"It was you," I yell. "You kidnapped her."

"True," he growls. "Doesn't that make you mad, Howell. Come fight me! Take your revenge!"

Although the opening is getting smaller, all I can think of is rushing back down the passageway and leaping at Professor Lucian.

"Revenge," he shrieks. "Take your revenge." Behind him The Special-Special One and his gang gather, echoing his call for revenge.

I take two steps back down the tunnel when I hear her voice. "Do not give in to anger, my son," my mother whispers. "Leave now."

I rush back to the opening and push my arms, head and shoulders through the narrowing hole. Outside Dani and Leonel grab my arms and pull. At the same time, from within the darkened passageway, Professor Lucian and the others grasp my ankles.

"Do you think you'll leave us in this place?" the Professor screams. "Never!"

The bricks tighten against my hips. Soon I'll be trapped.

A word I have never heard before enters my head. I whisper it. As I do, bolts of electricity shoot through me. My feet slam backward, punching against Professor Lucian, hurling him backwards.

I'm dragged out an instant before the last bricks slip back into place and the bricked-up wall closes completely.

Muffled howls of rage reverberate up and down the darkened passageways, shaking the wall and ground beneath us.

Outside a fierce battle. A grey wolf, jaguar and wild dog rip and tear at fleeing Drygoni, while overhead a red dragon hurls down fireballs scattering all Drygoni further and further into the sweltering desert.

An instant and our protectors are gone replaced by Esther Evening Star, *Señor* Quit, *Madame* Bouzius and Uncle Tal.

66. Why? What? When?

A wave of *Señor* Quit's hands and we are all, once again, mountain lions rushing away down the canyon, not stopping until we reach Camp *Corwynt*.

None of us can rest. Questions, questions. What about Professor Lucian, The Special-Special One and his gang? Are they locked in the dark passageways? And what is next for the six of us?

The four adults hug us, congratulating each of us on our return.

"First a good meal and then answers," Uncle Tal announces before any of us could speak. "What you would like to eat?" Before any of us can respond, Uncle Tal held up his hand. "Think."

And what we think appeared before us: hamburgers, tacos, quesadillas, and pizza together with all the drinks we can manage. At last, a birthday feast with my friends.

"What else would you like?" Uncle Tal asks. "A restful sleep or answers?"

"Answers," we all agree.

"You all helped the transfer. Howell has received some his mother's Doeth power. In the years ahead, he will grow in that power. Maybe one day he will become a Nerth Doeth as she is. When each of you are in need of help to transfer you own Doeth power, Howell will be there to help you as each of you has helped him."

"How will the Jimis contact him? Phone? Texting? Skype?"

Uncle Tal looks at me. "He'll know when you need his help. As for Professor Lucian and the others, they will not escape the haunted kiva until the summer solstice. Not before. But there are other *Drygoni* out there encouraging *Safonals* to do evil. Those *Drygoni* will challenge you. They'll try to force you to make errors, to give up any Doeth power you have." Uncle Tal continues, "We adults must leave you now. We have work to do. Maybe soon we'll all meet again."

Leaving? What about us? What work do they have?

Before any of us can ask any more questions, Uncle Tal waves his hand and the six of us fall into a deep sleep.

When we wake, we are sitting in the school bus with the grumpy driver. "Not many returning," he complains. "Always the same. Many in, few out. Still they'll still make me write up a report. Tell them only six coming back, I'll write. But they already know that. Question is: Why do they want me to tell them how many are returning when they already know? Still, they'll want me to write it all down. Maybe they'll be happy at that number, maybe not. Time will tell."

And off we ride, bumping across the desert.

Suddenly the grumpy bus driver calls out. “Here we go. Be ready.” Before we can ask, “Be ready for what?” the bus hits a huge bump. We’re thrown up, out of our seats, flying in different directions.

And that’s the last I saw of my friends that day. Flying through the air.

But I know I’ll see them again—soon.

67. "Sometimes Here Is There, and Sometimes It's the Other Way Around."

Splat! A stream of cold water hits me in my face. "Got you, dweeb. You're a dead man."

I open my eyes as another stream smacks me in the eyes. "Got you again!"

Sister Sarah stands over me, water pistol in hand. "Mother told me to wake you. She's making breakfast."

She swaggers out of my bedroom. Annie's girl is back!

I lie in bed gazing up at the painting of the lady in a long white dress, riding across the fairy mound on a pure white stallion.

Splat! Another burst of water in my face. Sister Sarah is enjoying this. "Breakfast and school," she shouts. "Does my little brother need his big sister to protect him?"

No! I won't need the protection of Annie's girls. No more.

As I shower and dress, I ponder some questions.

Do I say anything to my mother about Uncle Tal and the transfer? Where's Tommy Foxglove?

My father is buried in his morning paper as I enter the kitchen.

My mother sets food upon the table. She hugs me and puts her fingers to her lips. Silence.

"Your mother had quite an adventure when coming back from New Mexico, son," my father calls out.

"Let me tell him," Sister Sarah interrupts. "Mother saw this car had broken through a barrier on a mountain road. She got out of her car and rushed down the side of the mountain and helped the woman to safety. Then she called for the police and an ambulance. Isn't that great? Can't wait to tell my friends."

My mother stares at me, smiles, shakes her head back and forth as she touches her finger to her lips.

Let that be the story.

Sister Sarah runs out of the room ready to get dressed for school.

I look around the room before whispering to my mother. "What happened to Tommy Foxglove while I was gone?"

Again, my mother puts her finger to her lips.

"Disappeared. Sister Sarah made up some excuse about him being too possessive," my father whispers. "He wanted her all to himself. No other friends."

Another comfortable answer for Sister Sarah and my father. My mother and I know the real reason.

Sister Sarah, dressed as one of Annie's girls, enters the room "Better saddle up and get dressed if you need my protection, little brother?"

I smile and shake my head.

My mother smiles at me. "Howell won't need protecting. He will know what to do and when to do it."

"Just don't blame me," Sister Sarah responds, "if he comes home with a bloody nose from Bully Harold Bully."

As she leaves the house, I turn to my father. "Any news from Uncle Tal?"

"Tal? We haven't heard from him in years, right, Rhiannon?"

"Right," my mother answers.

She takes a notepad, writes on it and hands the paper to me. "Sometimes here is there, or not here, and sometimes it's the other way around."

I take her hand and smile. "The Crossingway," I mouth.

Before I leave the house, my mother catches my arm. "You have seen much, and now you will see more. The Drygoni are everywhere. They seek out Safonals who think bad things, do bad things. Many you can't prevent. Be vigilant. Learn to know when that badness grows, develops into wicked and evil thoughts and acts. Those that will hurt others. When you see this, you will know what to do and when to do it."

She bends down and kisses the top of my head before returning to the house.

68. "Howell Will Know What to Do and When to Do It"

They are everywhere. The dark-grey *Drygoni* figures, unseen by the *Safonals*, scuttle across the streets, fly through the air, growling and chuckling. Sometimes one will stretch itself out and walk next to a person. Sometimes a roly-poly shape will land on someone's shoulder. When I walk near that person, the form screeches and scuttles away. A smile. "What a beautiful day!" I say. The person smiles back.

This is what my mother sees all the time, I say to myself. *Why some, surrounded and smothered by* Drygoni, *avoid her and cross the street. What will happen if, when, I meet someone like that?*

And that's when I see him: Bully Harold Bully's father staggering along the sidewalk, drunk even at this time of the morning. Dark-grey forms circle and surround him, clutching his legs, his body, wrapping themselves around his head, walking in front, alongside and beside him and dancing on his shoulders. *Drygoni* sticking to him like flies to honey. His face is a permanent scowl. He screams cruel and obscene remarks at anyone who dares cross his path. His shoulders are slightly hunched, fists clenched. A fighting stance. His head and eyes shift from side to side as he waits for someone to glance his way, to say something/anything to him so he can snarl, yell and threaten them. I wait for him to scowl at me, to hiss a threatening, "What are you looking at?" But he doesn't. Instead he quickly crosses the street, snarling and avoiding eye contact with me, guided by the *Drygoni*.

I walk through the downtown park. I see my schoolmates chattering, telling each other about their upcoming winter vacation. Not many dark-grey shapes here. A few fly above a cluster of girls, whispering to each other and snickering as they point to various boys. Gossips.

Bully Harold Bully and his two friends hide behind a large mound of earth. Each has a catapult at the ready, aimed at my school friends. The dark-grey figures dance around them, encouraging them to harm others.

I stand in front of them. The dark-grey figures around them form and reform themselves, hissing and moving away as I move closer. Suddenly they leap up and run off, yelling and slapping their hands. "Watch out! He'll set the dogs on us!"

"I don't have any dogs!" I call out.

Throughout the morning, my mother's words ring in my ears, "You will know what to do and when to do it."

Things are different. I can interfere so many times. But I mustn't.

I sit in the school library looking at my classmates sitting before computers. *Drygoni* fly everywhere, looking for somewhere to settle. Then I see her: a girl, Mary Jackson, wiping tears from her eyes. An image appears in my head. It's the screen Mary Jackson has before her: a photoshop of her, dressed in her Salvation Army hand-me-downs, with a dog's head. I look around the room. Who could be so cruel? A slight wave of my hand and the image returns to a cluster of boys, sitting in the corner, snickering to themselves. *Drygoni* surround them. They glance up at the girl and giggle.

Should I interfere? Could I do it without raising suspicion that it's me?

A slight movement of my finger and the reflection of the boys' computer screen appears before me. On it is a list of girls ranging from goody-goody to easy to real dogs, complete with vile and disgusting emojis. The boys giggle as they add names to their categories.

A slight movement of my finger. A message is plastered across the boys' screen: "Delete this image immediately and apologise to Mary Jackson. Otherwise, in ten seconds, your list with your names attached will be sent to your teacher, the principal and your parents."

The boys look around the class, panicked, then back to their computer. One boy slams the lid shut as another leaps forward and pulls the plug on the computer. A second before they open the lid again. 5-4-3. They frantically delete the image, leap to their feet and scramble across to the Mary Jackson. Mumbled apologies.

After school I walk home through the park with Erin Powell. "Did you see that hear about those mean boys?" she asks. "Trying to convince us that a threatening message suddenly appeared on their computer? Of course, no one believes them."

I smile and remain silent.

"What a pity we all missed your birthday," she continues. "Your mother said you had a fever. Do you think your parents plan a late birthday party for you?"

I shrug my shoulders. "Perhaps."

69. Two Kites

As I walk beside her, I can't help thinking about my new friends. *Where are they? What are they doing? Will I see them again soon?*

"Look at that," Erin suddenly calls out. Two dragon kites swoop back and forth in the sky. "They're identical. Like twin kites." At that moment, the string on one of the kites breaks and it hurtles to the ground landing at my feet. I pick it up. "What a pity," Erin says. "Still one kite remains."

That's it! The question posed by Elder Jimi One and Elder Jimi Two leaps into my head. *"'When does one minus one leave one?'" The twins are a pair, like the dragon kites. Something has happened to one of them, leaving the other alone. The answer to the Elder Jimi One and Elder Jimi Two's riddle.*

Erin picks up the kite at my feet. "Something is written on it," she says. "It looks like '*Yon pa ale lakay ou.*' What language is that?"

"Does it say anything else?"

"'One not go home.' Somebody can't write English."

"I have to get home myself quickly," I yell.

"See you tomorrow?" Erin calls out.

"Maybe." I race through the streets.

One of the Jimis is missing. How will I find him?

I rush through the front door, straight into the arms of my father. "Howell, what is going on? That Harold boy's mother was here. She told me some dogs chased Harold, and his friends. They blamed you. I told her we don't have dogs. It couldn't be Howell. She grumbled and left. What is going on?"

I look at my mother. "Perhaps Harold and his friends are seeing things."

She knows.

"True," my father answers. "Probably a strange pack of dogs is roaming the neighbourhood. Keep an eye out, Howell."

I promise I will.

"You have some work to do, Howell," my mother says. "Upstairs now and clean your bedroom."

I rush upstairs.

"Which Jimi didn't return home? And why?"

I dig around in the bottom drawer. Maybe the broken compass will guide me. No, the arrow on the compass doesn't flicker. What else? I plunge my hand into the mass of objects.

Something warms in my hand. Deep in the corner of the drawer lies a battered credit card. Another of Uncle Tal's 'useless' presents. The credit card glows. I look at the back and front of the card. Something is written in tiny print. I hold the credit card up to the light.

"Press me against your forehead if you want to find out how where there is from here."

I hold up the battered credit card and press it against my forehead.

CPSIA information can be obtained
at www.ICGtesting.com
Printed in the USA
LVHW041826201020
669275LV00008B/202